Three Chords and the Truth

Three Chords and the Truth

Cas Sigers

www.urbanbooks.net

Urban Books, LLC
78 East Industry Court
Deer Park, NY 11729

Three Chords and the Truth Copyright © 2011 Cas Sigers

ISBN 13: 978-1-60162-298-3
ISBN 10: 1-60162-298-8

First Trade Paperback Printing May 2011
Printed in the United States of America

10 9 8 7 6 5 4 3 2 1

Distributed by Kensington Publishing Corp.
Submit Wholesale Orders to:
Kensington Publishing Corp.
C/O Penguin Group (USA) Inc.
Attention: Order Processing
405 Murray Hill Parkway
East Rutherford, NJ 07073-2316
Phone: 1-800-526-0275
Fax: 1-800-227-9604

Dedication

For Anthony, thank you for taking my three chords and creating a beautiful melody.

Prologue

"Only the Strong Survive" (Jerry Butler, 1969)

With Bach's Symphony No. 4 playing loudly through her iPod earbuds, Henna James rushed down the hall to dressing room A of the Copenhagen Opera House. Three steps behind her heels was Ahmad, her manager/ex-boyfriend, loudly calling her name.

"Henna! Henna, this is childish!"

Henna slammed the dressing-room door, almost clipping Ahmad in the nose. She panted as though she'd sprinted the thirty-yard dash and then let out a growling scream, as if she were challenging a big black bear face-to-face. Yet, the only person she was confronting was herself.

"Why did I tell him it was okay to come to Denmark?" she asked her reflection. It didn't answer back, and it didn't have to for Henna to know the answer. There were three loud bangs at the door, but Henna didn't flinch. She continued to stare at herself and concentrated to block out the noise. After a few seconds of silence, a softer voice pierced through the dressing-room door.

"Henna, open up. It's Haydu."

Henna turned and peered at the door, but she didn't move from her seat.

"Haydu, I'm okay. Go get ready for the show," said Henna.

"Not until I see you."

Henna rose and opened the door. She curiously looked down the hall but all she saw was her very stylish, extremely nosy, bass guitar player, Haydu.

"I sent him away," he said just before stepping into the room.

"I'm sorry you guys had to see me like that. I normally keep it cool, but, I swear, that man makes me crazy. He got word that I wasn't doing the second leg of the tour, and I wouldn't return his phone calls."

"We aren't doing the second leg?" Haydu asked.

"Yeah, about that. I don't think I can do it. I'm tired. We've been on the road for six months, and I want to go home. But Ahmad thinks it has something to do with us, and it doesn't."

Haydu moved close to Henna and placed his hands on her shoulder. "I thought you were over him?"

"What are you talking about?"

"I heard you guys arguing."

Henna lowered her tone when she replied. "Haydu, he brought her with him. He didn't have to bring her to Denmark just to tell me I needed to finish out the tour. It's just disrespectful."

"You can't let him get to you. You still have to go onstage and give a great performance tonight."

"I know."

"So this is the last show?"

"For a while, yeah. I'm sorry, I should have told you guys, but I really just decided a few nights ago."

"You have to do what's best for you. And, girlfriend, Ahmad is not what's best for you, so I'm glad you are not doing him anymore."

"Amen to that," Henna said, giggling. She walked over to the mirror, grabbed her brush, and started grooming her long, dark brown hair. "I really thought we'd get back together after the tour. I didn't think he'd move on." She stared at the dark brown flecks in her light cocoa-brown eyes.

"Still looking for yourself, huh?" he said.

"Yep, and one day I'm going to find me," she replied. After a little bit more time spent on brushing, Henna continued speaking. "The opera house is beautiful, isn't it?" Haydu nodded. "It's really cool that we booked this venue."

"That's because you are 'The Bomb-ay'!"

"No, it's because Ahmad is a hell of a manager. He could sell me singing 'The Alphabet Song' to the King of Siam."

"That's because you are timeless and classic."

Four loud thuds erupted. Henna rolled her eyes and turned in the opposite direction from the door. "Forty minutes until showtime," said Ahmad loudly through the door. "Henna, did you hear me?" he yelled.

She glanced at Haydu, and he knew exactly what to do. "I'll handle it. You just get ready."

Haydu gently kissed Henna's cheek and gyrated his lanky body out of the room. He was Henna's tour buddy—the one she ate with, confided in, and shopped with. He had picked out the sexy, long, slate gray dress she was going to wear tonight. It, too, was timeless, and classic, with a V-neckline that dropped down to its Empire waistline. It exposed a little cleavage; but since Henna was only a B cup, it was still very tasteful. The bottom half of the silk dress was cut on the bias, and it danced with every step she made. It looked like a gown that should have graced the Givenchy Couture collection, although they found it in a small boutique in Ontario. As soon as Haydu made her try it on, she knew this would be her finale dress. She glanced at it, hanging on the closet door, and then back at her makeup table, where she saw the brown velvet pouch that was given to her by Ahmad. Taking her pinkie finger, she outlined her initials, HMJ, that were embroidered in white satin stitching.

"This was my favorite bag," she whispered just before emptying its contents on the table. Henna then grabbed her silver lighter, flicked it, and placed the flame at the corner of the pouch. It quickly lit, and so she held it away from her face and continued to watch it burn.

Just then, Haydu returned to the dressing room. This time he entered as he was knocking. "Oh, I forgot . . ." He stopped talking as he noticed the burning bag. "You're supposed to be getting ready."

Henna walked to the granite sink and tossed in the quickly burning pouch. Haydu didn't say anything as they watched the velvet disintegrate into a tiny puddle of dark ash.

"What did you forget?" she asked.

"Huh?"

"When you came in, you said, 'Oh, I forgot . . .'"

"I just wanted to tell you that Ahmad may be a great manager, but you are the star." Haydu gave her a hug and left the room.

Henna then skirted back to the dressing-room mirror, grabbed her hairbrush, ran a few drops of warm water on the soft bristles, and pulled her hair back into a ponytail. She applied clear hair gel to slick back her wispy ends, and in two steps placed her dangling locks into a very tight bun.

"The last show, the last show, the last show," she softly repeated before slipping into her dress. After five albums and ten years of touring, Henna was seriously considering this not only to be her last show for the year, but for good. She hadn't dared to mention that to anyone yet. Her voice fed a lot of people, and sometimes she felt the pressure of continuing because people relied on her. She was never that fond of fame, and she really disliked the responsibility that often came with it. Her entourage was small. There was no "glam squad" or stylist. Henna did her own makeup and hair. However, she was committed to her band; they were like family and she wanted to make sure they would all find great gigs if she quit.

"The last show, the last show, the last show," she kept repeating as she put the final touch of gloss on her lips.

Her walk from the dressing room to the stage felt like an out-of-body experience. As though she were gliding in slow motion, she felt a release with each step she took. Just knowing this was the last show was giving her a sense of peace.

The performance that evening lasted for two hours and twenty minutes, thirty minutes longer than the rehearsed show. Henna did a three-song a cappella set, and even sang "Happy Birthday" to the prime minister's wife. She was definitely in rare form. Finally it was over, and she ended with her trademark closing:

"I'm Henna James. Peace and blessings to you, thanks and good night."

Ms. James bowed her head, and slinked offstage, just as the twenty-foot blood-red curtains closed. The audience had no idea that this grand exit might truly be her final bow.

Chapter 1

"Lonely Teardrops" (Jackie Wilson, 1958)

Henna was excited to be back in Brooklyn, New York, and to sleep in her own bed. The tour had exhausted her, both physically and mentally. Two weeks before it had started, Ahmad admitted that he was conflicted about managing her, since he was seeing another woman and felt it was in poor taste for him to manage his ex. But Henna went against her gut and asked him to stay on, at least until after the tour, thinking she'd be strong enough to handle it. Not only was she a professional, but she figured the tour would be an escape. By the time she returned from it, she hoped, her heart would have started to mend. Yet, each night was a reminder, each song was a memory, and for the last 173 days, Henna had to relive this heartbreak onstage in front of thousands of strangers. The man whom she'd trusted with her heart and her art, which was equally as precious, had abandoned her.

"They have no idea," Henna would often whisper to herself in between songs as the audience applauded in amazement.

As she settled back into her brownstone in Fort Greene, she could still feel Ahmad's lingering presence. Henna took the remainder of Ahmad's clothes, bundled them in a bag, and placed them in her designated storage space located in the garage. She spent her first day back in bed, returning e-mails and updating her calendar and phone address book. One by one, Henna deleted old numbers of people she no longer wanted to be in contact with and those she could no longer remember. When she was done, her phone list was twenty-two people lighter.

"If only we could truly delete people as easily," she murmured.

Before she went to sleep, Henna thought about Monica Cole, her close friend and roommate from Alcorn State. The two met freshman year after Henna had decided to return to her roots in Mississippi to attend college and major in communications. For four years the girls were inseparable but right after college, Henna moved back to New York and Monica took a job in Atlanta. Though they made a point over the years to schedule an annual "girls weekend", their quality time has been few-and-far between. In the past two years, e-mails and phone calls had been their only communication. But now that the tour was over, and she wasn't recording, Henna had nothing but free time. A visit to Monica was well overdue, so she dialed her number. Monica picked up on the first ring.

"Are you back in the country?"

"Yes, and I'm coming to see you."

Monica responded with elation. "Great! When?"

Henna thought about her answer for several seconds. Monica was a stickler on promises, and Henna was extremely fickle. Ninety percent was as sure as Henna ever was about any decision. If she gave Monica a date, she would have to stick with it, or never hear the end of it.

"Before the end of next month. I promise."

"I'm putting you in my calendar for next weekend."

"No. It may be the end of the month," replied Henna.

"Too late. Next weekend, it is. If I don't make you commit, I may not see you for another year."

"Fine. You sound busy too."

"Just having dinner with Julian. You okay?" Monica asked.

"I am. Glad to be home, and glad to hear you are still with Julian, even though I don't know that much about him," Henna responded.

"Well, you'll get to meet him when you come down, next weekend," Monica emphasized.

"Okay, well, go eat. I'll call you in a few days."

"My door is always open. I love you and miss you."

"Love and miss you too," Henna responded before hanging up.

Monica was always a breath of fresh air. She was the friend who always put a positive spin on everything, which was just what Henna needed. But Monica was also the friend who overanalyzed situations, and Henna knew she'd have to talk about Ahmad. This was something she didn't want to deal with. Honestly, she didn't want to talk about anything. She simply wanted to take a few days in familiar surroundings, cook her own meals, and smell her citrus-scented fabric softener. Henna retired to bed that evening before seven o'clock, but the ringing of her house phone interrupted her sleep. Though many of her friends had gotten rid of their home phones and relied strictly on their mobile devices, Henna couldn't part with hers. But on this evening, she wished she had. It was Ahmad. She let him speak first.

"I wanted to make sure you made it back safely."

"Whatcha need?" Henna said curtly.

"Want to meet at Moe's?" Henna was silent, and so Ahmad continued. "I can meet you tonight, in an hour, if that's good."

"Fine," Henna blurted out, and then quickly hung up. After several minutes of pacing and cursing, she realized that seeing Ahmad would be good. She didn't talk with him but a few times on the tour, and then there was the Denmark fiasco. She needed to see him for closure. So after taking several deep breaths, Henna slipped on a long black skirt, a T-shirt, and flats. She grabbed the old school leather Adidas duffel bag, she'd purchased for him, that was filled with his clothing, and tossed it in the backseat of her car. Getting rid of his last items of clothing was one step closer to that final good-bye. Again, she knew this was the best thing.

Moe's was her testing ground for new songs, and her hangout spot when she needed a drink. It was a few blocks from her home, and normally she walked but since she was carrying a heavy duffel bag filled with clothing, she decided to drive. Henna got there in no time and surveyed the area for his truck. It wasn't there, so she stayed in the car until she saw him walk inside. Henna wanted to see him first to make sure that this was something she'd be able to do without breaking down. It would be better to stand him up than to let him see her cry. But amazingly, not one tear fell. Not that she was over him; she was simply used to hiding the truth. After six years of being with a man who couldn't make a permanent commitment, Henna was always on guard for him to walk out. In truth, his departure was something she'd imagined and even visualized repeatedly. Ahmad was unpredictable and impulsive, which was part of the attraction. On the other hand, he was selfish and uncompromising, and if something didn't suit him, it wasn't going to fly. This was what she hated. She wanted marriage, but he said marriage didn't define the connection they had. She didn't buy it in the beginning, but after four years, she not only bought into his fairy tale, but also found herself saying their connection was beyond a few vows. It wasn't the best relationship, but he was a terrific manager, and so she stayed in it, partly for convenience and mostly because Henna was a creature of habit.

After sitting in the car an additional five minutes, Henna grabbed the duffel bag and walked into the lounge. Immediately she was greeted by a host of friendly faces. Maria, the very busty, and very nosy, Colombian owner, came from around the bar to give her a hug. The gossip immediately and rapidly spilled from her tongue.

"Man, we've missed you. So much has happened. Philippe finally got busted for trafficking. Yvette is in AA, Coco had her baby, and Alexa had a Botox job, which went terribly wrong. You should see her. It's a mess. How was the tour? You look so good." Maria took Henna by the hand and pulled her over to the bar. "Charlie, a glass for Henna," Maria said.

The bartender didn't even ask what she wanted; he grabbed a bottle and poured her favorite brand of red wine, Schlink Haus. She took several minutes to sip her drink and give a few details of the tour before Ahmad made eye contact and motioned for her to come over. He was sitting at "their" table.

"How sentimental," she whispered as she approached slowly. Ahmad attempted to hug her before she sat, but Henna quickly placed the duffel bag between their bodies and took her seat. With neither party knowing what to say, they sat in silence for several minutes, randomly gazing around the lounge.

At last, Henna spoke. "You look good, Ahmad."

"I don't want us to end like this," he blatantly replied.

"How do you wish for us to end?"

"Not like this," he answered.

Ahmad then rose and went to the bar for another beer. When he returned, one of the cocktail waitresses bounced over to the table and spoke with excitement. "So I heard you two are finally tying the knot." They both gave her an odd glare, which didn't stop her from pursuing the conversation. "You are getting married aren't you?"

Henna shook her head, and Ahmad disfigured his face as though the word "marriage" gave him diarrhea. Eventually the waitress got the feeling that something was awry and walked away.

Desperately ready to leave, Henna decided to wrap up the conversation. "That's all of your things," she said, motioning toward the bag. "I'm not mad at you or anything, but since the tour is over, and you're no longer my manager, there really is no need for us to talk anymore." Henna rose and walked toward the front door. But before she could make her exit, she was compelled to return to where Ahmad sat at the table, still sipping his Duvel.

Henna walked back, leaned over, and stared at him. Without a blink, she asked, "Why? Is it something I did? Something I didn't do? Something I didn't know how to do? What?"

Ahmad saw the hurt, and he knew his answer would only drive the stake deeper, but he felt he owed Henna an honest response, and so he replied, "You just weren't enough for me to give you my forever."

Although that was a variation of what she expected to hear, the words still stung like a thousand wasps attacking her face. One by one, her faculties shut down. First her heart dropped; then her legs locked; finally her vocal cords gave out. The only ability still operating was her mind, and it was screaming at her, "Run right now before the meltdown," but her body couldn't respond.

"I'm sorry," he continued, "but that's the truth."

Henna closed her eyes and finally managed to control her neck muscles enough to turn away. After three deep breaths, she gained feeling throughout the rest of her body and was able to put one foot in front of the other. But before she walked away, she took the duffel bag and emptied his contents onto the table. As clothing poured out onto the wood, one of his sneakers knocked his glass of beer into his lap. As Ahmad jumped up, Henna clutched the bag and didn't speak a word as she exited the bar. She rushed to the car, turned on the ignition, and revved up the engine. She looked at the bar and desperately wanted to run her car right through the front door, aiming her bumper at Ahmad's forehead. And though that was extreme, she truly wanted to walk back in and punch him dead in the face. However, she knew that would end up in tomorrow's tabloids, another drawback of fame. You could never be your true self in public. With each second she sat, the anger built more and more. She was pissed that he would say something like that, and more pissed that she couldn't retaliate. She glanced over at the empty Adidas bag and a tiny smirk emerged but the anger immediately returned and finally she combusted into full-blown tears—tears that turned into loud, uncontrollable bawling, which didn't stop until she was home and in bed.

Sleep, however, was nowhere on the agenda that night. Henna sat in the center of her bed and evaluated Ahmad's answer at least a hundred times. It was killing her. Finally she picked up the phone and called Ahmad.

"You okay?" he asked, assuming there was a problem, since it was almost 2:00 A.M.

"Was my talent not enough? Was I a bad lover? Was I not giving enough? Was I not strong enough? Was I not submissive enough? Was I not pretty enough? Did I travel too much? What in the hell was it?" she yelled.

"I don't want to do this."

"But you started it, and I have to know."

"I already told you."

"With a very dramatic line. I heard you, but it has to be more. Something specific."

"I don't know who you are anymore. You've become so closed-in. It's like you've lost yourself in your work, and Henna is gone."

"You once told me that I had to immerse myself in my art to create something genuine."

"You took it too far. I liked you better before you were famous. You used to be happy. You used to have peace."

"You know what, Ahmad? Fuck you! You created this monster. You created this star! And now you can't deal with what you've created. And if you don't know who I am, there is no way you can manage me."

"You're right."

"I know I'm right," Henna emphasized.

"This is what—"

"I'm done talking to you. I've heard enough." Henna hung up immediately. She knew she was in the wrong, and should have handled it better, but she was getting extremely mad. Ahmad had been her manager since he discovered her singing in a lounge in SoHo. He taught her the business. He taught her to bury herself in her work and in her music; to spend every waking moment breathing her art; taught her that nothing else mattered. Before him, she was Henna Marie Jameston. Ahmad created Henna James, a persona she didn't even like at first. Yet he insisted that she love her. So she did.

He used to say, "I love Henna James, and the world is going to love her too," and he was right. The world did love Henna James; and the more they loved, the bigger Henna James became. And the bigger Henna James became, the smaller Henna Jameston got. Ahmad was right again. She wasn't herself anymore, and there was no peace. Henna knew she was fading away a long time ago, but she never thought she'd lose her man in the process.

"Maybe it was supposed to be for a season?" Henna questioned aloud. "It still hurts, though," she whispered as she placed her head on her pillow and tried to sleep. Her mind continued to play the conversation, until the phone rang. She knew it was Ahmad, and at first wasn't going to answer, but she picked up just before the voice mail.

"I'm sorry," he said before she could speak.

"Good night," Henna replied with exhaustion in her voice. She rose from bed, went to her living room, and began an all-night writing session.

Chapter 2

"Take This Job and Shove It"
(David Allan Coe, 1978)

That morning, around nine o'clock, Henna fell asleep and stayed in bed for the next two days. She came in and out of snoozes every few hours, but the pain in her heart fatigued her body and weakened her muscles. She literally couldn't rise from the mattress. Henna didn't shower, communicate with others, or eat. But after three days of ignoring persistent phone calls from the music label, she finally returned their call. As suspected, her rep wanted to discuss her next project. Henna had released two independent CDs before getting signed to a four-CD deal. With three down, her domestic sales were steadily declining, and she knew the label wanted her to go in a different direction and produce something more commercial. They wanted Henna to move from the jazz adult-contemporary lane into the neo-soul arena. It was mentioned on album two, requested on number three, and sure to be a demand for album four. Therefore, she showered off three days of mental funk, got dressed, and went into Manhattan.

Standing outside 550 Madison Avenue, Henna peered from underneath the brim of her black Yankees cap, gazed up the side of the towering building, lit her cigarette, and took three large puffs before walking in. On her ride up to the twenty-fourth floor, she braced herself for the worst. According to her contract, the label could choose to indefinitely shelve her next CD, which wasn't even complete, if they felt it wasn't ready to be released. However, that wasn't her concern. She couldn't be signed to any other label until she produced the fourth CD, and going into the studio to push out another Henna James creation was the last thing she wanted to think about. She walked into the lobby and spoke with the receptionist for a few seconds; then Phillip Moreano floated around the corner. Phillip had been in the music business for twenty years. He'd birthed numerous talents, and destroyed twice as many.

"Phillip, hi. I thought I was meeting with Thalia?" Henna said.

"She called you for me," he replied, gesturing toward his office.

They walked into his large corner space, which was overflowing with plaques, platinum records, autographed pictures, and magazine tears of various articles.

"Coffee, tea, water?" he offered.

"No, thank you," Henna replied.

Phillip's voice was nasal, loud, and abrasive, and Henna hated to hear him talk. She often tuned him out, but today he got right in her face and spoke. She wasn't going to be as lucky.

"I'm not going to beat around the bush. We love Henna James, but the U.S. is not so fond of her right now."

Henna immediately rose to her defense. "I'm so much bigger than the U.S. I sell well overseas."

"Well, pack your bags, honey, and move to Russia. Take up a couple of languages while you're there."

Henna quieted down. She was in foreign territory. Normally, Ahmad fought these battles for her. But she no longer had a manager, and she knew the label was going to use this to their advantage.

"The truth is, your sound is old. Your niche has transformed into something we can't market. We went along with you and 'your voice' for this last project, but we cannot afford to buy into it again. If you want to continue a career with Sony, specifically Columbia, then you have to change your sound."

Henna took his insults with grace and gave a gutsy response. "Well, maybe Columbia is not the label for me."

Phillip sighed and replied, "I hate when you artists do this." He rose, walked around the front of the desk, and stood next to Henna. "If you want to go sell your music on the A train during the lunch express, then you can. But you will do it after you complete this fourth project, which I am in charge of. We want to see the numbers we know you can do." Suddenly his approach softened and his tone had much more of an inflection of sincerity. It was still all an act, and Henna knew it well. Phillip walked to his shelf of CDs and pulled out Henna's first Grammy-nominated project with Columbia. He embraced it like an adorable newborn. "Remember her?" he said, pointing to a picture of Henna on the front cover. "She was light and soulful. She was passionate and uplifting. This is the Henna we love. This is the Henna they want. What happened?"

Henna pushed back from the desk, looked him square in the eyes, and replied, "Life."

She grabbed her purse and turned to leave the office. Phillip quickly pulled her arm and attempted to lure her back to the desk. Yet, she stood still with contempt raked across her face and listened to his suggestion.

"You just need a little inspiration. There is a new artist we've been looking at signing. However, Thalia made the suggestion that maybe her sound would be good for you. Why sign someone whom we may already have?" he stated, with a baiting smile.

Henna frowned. "So you want me to copy someone else's style of music?"

"Of course not. We want you to get inspired from her and apply that inspiration to your own style." He handed Henna two tickets. "She's performing tonight. Go see her."

She took the tickets and read the name. "Crimson?" She glared back at Phillip. "You are kidding, right? She's a child. I'm thirty-four years old! I can't make teen music."

"I like you, Henna, and I think you can turn things around. I'm just not ready to see you go."

Though she knew the industry was filled with bloodsuckers, Phillip Moreano was the vampire you wanted on your side. She looked at the tickets once more, then let out an exasperated and defeated "okay."

"Great!" Phillip said, with a loud clasp of his greedy little hands. Henna then turned again and began to leave the office, but Phillip wasn't done.

"I spoke with Ahmad. So you're in the market for a new manager, huh?"

She glanced back around and gave Phillip a pleasant smile, but she didn't respond. She simply walked out of the office.

By the time she hit the elevator, Henna was already digging though her purse for that nicotine fix. She swiftly paced through the lobby, hit the fresh air, and sucked in a puff of packaged tar. Once more, Henna looked up the side of this enormous building, and imagined Phillip Moreano going bankrupt, jumping out of his luxurious office, and landing somewhere on the sidewalk between the cracks and the muck. This thought gave her a simple bit of pleasure, enough contentment to bring a tiny curl to her mauve-painted lips. She took a few more smoke inhales and walked down Madison toward Fifty-seventh street. At the corner of Fifty-seventh and Park, Henna walked into her favorite pizza parlor and got two large slices of cheese pizza. She sat in the window, while eating her hot cheese and dough, and gazed at the folks passing by, one of her favorite pastimes. As the hour passed, she thought about her conversation with Phillip. If she was no longer with Columbia, would another record label choose her? And, if another label didn't pick her up, what would she do?

Henna put down her pizza, removed a tiny notebook from her purse, and began jotting down a few options to her last question. The first answer was, tour old songs overseas for the next three years. This would give enough savings for at least an additional four years after she stopped touring. The last option was to sell CDs on the D train. She refused to give Phillip the satisfaction of telling her what subway train she'd be reduced to, but he'd planted the seed, nonetheless. Ultimately she had one more CD to produce. Henna figured if she could muster the energy to give the label a hit, then maybe she'd have more bargaining power for her next deal. She pulled out the tickets and read the address for the show that night.

"Crimson," she griped with hostility. "If you have the audacity to go by one name, why not just make it a regular name?"

Henna finished her pizza, hopped on the train, and headed back to Brooklyn. Normally, she would have hailed a cab, but she had missed New York so much, she wanted to soak up every bit of her city's essence. So with her baseball cap pulled down low, Henna sat down in her little orange seat and took in a deep whiff of the subway stench.

"I'm definitely back home," she whispered.

Seconds later, a young musician came through selling his CDs. Henna normally paid no attention to the millions of starving artists hustling their products amid the underground train system, but today her story was different. She imagined herself in that position. And though she figured going from Grammy nomination to subway promotion was a stretch, there was some connection with this guy. Therefore, she reached in her bag and purchased all ten of the CDs he was carrying. With a purse packed with unfamiliar music, Henna exited the train and walked a few blocks over to her home.

Once settled, she called Haydu and invited him to see Crimson sing that evening. He obliged, and close to ten o'clock, they walked into the Blue Owl. The show didn't start until eleven-thirty, and Crimson didn't go on until midnight. At least her hair matches her name, Henna thought as the young girl graced the stage. But before she really got started, Henna was over it. If it weren't for Haydu flirting with the bartender, she would have left thirty minutes after arriving.

The Blue Owl gave great atmosphere. There really wasn't a stage—only an area with a tiny platform in the corner—and the crowd was obnoxious, which said a lot, coming from a New Yorker. After Crimson introduced herself, she belted out her first song. It was cute, and very trendy. It was something about the paparazzi, but that's all Henna could remember. The second song, however, was extremely catchy. Henna liked it—although it wasn't her style.

Crimson was a typical commercial artist, and Henna was not. Henna's lyrics had meaning and depth, and her sound couldn't be defined by one genre. She wasn't Beyoncé, or Celine Dion, or India.Arie. Henna was a female Kem, with a flare of old blues; a modern-day Billie Holiday, without the tormented soul. She was like Sade, but there could only be one Sade, so she was . . . Suddenly she didn't know who she was. Yet, she was sure that she was not Crimson.

"I'm ready to go," Henna told Haydu.

"I like her," he replied.

She gave him a look of disappointment and reiterated her statement; this time she said it with forceful, choppy diction. Haydu took his friend by the hand and led her from the Blue Owl, back to the busy streets of the East Village. The two hopped over to a couple of other bars, and had a few drinks, but Henna wasn't in the mood for conversation. She drank, he talked, and soon Haydu grew tired of her one-word responses. Hence, the two retired back to Brooklyn.

As soon as Henna walked into her place, she opened her computer, went online, and searched for a ticket to Atlanta. She booked her flight, left a message with Monica, and took a shower. Before she went to bed, she opened a CD from the anonymous subway musician. It was good. It was very good. His voice was reminiscent of Andy Gibb's, but his music had the composition of something created by the Roots. It was awkward; yet the combination worked. She finally looked at the terrible script font on the front cover.

"'Judge'?"

Henna displayed a look of confusion, as if she'd read the name wrong. She silently read it once more, and confirmed her doubt. She then carelessly tossed the case onto her nightstand. "Freakin' vague one-name artists."

Just before she got in bed, she checked her voice mail. She only had two messages, one from her mom and one from Haydu. But as she looked at the caller ID, she noticed Ahmad had called twice. Their last conversations had cut so deep, she couldn't bear to hear anything else he had to say. Yet, she spent an hour wondering why he called. She pulled out her phone and put a new item in her calendar for tomorrow. "Get a new phone number," she mumbled while typing. Henna got under the bedcovers, turned on her belly, and finally went to sleep.

Chapter 3

"The Thrill Is Gone" (B.B. King, 1970)

Henna James arrived in Atlanta, Georgia, at 10:20 A.M. She called Monica to see where she was.

"I couldn't get away, my brother should be there in about thirty minutes," said Monica.

"Your half-brother, the one that lives in California?"

"I don't call him my half-brother but yes. He lives in Atlanta now."

"Well I don't want to wait. I'll just take a cab." She asked Monica to cancel her brother, and Henna placed her three oversize Diane von Furstenberg's vintage collection bags into a yellow taxi. Her eyes immediately began to itch from the pollen-infested air, and so she blinked ferociously to combat the irritation. Henna didn't have a return date; but if her allergies continued to bother her, she would be leaving sooner rather than later. She called Monica once again while riding, this time with a rather peculiar request.

"I want a slice of pecan pie," Henna commented.

"Ooh, you should stop by Julian's place."

"Who?" Henna asked.

"My man, Julian."

"Oh yes, the mysterious Julian," Henna joked.

"He owns a dessert place and they have a delicious pecan pie."

Monica gave her directions, which Henna relayed to the cabdriver, and they soon arrived at the dessert café known as Sweet J's. She asked the driver to wait while she picked up her pie. Henna rushed in and walked over to the counter, where the cakes and desserts were displayed. Her eyes grew wide with excitement. Though Henna was skinny as a rail, she loved desserts, all kinds. Her favorite cake was coconut; her favorite pie was pecan.

"I want you," she said, placing her long fingers against the glass as she eyed a lonely slice of pecan pie sitting in the corner of the shelf. The glaze on the pecans was thick, and Henna couldn't wait to taste the sweet dessert.

She glanced over at the man standing next to her, whose grin caught Henna off guard. He was incredibly sexy. Standing close to six feet two inches, he had very strong, high cheekbones and honey-colored skin that appeared smooth and clean-cut, as though he had just shaved minutes ago. She didn't remove her large oval shades but still found herself gazing into his deep-set eyes.

He looks young, she thought, but she still couldn't help giving him a flirtatious smile. However, as she tilted her head and continued to grin, the man ordered.

"A slice of pecan pie."

Henna gasped, as though he'd ordered her head on a platter.

"No, no, no. I want that slice. Didn't you hear me say I wanted that slice?"

He callously shrugged his shoulders.

"Is there anymore in the back?" she asked the server, who then offered to go check.

It was suddenly a stare down between the two lovers of pecan pie. As the clerk came back into view, Henna couldn't tell by her expression whether or not she'd have to go to war, but the clerk delivered bad news seconds later.

"No more, sorry."

Henna quickly went from distress to "dis is gonna be my pie." She turned on the charm, lowered her head, batted her naturally long eyelashes, and spoke in a demure, sweet voice.

"I just got in town, and I've been craving pecan pie all day. Please let me have that slice."

He smiled, gave her a once-over, and turned to the server.

"Two forks, please. Have we met?"

Henna's charm went out the window. "I don't think so. Um, I don't want to share the slice."

"Oh, you want the whole piece?" he asked, not believing her impudence.

Like Sally Field in Sybil, Henna suddenly changed back. This time she gave him an arm rub with her charisma.

"Please. Don't I look like I need some pie?" Henna turned slightly and swiveled her hips from right to left.

He smirked and looked her up and down once more. "You look like you need something," he said, with a smug look.

Not understanding his vague expression or his comment, Henna bluntly replied, "Can I have the pie, or what?"

"You can share it with me, but I'm not giving you my whole slice."

"But my cab is waiting, and that slice is too tiny to share."

By now, the server had moved on to the next customer. Still, the two stood there a few seconds longer, debating with silent expressions. Finally he moved to the cashier and paid for his slice. Henna looked at the other desserts. Though they looked good, nothing was going to fill her desire for that pecan sweetness. She mumbled and griped; then she retreated from the counter and headed toward the exit. As she passed her pastry foe, who was grabbing napkins, Henna bumped his elbow.

"I'm sorry," Henna softly stated.

The force was just hard enough to make his pie slice fall to the floor. She gave a bogus look of remorse, then rapidly turned around and trotted out the door. The guy stood there and watched her walk to her cab. Henna glanced back to see if he was watching. Once she caught his eye, she shrugged her shoulders and showed a very sly grin. His look of contempt nearly burned a hole through the glass, but Henna didn't care. She plopped back into her cab and headed down the street.

Once she arrived at Monica's job, she paid the cabdriver as he removed her bags from the trunk. With her large duffel strapped around her body, Henna rolled the other two bags and went into the executive office building. Though she was dressed down, her long figure, huge shades, and designer bags made her an instant standout in this corporate world of black and gray suits. People were nearly bumping into each other as they stared at Henna as she walked to the set of elevators. She rode up to the thirty-second floor, and walked into Schweitzer Marketing and Associates.

"Monica Cole, please," she said to the receptionist, who gave her an odd peer.

Three minutes later, Monica came buzzing around the corner, anxious to see her friend. She reached for Henna, who was still clinging to her bags.

"It took you forever to come get me," Henna pouted.

"I was on a conference call. It took . . . You know what, put your stuff down and hug me, girl."

Henna smiled and gave Monica a very tight embrace.

"I've missed you," Henna whispered while laying her head on Monica's shoulder.

Monica glanced down at her bags. "What is all that?"

"My stuff."

"Where's your cab?" Monica asked.

"Gone. I thought I'd be riding home with you."

"I said, come and get the key and I would meet you there. I can't leave work. It's the middle of the day!"

"But I'm here. Doesn't that mean something?" Henna was quite spoiled.

"Not to my boss," Monica replied. "And I'm sorry about my brother. He's always late."

Henna changed the subject. "Why are you working here, anyway? You should be on the road with me."

Monica noticed that the receptionist was taking mental notes on this conversation, and that she and Henna would soon be break room talk for the next two days. Therefore, she grabbed one of Henna's bags, rolled it into her office, and closed the door behind them.

Henna immediately walked over to the window and commented, "Nice view. I guess you are important around here."

"Not as valuable as my friend Henna James, who travels the world spreading her song," Monica said, with a huge smile.

Henna turned from the view and, with a distressed look, replied, "Girl, please, I'm so tired of this singing shit. I don't know what to do."

"But you just said I should be on the road with you."

"If we were on the road together, it would be different. But right now, I'm sick of music."

"Say it ain't so," Monica jokingly gasped.

Henna turned back around and gazed at the view. She was quiet for a few seconds as Monica flipped through some paperwork, but as soon as Henna started talking, she didn't stop.

"So I went to get a piece of pie from Sweet J's, which is a tacky name, by the way—"

"But the pie was good, right?" Monica interrupted.

"I don't know, because this asshole ordered the last slice."

"Maybe he didn't know it was the last slice."

"He knew, and when I asked him for it, he tried to share. Why are all the sexy men such assholes?"

"Because they can be." Monica laughed, first very softly, but then a loud cackle followed.

"This is amusing to you?" Henna asked.

"Yes, Henna, it is. Why should some stranger give you his last piece of pie? I wouldn't have given it to you."

"I wouldn't have asked you. You are not a man. A real man would have given the pie to me, because it was the chivalrous thing to do."

Monica simply stared, with a silly grin, at her friend. "I've forgotten how self-absorbed you really are. Oh, was Cola there? She's so mean to me. Was she mean to you?"

"Who is Cola? What are you talking about?"

"The lady behind the counter. Julian needs to get rid of her. Some people aren't cut out for customer service."

"There was an older lady, curly salt-and-pepper hair."

"That's her." Monica grimaced.

"She was pleasant. Maybe she just doesn't like you."

"But everyone likes me! You know what, never mind."

Henna continued to walk around the office, perusing the books and magazines. "I think I'm going to have a fling while I'm here."

"What?" Monica yelped.

"Why not? I've been with Ahmad for the last five years and I just want to have a little fun."

"This is so unlike you," Monica stated.

"Exactly. Even just now, when I was flirting with the asshole pecan-pie guy, it felt good, invigorating. I'm too uptight. It may help me forget my problems."

"Chile, what problems do you have?" asked Monica.

"How much time you got?" replied Henna.

"I got all night." Monica lit up with excitement. "So maybe we can go out tonight and look for you a man?"

"No, I don't want a premeditated night of passion. A fling just has to happen," replied Henna.

"It's already premeditated, because you've put it out there."

Henna made a silly, childish facial expression and went into her purse to grab a cigarette. Monica quickly snatched the rolled tobacco from her hand.

"You can't smoke in here. I can't even believe you're still smoking. Who smokes these days?"

"Millions of New Yorkers. We're a very elite club," Henna joked.

"An elite club of fools. You're quitting."

Henna overdramatically snatched the packet of cigs from Monica's hand. "I need them!" she groaned. "They are all I have left. My man is gone. My music is gone. Please don't take my smokes."

Monica frowned and tried to snatch them back; instead, the cigarettes fell from the pack and onto the floor. Henna quickly bent down and desperately picked them up.

"You look like a crackhead," said Monica.

Henna gave a sincere expression. "Mo, you don't understand what I go through. Just let me have this." Monica handed her the empty packet, and Henna placed the cigarettes in, one by one.

Monica leaned against her desk and looked at Henna's wiry frame. "Are you okay? You're losing weight."

"I'm good. I just needed a vacation." Henna gave Monica a phony smile as she flipped the unlit cigarette between two fingers.

"I know you're lying, but it's good to see you, anyway."

Henna reached for Monica and hugged her again. With her head still propped on Monica's shoulder, Henna spoke in a mushy, baby-sounding voice. "Can't you leave work now?"

Monica sighed and looked into her weary friend's eyes. "I will see."

Henna quickly perked up as Monica made a couple of phone calls. Thirty minutes later, they were walking out of the office building and into the parking garage. Yet, as they walked, Monica sassed, "Don't think I'm going to be playing hooky with your tail every day. How long are you staying, anyway?"

"How long can you put up with me?"

"Oh, about two days."

Henna stopped walking and lowered her head.

"Girl, come on and get your behind in this car," Monica laughingly ordered. "You know you can stay as long as you want."

Henna tossed her bags in the trunk; then the two women pulled out of the garage.

Because Henna was extremely spoiled, Monica normally gave in to whatever her friend wanted. This give-give relationship dated back to the girls' freshman year when Henna and Monica became roommates. Henna wanted the top bunk, and though Monica hated the bottom one, she gave in. If they saw two boys, Henna got first pick at which boy she liked. From that point, it was second nature. Most people gave in to Henna.

It was something about her. She had this special aura that made people want to surrender. Henna was used to this behavior; so when she didn't get it, she figured it had to be something wrong with the other person. There surely couldn't be anything wrong with her. She was Henna James. And, though she was spoiled and a little selfish, Henna was extremely kindhearted, and for her friends, she'd do anything. Henna was complicated, and guarded before the career, and it tripled afterward, but once anyone got a glimpse at her true nature, they'd fall in love. Monica was just one of her many victims.

They stopped by the market to grab a few grocery items, and Henna insisted that she cook Monica's dinner that evening. Cooking was the only domestic bone in Henna's little body. She hated cleaning, washing clothes, and any other household chore. In the kitchen, though, she was a whiz. It relaxed her. So Henna breezed through the aisles, grabbing asparagus, lemons, Cornish hens, sweet potatoes, and several spices. Monica just tagged behind, picking up a couple of toiletries. She and Julian ate out nearly every day, and when she ate at home, he usually cooked. Monica was looking forward to Henna's meal, and Henna was excited about having someone to cook for.

As soon as they arrived home, Henna changed into her sweats and started preparing. However, Monica didn't have a single good knife in the raggedy bunch that sat atop her counter. Henna started chopping the asparagus, but the worn-down knives couldn't make a clean cut.

"How am I supposed to make a meal in a kitchen filled with butter knives!" Henna yelled.

Monica rushed to her side and began pulling knives from everywhere, but they were all dull.

"I will get them sharpened tomorrow," Monica claimed.

"Sharpened? Honey, you need new knives. These are cheap," Henna said while taking several and tossing them in an empty box sitting by the trash.

"No," Monica yelped as she quickly retrieved her inexpensive cutlery. "Don't throw them away."

"You don't use them," Henna retorted.

"So. They're mine," Monica responded with a child-like temperament.

Henna looked at her veggies sprawled on top of the counter and sighed. "I will do the best I can."

"Just cook," Monica said with slight laughter.

Henna walked toward the refrigerator and noticed several pictures hung by magnets on the door. At this time Monica was sifting through her mail on the counter.

"Who's this?" Henna asked, pointing to a picture of a young woman.

"That's Nia. She's like my little sister."

Monica continued looking at the five pictures and counted three with Monica and an older gentleman. Henna removed one of the pictures and stared at it for a moment.

"Mo!" she called out. "Did your dad grow a beard? He looks different."

"What?" Monica replied, turning to see what Henna was talking about. She saw the picture in Henna's hand and made a peculiar face.

"Is this your dad?" Henna asked, wrinkling up her face.

"No!" Monica snapped. "That's Julian," she said, snatching the picture from Henna's hand.

Henna immediately burst into laughter, and attempted to seize the picture from Monica's hand. She wasn't quick enough, though, as Monica rapidly moved the photo to and fro.

"Stop laughing," Monica pleaded.

"Okay, okay, just let me see it again. All this time you talked about Julian, you never said he was a more mature man."

"That's because you judge. Like you're doing right now."

Slowly Monica placed the picture in Henna's palm, while Henna held her lips together very tightly to hold in the giggles. But Monica could see the expression about to burst through, so she seized the picture once more.

"He's very sexy in person!" Monica shouted.

"I'm sure he is," Henna answered with sarcasm, "in a nursing-home type of way."

Monica didn't find it funny. At first, she thought she could handle the age difference, but when everyone kept mistaking him for her father, it became embarrassing. Her skin hadn't thickened enough to handle insensitive age comments, but Henna had no idea. Therefore, after a few glares, Monica delivered a punch just as bitter. "At least I have a man."

Henna stopped laughing, and frowned. "That's mean."

"Well, you're being mean. I really like him. I can't help that I fell for an older man."

Henna apologized and asked to see the picture again. She looked at Julian's picture and smiled. "Does he treat you well?"

"Very well," Monica replied.

"Then I look forward to meeting him. I'm sorry I joked about it." Henna kept looking at the picture, and then she made an interesting face, which wrinkled her nose as though she was holding back a sneeze. "I don't want you to get mad, but do all his parts work?"

Monica, shocked at Henna's candor, huffed and took the picture away from Henna's grasp. Monica placed the photo to her chest and held it like a long-lost love letter. "Of course they work!" she exclaimed.

"I was just wondering, 'cause—"

"No more talk about Julian. When you meet him, you will see."

"Okay," Henna said, tossing up her hands to admit defeat. "I'll leave it alone."

Monica walked back to the fridge and placed her picture back on the stainless-steel door. She glanced at Henna, who was seasoning her Cornish hens. "This is the problem with women today. They feel like men are supposed to have money, nice cars, great careers, great personalities, and still look like an Armani fashion model. Julian is a great catch."

"I thought there was to be no more talk about Julian," Henna mocked. "If you like him, I love him. Like you said, at least you have a man."

"I didn't mean it that way," Monica said as she consoled Henna with a soft shoulder rub.

"It's okay. I'm over it."

"You sure?" questioned Monica.

"Yes," Henna said as she snapped around and pointed the knife in the air. "I don't want to be with anyone who doesn't want to be with me. So I say good riddance."

Monica dodged the swerving knife as Henna talked. "Watch that knife."

"Please, I could stab myself in the eye with this knife and still finish dinner. Buy some new cutlery."

Henna rinsed her hands and went to her purse for a cigarette break. She opened the patio door, went outside, and smoked. As Monica watched her waif friend, she knew that she was still hurting, but there was nothing she could say. Henna never admitted to any hurt, because she wanted people to think she was immune to those types of emotions. She was really good at it too. Most of the time, she was excellent at keeping her feelings at bay. But occasionally there were slipups, as Henna called them. If she got caught truly caring about a man, she considered it an accident, like a bear trap she fell in, and desperately needed to claw her way out. Ahmad was her biggest "slipup" to date.

When Henna walked back in, Monica commented again on her weight. "You're too thin."

"I'm an entertainer—there is no such thing as too thin," Henna said, twirling around the kitchen.

"I'm serious."

"I eat. All of the time," Henna claimed.

"Are you stressed?"

"Nope."

"Are you on a diet?" Monica asked.

"Nope."

"Are you happy?"

"Nope," Henna replied again, as she kept her focus on preparing the sweet potatoes. There was silence for an entire minute, but she could feel Monica staring, so she turned around. Monica's look of concern compelled Henna to defend herself.

"Happy is an emotion. You can't expect to be happy all of the time," added Henna, but Monica's expression remained the same. Henna suddenly put on a wide grin, exposing all of her perfectly aligned pearly whites.

"Stop being silly. I'm serious," Monica whined.

Henna wiped her hands on her apron and took a seat at the bar. "I'm in a weird place with my music. The sales didn't go as well as the label would have liked, so they want me to change my style. Perhaps, Ahmad and I weren't meant to be together, but he was like a rock that I could lean on, and he's no longer there. And I'm getting older. I can't get over with my looks, like I used to."

"You're only thirty-four."

"In an industry filled with teens."

"But they don't have your wisdom," Monica added.

"Wisdom doesn't sell records, booty does. And I don't have too much of that either," Henna answered as she stood and turned around to show off her tush. Monica chuckled but had no reply.

"So that's it. I sense there's more," Monica said.

"More like what?"

"More like more. It's like I look into your eyes, when you actually make eye contact, and there's something wrong."

Henna lowered her head. "I'm just searching for something. I don't know what it is, but when I find it, I will let you know."

"Something like what?"

"You and these damn questions. Something like me. I used to smile, I used to laugh, I used to crack jokes, and I used to love making music. I miss me. Now I don't want to talk about it anymore. Ya dig?" Henna glanced at the fridge and redirected the conversation. "So tell me about Julian. How long has it been? Have you two said the 'L word' yet? Catch me up."

"Yes, we have, and it's been about six months. He's a pastry chef, but he can cook just about anything."

"How old is he?"

Monica frowned.

"I just want to know," insisted Henna.

"He's fifty-four."

"Not bad."

"And he has a second home in Paris."

"Even better," Henna said, smiling. "Does he have a grandson or someone he could hook me up with?"

Monica playfully slapped Henna with the roll of paper towels. "Get over there and cook my dinner. Earn your keep, wiseass."

Close to ten that evening, the girls were attempting to get dressed to go to Cat's Corner, a local lounge that was always buzzing with visiting celebrities. Monica was in her jeans and a sexy fuchsia blouse that wrapped around her waist. Henna was still walking around in her gray cotton Old Navy underwear. Her clothing was spread across the bed, and hanging on the corner of the dresser. Monica, twirling her car keys, walked in the room, thinking Henna was dressed and ready to go.

"What are you doing?"

Henna turned around with tears in her eyes.

"What happened?" Monica asked with concern.

Henna could barely form a sentence. She sounded like a hurt infant. "I don't look right in anything. All I have is stage clothes and sweats. I don't have anything to wear out."

Monica swept through the room, picking up random textiles and placing tops to bottoms. "This is cute. This is nice too," Monica said, hoping to convince her friend. Then suddenly Monica noticed that every piece of Henna's clothing was either black or very dark gray. "This is why you are unhappy. You have no color in your life."

"I look good in black."

"If that's the case, then why are you in here crying like somebody stole your baby doll?"

Still whining, Henna replied, "'Cause I don't look good in any of these black clothes." She held up a pair of skinny jeans. "I'm too skinny for skinny jeans, I look funny. I'm too old for these short skirts. I'm too—"

Monica interrupted her. "Stop it right now! I am not having this pity party with you. You are Henna James! Have you forgotten? You could walk in Cat's Corner wearing a futon cover and the people would applaud. Put these jeans on." Monica tossed Henna a pair of denims. "Put this T-shirt on, and let's go. The more casual you are, the more comfortable you will feel."

Henna slowly put on her jeans. She looked at herself in the mirror, and then she turned to look at her butt. "At least my little butt looks good," remarked Henna.

"Those cigarettes are going to kill you, so it won't make much difference unless they bury you facedown. . . ."

"Which could be interesting," Henna added with a chuckle.

Monica joined in the merriment, and soon Henna was dressed. Monica had no idea that her friend was this fragile. She wasn't used to this Henna, who was apparently on an emotional roller coaster; it seemed that Henna wasn't used to this behavior either. As soon as they got in the car, she apologized.

"I don't know what came over me. I tried on one outfit and it just didn't seem sexy or cute, and it went downhill from there."

"Don't apologize. We all have those moments," Monica responded, and they drove to the lounge.

Seconds after they walked in the door, people started buzzing about Henna's arrival. At first, it was obvious stares, and then whispers. Eventually people walked up to Monica and talked until they were finally introduced. Henna and Monica found a seat in a semidark, cozy corner near the far right side of the stage. Monica soon went to the bar and returned minutes later with two peach martinis.

"Do you think I can smoke in here?" asked Henna.

"No."

"Are you just saying that, or do you know for sure?" Henna questioned.

Just then, the owner of Cat's Corner walked up to the table. Catherine Mills was an old-disco singer and retired Broadway diva who left the glitz and glamour of

New York, to settle down in the South with a man and have three beautiful girls. Once in Atlanta, she opened a jazz lounge, which became the hottest spot to hang at in the 1980s. After the '96 Olympics, she opened Cat's Corner. It was more upscale than the first lounge, and it had been operating for over a decade. Cat was somewhat of a legend and she and Henna had previous run-ins at various music events.

"Well, well, who do we have here?"

"Hi, Cat," said Henna. She stood up and gave Cat a hug, and then she quickly stated, "I'm not singing tonight."

"Damn, I had my spiel ready and everything. You sure?"

"I just got off tour," Henna stated.

"Oh well, honey, I understand. I slept for weeks every time I got off the road."

"See . . ." added Henna as she eyed Monica.

"But that's no excuse for sneaking into town and not coming by to perform," countered Cat.

"I promise to perform before I leave. I will be here for at least a week."

Henna and Cat embraced again, and moments later, the host for the evening was introducing the main act for the night. After two more drinks, Henna actually began enjoying herself. She and Monica laughed, talked about people, and caught up on everything that had happened in the last year.

At the end of the evening, while Henna and Monica were walking to the car, Henna noticed she had three missed phone calls. She didn't recognize the number, and they didn't leave a message, so she didn't bother returning the call. However, as soon as they started en route to the house, her phone rang again. This time she answered it. It was Ahmad. Henna held the phone away from her ear for a few seconds as she contemplated hanging up, but then she put it back to her ear and listened.

"I know you don't want to hear from me, but I had to call you."

"Why? What do you want now?" she asked with definite disgust.

During the entire phone call, Monica was calling him names in the background. She even tried to snatch the cellular from Henna a few times, but Henna kept forcefully pointing to the steering wheel. After a few rambling remarks, Henna cut the conversation short.

"I have to go."

Henna hung up the phone and turned it off. Although Monica commented and questioned Henna repeatedly the remainder of the ride, she was silent. Monica, however, was persistent, and when they walked in the house, she cornered Henna and demanded she say something.

"Ahmad is getting married," Henna said with a pleasant yet empty smile.

"The bastard, he said he would never get married," Monica stated.

"No, it's okay. This is actually good, because now I don't have to wonder if we are going to get back together."

"You would have gotten back with him?"

"Probably not, but you never know. People do crazy things in lonely times." Henna grabbed a glass from the cabinet as Monica intently followed her every move. "Honestly, this is a good thing." Henna filled her glass with crushed ice and then with water. She stood against the steel door and drank. Monica stared as though her friend could have a mental breakdown at any moment. Henna continued to smile and drink as though nothing had happened. Then both women quickly turned their heads as they heard keys coming in the front door.

"Hello . . ." the voice called from the other room.

Monica's face lit up as she rushed from the kitchen. Henna followed. Julian shut the front door and met Monica halfway. She eagerly greeted him with a kiss.

"Babe, this is Henna. Henna, this is Julian."

Julian extended his arms and Henna gave him a quick embrace. As she pulled away, she took in a deep breath.

"You smell good." She sniffed again. "Good . . . like pecan pie."

Julian laughed. "I baked three today," he said.

"Please tell me you have some with you."

"They were orders."

"Damn it!" Henna yelled.

Julian and Monica both laughed, and he promised to get her a pie before she left town. They all settled into the kitchen and talked for the next two hours. By the time Henna retired upstairs, it was after 3:00 A.M. However, she wasn't tired. Instead of resting, she pulled out her writing journal and began working on some music. She hummed a few bars, and just as she began hearing lyrics, Monica popped her head in the door.

"He's cute, isn't he?" Monica whispered.

Henna giggled and answered, "In a mature way."

"Well, that's an upgrade from a nursing-home way," said Monica.

"As long as you're happy."

"He's very good to me."

"Again, as long as you're happy," Henna restated.

Monica popped back out, and Henna continued working for another hour. She didn't make much progress with the lyrics, but she came up with a couple of good melodies before she got into bed.

Henna glanced at her cell phone and turned it back on. The screen read four missed calls, all from Ahmad.

"Why do I want to talk to him?" she asked herself aloud. Henna picked up the phone and started dialing his number. Before the line connected, she hit the off button and gently placed the phone on the pillow beside her head.

"It's all good. It's all good," Henna kept whispering. She stared at the phone until her eyelids could no longer stay open. Henna prayed that her last words would actually be true by sunrise.

Chapter 4

"Hello Stranger" (Barbara Lewis, 1963)

At exactly three minutes after eight the next morning, Henna's eyes popped open. She'd only had a few hours' sleep, but for some reason she was wide awake, and so she tossed on her robe and went downstairs for coffee. Monica was already up and preparing grits and eggs in the kitchen.

"Good morning, sleepyhead," greeted Monica.

"Why are you up so early? It's Sunday."

"I know. I'm going to church."

"Why?" Henna asked.

Monica turned and gave a look of disbelief. "You're kidding, right?"

Henna shook her head.

"You smoke, you drink, you hang out all times of the night, and you don't go to church. You've become a regular rock star, haven't you?" Monica joked.

Henna formed the iconic rock-star hand symbol, with her pinkie and pointer extended, threw her hands in the air, and jutted out her tongue as though she were in the front row of a 1980s KISS concert. She let out a huge laugh, then replied, "Hold up. You drink and hang out. In fact, I was only hanging out because of you."

"But I go to church to repent for all of my bad behavior. What do you do?" Monica asked.

Henna stood there for a minute and seriously contemplated her response. Finally she answered, smiling
widely. "I volunteer, teaching music classes at the Boys
and Girls Club. God loves the children, and therefore
He will love me."

Monica chuckled and continued breakfast. "You want
some?" she asked.

Henna shook her head, opened the refrigerator, and
removed a grapefruit. "I'll just eat this. Where's Sweet
J?"

"He had a wedding to cater today."

Henna sat down, poured sugar over her grapefruit
half, and scooped out individual slices. Monica joined
her, but they didn't speak much. It was almost as
though they'd caught up on the last few years overnight
and no longer had anything else to say. Monica invited
Henna to church, but she declined and went back upstairs after she ate her fruit.

About thirty minutes after Monica left, Henna pulled
out her digital recorder and hummed the tunes she'd
created last night. She put on a long, flowing black skirt,
pulled her hair into a ponytail, and walked out onto the
porch. The pollen was still affecting her a bit, so she took
an allergy pill and chased it with a bottle of Penta water.
Monica's home was located in historic Grant Park. It
was an older home that had been renovated years ago. It
had a huge wraparound porch, which Henna loved, and
to top it off, a large roped hammock hung from the top
of the porch. Porches weren't common in Brooklyn, and
stoops didn't count. So Henna was going to enjoy this
beautiful day and soak up the sunshine. It was a mild
seventy-five degrees, with a slight breeze, so she crawled
into the hammock, with her journal, iPod, and bottled
water, and then wrote a few lyrics. But before long,
Henna closed her book and her eyes, and simply rested.

About ten minutes into Henna's nap, a pickup truck pulled into the driveway. Craig, Monica's brother, who had left her hanging at the airport, hopped out and walked toward the house. Before he could get to the porch, he spotted Henna resting in the hammock. He tiptoed closer and peered at her face.

"I don't believe it," he whispered.

Henna must have felt his energy beaming in her direction, because her eyes flicked open, and she leaned up to take a better glance.

"The pecan pie–stealing asshole," she muttered before calling out, "What are you doing here?"

"What are you doing here?" he countered.

Neither of them gave an answer. Craig walked onto the porch. Henna kept her eyes on him, but she left her iPod earplugs in and her music on.

"I'm Monica's brother."

"Her half brother from California? I saw a picture of him once. He didn't look like you. He was skinny," Henna commented.

"He's been lifting weights." Craig posed for Henna. "Wanna take a new picture?"

She looked at him, rolled her eyes, and opened her journal. Craig stood over Henna and watched as she began to write. He was determined to make her talk to him, and she was determined to ignore him until he went away. Apparently, he was more patient than she, and eventually she spoke.

"Do you mind?"

"Actually, I do," he said. "You know, I thought you looked familiar the other day, but I wasn't sure, since you were wearing your big superstar shades." Henna continued to ignore him until he formally introduced himself. "I'm Craig. Nice to see you," he said while offering a handshake. Henna looked at his hand and then cut her eyes in his direction. "This is when you're supposed to say, 'I'm Hannah.'"

"You know who I am already, and it's Henna, like the dye. Not Hannah, like Montana"

"That's what I said."

"No, you didn't."

"Fine, Henna, like the dye. Are you enjoying your day?" Craig changed his tone from irritation to flirtation, but Henna simply smirked and kept writing. After a few more seconds of being ignored, Craig stopped trying.

"Well, I'm going into the house to get some of my things I left here."

Henna didn't bother looking up as he walked into the house. Minutes later, he came out, carrying two large boxes. By the time he'd reached the truck and placed both boxes in, he had worked up a sweat. He removed his T-shirt and placed it in the front seat. Underneath the shirt he wore a fitted white tank. This time as he passed by, she couldn't help but notice Craig's glistening skin. She peered from the top of her journal and watched him walk into the house, but she was careful not to turn or make any movement. She surely didn't want him to notice her interest. Craig came out once more, holding another box by its brim, which caused his bicep to bulge slightly. With quick, clever glances, Henna followed his every step.

She whispered, "Looks like somebody's all grown up."

When Craig turned his body in her direction, she quickly glanced down at her journal pages. But it was obvious that she was a bit flustered. He noticed, and it was just enough incentive for him to approach her again, once his work was done.

Craig placed his last box in the truck and then took a seat parallel to the top step of the porch. He leaned his back against the column and stretched his feet across the stair, while sipping from a bottle of water he'd retrieved from his pickup. With his body facing Henna, he was in position and determined that this was going to be his placement until she made notice of him and started a conversation. Unfortunately for Henna, Craig had all day. But it only took a matter of minutes before she closed her book and gave in to his quiet tantrum.

"Is there something else you need?" she asked.

"Nah, just enjoying the view."

Henna looked to her right, the same direction as Craig faced, but there was nothing but rows of houses. She shrugged her shoulders, suggesting that there was nothing to look at. He was quick to reply.

"I'm not talking about the view on the street."

Henna noticed his flirting and began fumbling with her iPod.

"Uncomfortable with silence?"

"No, uncomfortable with your obvious and tacky flirting."

"Please, you were all over me yesterday," said Craig.

"That was only to get the pie, nothing more."

Henna ignored him and scrolled through her music play list.

Her callous attitude finally bothered Craig. He rose from the steps and mumbled a remark under his breath, but just loud enough for her to hear.

"I swear, Monica and her bougie-ass friends."

"Excuse me?"

"You heard me. I'm trying to be nice, but you're so stuck-up, you wouldn't recognize a nice guy if he fell in your lap."

Now, he finally had Henna going. She sat up in the hammock and spoke forcefully. "Nice? You took the last piece of pecan pie."

"I asked if you wanted to share. But your greedy ass wanted the whole thing."

"And if you were a gentleman, you would have given it to me."

"If I were a fool? Is that what you said?"

"I'm an all-or-nothing type of woman."

"And that's why you got nothing," he responded.

"And that's why your pie fell on the floor," she spoke childishly. Henna placed her earbuds back into her ears, put her iPod to her side, closed her eyes, and listened. Craig stood there for a few seconds and then removed her left earplug. Henna moved her head away.

"What are you doing?" she asked, annoyed.

"Door number one, or door number two?"

Henna gave him a puzzled look and then replied, "How old are you? Twelve?"

Craig smirked. "Actually, I'm twenty-four. Now, again, door number one or door number two?"

After a few grumbles, and a couple of sighs, Henna answered, "Door number one."

Craig gave a shifty smile and spoke. "And behind door number one . . ." He squirted his water bottle in her face, spewing cool water on her warm skin. Henna was pissed. Craig took off running toward his truck as she fumbled, trying to rise from the hammock. She wiped the water from her face.

"You're such an asshole!" Henna screamed.

"That's what you get for knocking my pie on the floor," he yelled while opening the door of his F-150.

Henna was still twisted in the hammock as he pulled off. Her fuming looks followed him down the street. But there was nothing she could do, except wring the excess water from her shirt, go inside, and change.

She switched into a pair of sweatpants and another tank top. Henna hated juvenile antics; she didn't find them cute or charming. Yet, she kept reminiscing about Craig carrying those boxes to the car. He was incredibly sexy, but very egotistical. The fact that he'd just ruined her afternoon rest made her angry, but the more heated she became, the more she was turned on. He was twenty-four, and immature, but he had a body and a face that could stop traffic. He was not the type of guy a thirty-four-year-old woman would enter a relationship with, but he was perfect for a fling.

Henna went into the kitchen and pulled out a couple of steaks. She tenderized and seasoned them. By the time she was actually ready to place the meat in the oven, she heard keys in the front door. From the kitchen Henna began yelling. "You will never believe what happened today!"

"What happened?" asked Craig, who completely threw Henna off guard.

"I thought you were Monica. What are you doing back here?" she said, meeting him in the foyer.

"I left one more thing in the attic, and I wanted to apologize," he said.

"So you just walk into Monica's house all of the time without knocking?" Henna asked, returning to the kitchen.

Following her, Craig replied, "I used to live here, so yes. Sorry if I shocked you." Craig continued to linger around the kitchen. His presence was making her nervous, and he felt it. Craig wasn't sure if it was sexual tension or dislike, but he planned to find out. He walked over and stood by her shoulder as she peeled a potato.

"You know you shouldn't really peel a potato like that," he said, gently removing the oval tuber from her hand.

"If your sister had a decent knife in here, I wouldn't have a problem."

Craig pulled a pocketknife from his jeans and began peeling the skin from the potato.

"You always carry knives around with you?" Henna asked.

"Sometimes, but lately I've been doing some construction, so it comes in handy."

Henna watched until he was done. Her angst was turning to interest, and she was trying hard not to show it, but Craig was onto her. He started his quest by moving into her personal space and circling her body.

"What do you think about me?" he inquired.

"I don't even know you," she said while boiling water for her potatoes.

Craig moved in closer. "I don't know you either, but I have thoughts about you. You're cautious, arrogant, but extremely passionate."

Henna stopped messing with the potatoes and posted against the counter. "Well, as a matter of fact, I have thoughts about you too. You're overconfident, stingy, and your gallantry needs work."

Craig chuckled. "Gallantry?" Her wording amused him.

"Do you even know what that means?" Henna asked, with a smug expression.

"Actually, I don't," he admitted.

"It means good manners . . . chivalry."

"So my chivalry needs work, huh? Well, my words were supposed to be taken as compliments. A little arrogance is sexy. And, lucky for you, sexy happens to be my weakness." Craig stood back, looked at her, and waited for her reply.

Henna gave none, but she did notice him waiting for something. So she finally asked, "What? You're waiting for some kind of answer to that tacky-ass compliment. You think I owe you some kind of praise or something?"

Henna sat at the counter and Craig stood on the opposite side of her. He was tired of making the first moves. He wanted to stay, but he wanted her to work for it. So he pretended to give up. "You know what? You're right. You don't know me." He turned to leave the kitchen, but Henna was completely intrigued by now. She couldn't let him go.

"Well, tell me about you then. This way I can justify my predetermined assessment."

Craig quietly repeated her last two words and sneered. He thought he had her right where he wanted, but in reality she was reeling him in.

"What is it you do?" Henna asked.

"I play guitar, toured with damn near everybody, and just came off tour about four months ago. I decided not to move back to California, but instead come here and buy a bar with my boy, Travis. Plus, growing up, my sister and I only spent summers together, and I thought it would be cool if we could spend more time with each other."

"I just got off tour too. Where did you go?" Henna was now giving him direct eye contact. Oddly, it came natural, where normally it was something she had to think about. She was bold and forward, and now it was Craig feeling somewhat reticent.

"All over Europe," answered Craig.

"What's your favorite city in Europe?" she asked.

Craig paused, thought for a moment, and then responded, "Prague."

Henna began smiling. "I thought you'd say something predictable, like Rome or London. Actually, I love Prague. You like the castles?"

"The beer," Craig said quickly, which made Henna laugh.

"Ah, she finally laughs," he said.

The sexual tension was broken, and now it was just pure, unadulterated attraction.

"So . . . your bar, is it open?" Henna asked.

"No, Travis and I are still renovating. But I'm excited about it. I'm there seven days a week, day and night, just trying to make sure everything is right, you know."

"When do you rest?" Henna asked as she unfolded her arms, which Craig saw as his opening. He moved to the same side of the counter to reply.

"When you're raising a baby, there's no time for rest."

Henna saw his approach, and she held her territory. She didn't back away but welcomed his advance. "I don't know anything about raising a baby," she answered.

"Well, my baby's getting older. Soon she'll be able to run without me watching over her. Who knows? Maybe I'll find a new baby to care for." Craig slightly grazed against Henna's arm and gave her a wink.

She played along. By now, she knew they'd be sleeping together. It was only a matter of time, and who would make the actual first move. But she couldn't be baited that easily.

"I don't like people who speak in metaphors."

"Really? You're a songwriter. I would think you'd love that."

"Well, you would think wrong."

"My bad."

Henna felt him backing off, so she had to keep the banter going.

"You think it's cute to say whatever is on your mind?" she asked.

"I do. Why beat around the bush when you can just get inside it." Henna simply shook her head and checked on her potatoes. Maybe he was going to be more than she bargained for. She wanted to be in control of this little fling, and Craig was going to be difficult to manage.

"You should wear your hair down." Craig followed her to the stove and tugged on her ponytail.

"My hair is fine." Henna nervously slicked back the edges with her hand.

"I'm only saying, if you wear your hair down, it would be sexy."

Henna faced Craig, pulled her ponytail down, and shook her head. Her long black hair fell perfectly in place. "Better?" she asked.

Craig and Henna were so close, their noses nearly touched. Both their hearts were pounding fast.

"You feel that?" Craig questioned, referring to the intensity in the air.

In the middle of exhaling, Henna replied, "Definitely." Craig continued to look into Henna's eyes, while 'kiss me' rang in her head. She just couldn't say those words aloud. However, there was no need, for Craig was obviously a student of telepathy. He leaned forward and softly placed his lips to hers. It was a short but fiery kiss. It wasn't open-mouthed, but a seductive pucker. Henna was the first to pull away. She leaned over and turned the oven off.

"You lose your appetite?" Craig inquired.

"No, I just don't want the steaks to burn while . . ." Henna never finished the sentence. She looked back at the stove and made sure it was off; then she walked to the door frame of the kitchen.

"While what?" Craig asked, playing dumb.

Henna glanced at him over her shoulder but didn't answer with words. She only gave a tiny, flirtatious smile, turned back around, and slowly walked out of the kitchen and sauntered upstairs. Henna was exerting her womanhood, and Craig was putty in her hands.

However, once the bedroom door closed, the tables instantly turned. Craig gained full power. It was a matter of seconds before he had ripped off Henna's blouse and was removing her bra. Henna, normally a control fanatic, let him have his way. He tossed her down on the bed and quickly removed his pants. Henna slid off her sweats, and the temperature in the room instantly went up ten degrees. Craig reached down on the floor and pulled a condom from his pocket.

"Condoms and pocket knives, wow, what else you got in those pants?"

Craig grinned as he knew he was about to answer her question. The sex was hot-blooded, sensual, and purely lustful; yet they didn't kiss one time. Afterward, Craig and Henna lay in bed, covered from head to toe in salty sweat. Craig let out a faint "Wow."

Henna turned to him and grinned. "Yeah, wow."

Yet, she quickly came to her senses. As though the last hour had been some sort of out-of-body experience, she sat up in the bed and looked at Craig. "What just happened?"

Craig laughed and gave her a peculiar stare.

"I mean, I know what happened, but what I'm saying is, I'm not trying to be with you or anything like that. You know that, right?"

Craig went for the dramatic approach. He inhaled and held his hand to his heart. "You mean you were just using me?"

Henna laughed. "Don't even try it. You know what this was, and it was oh, so good. But I'm going back to New York next week, and I want us to be clear."

"I enjoyed my afternoon, and I'm very clear. I won't be sweating you, I promise. I don't have time for someone like you in my life, anyway."

"Someone like me? What does that mean?" asked Henna.

"I know how you singers are. You toy with men's emotions, have us all wrapped up in your song—"

"Musicians do that," Henna interrupted. "Maybe I don't have time for someone like you?"

"Well, let's just say we don't have time for each other. But"—Craig paused and glanced at Henna's bare body, partially wrapped in sheets—"I do have more time today." He leaned over, grabbed her hand, and kissed her wrist.

Henna giggled like a pubescent girl. "We better get dressed before—"

"Oh shit, I think that's Monica pulling up."

Henna ran to the bathroom and Craig jumped up and got dressed. He met Monica downstairs in the foyer.

"What are you doing here?" she asked.

"I came to get the rest of my things."

"Where's Henna?"

"Upstairs."

Monica went into her room to change clothing. Craig went into the kitchen and poured himself a cold glass of water. Henna came down and, from the door of the kitchen, watched him drink. He slowly turned and smiled at her.

"This is between us."

"Most definitely," he agreed.

Henna walked in and checked her food. Craig looked at Henna's legs. "You have very nice legs. You ever danced?"

Henna was especially proud of her legs. She often thought they were her nicest attribute.

"I used to do dance when I was younger," Henna said casually.

"Ballet?"

"Ballroom stuff, tango, things like that," she replied.

"Oh yeah? I tango."

Henna doubted his every word, and her expression showed just that. She gave him a look of disbelief.

"What? You think because I am a brother, I can't tango. We should go dancing sometime. Oh, that's right. You're leaving next week. Well, you still have very nice legs."

Henna gave a tiny smile.

Craig seemed as though he was waiting for her to say something. "You don't have anything to say? No thank-you? No returned compliment?"

Henna paused for a minute and then responded, "You have nice taste in women's legs."

"Okay, okay, I give up," Craig said while laughing.

Henna was fatigued. She hadn't had wild sex like that in over a year. She could hardly stand. Still, she had this stupid grin on her face. It was the orgasmic glow, which she didn't want Craig to recognize.

Monica marched into the kitchen all smiles. "You should have been at service this morning. The Word was right on time."

"Remember the pecan pie asshole? Well, there he is," Henna said, motioning to Craig.

"Why didn't you say that when you first saw him? You've met Craig before. Our sophomore year, he helped me move in."

"We were nineteen. That was fifteen years ago. And how old was he then?"

"Nine," Craig blurted out.

"Exactly," Henna said, and then it hit her. "You were nine? Wow, you were a child."

"I'm grown now, that's all that matters," he said, with an explicit stare.

Henna quickly turned the other way. "I'm cooking steak."

"Oh, I just came home to change. I'm going to dinner with Julian. You guys should join us."

"I have to head to the bar," Craig replied.

"And I want to stay in," added Henna.

"Fine with me." Monica went into another room.

Craig moved toward Henna and whispered in her ear, "I enjoyed you."

Henna returned the whisper with an even softer murmur. "I'm sure you did."

Craig moved away and grinned. "Arrogant to the end."

"You said it was sexy," she said softly.

Craig looked Henna up and down and nodded. "Indeed." He exited the kitchen, and left the house.

Henna exhaled deeply and gave her body a tiny shiver and gyration, to shake off Craig's essence. She then stuck the potatoes with a fork to check their tenderness.

Monica came back into the kitchen. "Where's Craig?" she asked.

"He left."

Monica waltzed over to the stove and poked Monica in the side. "Don't tell me you didn't see it."

"See what?" asked Henna.

"My brother has a little crush on you."

Henna turned toward Monica and made an awkward expression. "Please. I would hurt that child."

"Oh, I'm not saying you should get with him. In fact, you should stay far away from him. Craig is not what you need in your life right now."

"Tell me about it," Henna mumbled.

"What did you say?" asked Monica.

"I said, um . . . I said, he's a man, and I want to stay clear of them for a while."

"What about your fling?" Monica asked.

"Girl, you know I was just talking. Ahmad started as a fling, and you see where that got me."

Monica walked toward the door while talking. "You sure you want to stay in? You've been here all day, I know it's been boring."

Henna placed a smile on her face. "Actually, today was refreshing. Trust me, I'm good."

Monica smiled and left. Henna continued with dinner and then chilled the rest of the evening. She watched television, played around with some music, and went to bed, feeling empowered and inspired. Can great sex make you feel this way? she thought.

"Or is it more?" she uttered.

Either way, she slept like a baby. When she awoke and went to the bathroom first thing that morning, Henna looked in the mirror.

"It's still there," she chuckled, referring to her stupid grin. She pulled down her panties and sat on the toilet. "A real good pee should get him completely out of my system." Henna nodded and smiled to herself, as if her theory made sense; then she sat on the toilet an additional five seconds, for good measure. It was bound to be an interesting week.

CHAPTER 5

"It's Gonna Work Out Fine"
(Ike and Tina Turner, 1961)

When Monica got off work on Monday, she once again had dinner plans. This time it was with Mick. But she was determined to get Henna out of the house.

"You have to get dressed and go with me to dinner tonight," she told Henna as soon as she walked in the door.

"You and Julian?"

"No, Mick."

"Who?" Henna asked.

"I'm applying for a loan, and Mick is my financial consultant."

"You need some money? I can give you a loan," commented Henna.

"No. I'm getting a loan to help Craig with his club."

"Oh, in that case you're on your own. So what am I supposed to do with the other turkey leg?"

"Put it up until tomorrow," Monica stated. "Mick has some nice friends. We could all go out afterward—"

Henna quickly interrupted her friend. "No hookups."

"Well, I have this other friend. He's really nice, Henna. He works with me. His name is Alphonzo. He's attractive, smart, and just an all-around good guy. He could even be your fling."

"I don't want the fling anymore, and I don't want an all-around good guy. I don't want a guy at all."

"Fine, just sit around here and mope," Monica fussed.

Henna headed to the bathroom, and as she passed by, she muttered, "I'm not moping. I'm chilling."

Monica went upstairs then and took a catnap for a couple of hours, while Henna put on her leggings and sneakers and took a run around the neighborhood. When she returned, she took a shower and stretched across the bed. Henna dozed off for thirty minutes, but then Monica woke her up to come downstairs and meet Alphonzo. Monica inadvertently left out that Alphonzo would be coming over to bring her some paperwork. Henna bucked at first, but Monica reminded her that it was her home, and she didn't mind bringing Alphonzo upstairs to see her.

"You wouldn't dare bring him upstairs."

"No, but I already told him that you were here," she added. "So go and get yourself together."

After a few more curse words, Henna got up and walked into the bathroom to freshen up. Five minutes later, she walked downstairs to greet Alphonzo. He stood five feet ten inches, and had the physique of a football player. He was cute, but that didn't matter, because Henna was over men. Now that she'd had her fling fix, the thought of dating made her stomach hurt. Yet, Monica wasn't hearing it. As soon as Henna graced the living room with her presence, Monica went to work.

"So, Henna, Alphonzo hasn't had dinner, so I invited him out with Mick and me."

Henna knew what she was up to. "I thought you were meeting about finances. Isn't that personal?"

"We've already talked about the personal part. We are discussing the renovations and how the moneys will be spent."

Alphonzo joined in. "Henna, would you join us?"

"I already cooked," she quickly replied.

"But we can have that tomorrow," Monica retorted in the same hasty manner.

Though Henna was losing the battle, she kept going. "I'm not dressed. Maybe next time."

"We can wait. Go ahead and put something on. I will help," Monica rebutted. She pulled Henna upstairs as they both quietly fussed.

"Why are you being funny?" Monica argued.

"'Cause I don't want to be bothered," Henna countered.

"Well, too bad. If you didn't want to be bothered, then you should have stayed in New York."

"Maybe I should have," said Henna.

Monica stopped walking. "You don't mean that, do you?"

Henna tightly pressed her lips together and shook her head. "Of course not. I'm just not in the mood for any man contact."

"I think interaction with men is just what you need. You are the queen of bounce back. Now get your ass in there, Tigger, and get to bouncing."

Monica popped Henna on her bottom and pushed her into the bedroom. Henna threw on a black wrap-around dress. She liked to wear heels, but since Henna was five foot eight, and didn't want to be taller than Alphonzo, she threw on a pair of flats. Monica also tried to persuade Henna to ride with him to the restaurant, but she realized she was pushing it when Henna threatened to go back into the house.

Henna was still enjoying the afterthought of Craig and wanted to share her sexual encounter with Monica, but she couldn't. Spending an evening with another man was just something she didn't want to do. She had experienced her overdue release, and now all she wanted to do was relax. But Monica wasn't having it.

They arrived at TWO Urban Licks, where Mick was already waiting for them. Mick was six feet three inches tall, dark in complexion, and sported a bald head, with a five o'clock shadow. His skin was smooth, like a dark chocolate Dove Bar. His small eyes slightly slanted upward. He was definitely easy on the eyes. Monica introduced everyone and they went to their table. As they walked through the restaurant, Henna leaned over and whispered in Monica's ear, "Now I'm sure all of his parts work."

Monica giggled quietly and pushed Henna to keep walking ahead. The four ordered a bottle of wine, and conversation immediately erupted. Mick had been in finance for six years; before that, he worked for the New York Exchange. He moved to Atlanta because the stress from NYE was giving him high blood pressure.

Alphonzo was not a numbers man. He worked in the graphic design department of Monica's advertising firm. His specialty was corporate logos, banners, and signage. He was originally from Texas, and his roots were Mexican and African. His mother was from Guadalajara, and his father was from Kenya. Alphonzo had the innocent smile of a six-year-old, just happy to be home from school, and the more Henna looked at him, the more attractive he became. He had a regular upbringing, nothing exciting, and he seemed content to be working in corporate America. Normally, this would have bored Henna to tears, but after years of living on the edge with men who always had her dangling over a rocky cliff, this regular man standing on solid soil might be good. These thoughts led to quiet reflection most of the evening. Monica noticed, but let it go. She was simply happy that Henna had come out.

"So, Henna, I'm embarrassed to say that I've never purchased your music."

"It's cool. I have an eclectic, but loyal, fan base."

"Man, you've never heard her music?" commented Mick. "I love your stuff. If I'd known you were coming, I would have brought my CD for you to sign."

Henna smiled again and thanked him for the compliment.

"What kind of music do you sing?" asked Alphonzo. "I don't listen to much music."

"Yes, you do," commented Monica. "You love country music."

Henna perked up. "I like country music too. Blues is my favorite, but they're similar."

Alphonzo agreed and smiled. It was obvious that the music connection was a link that was going to open up further communication. He was attracted to Henna, and he let it be known by certain glances and grins throughout dinner. Monica's job was done; now she could concentrate on what she came for. She pulled some papers from her bag and showed them to Mick. The sketches detailed the club renovations. Attached was a line item list of things she would purchase with the loan. Now, loan officers normally could care less about budgetary expenditures and more about credit scores, but Mick was a specialist. He was there to make sure Monica got "the most bang for her buck."

As Henna noticed his intriguing interaction with Monica, she knew Mick was willing to take this saying to another level that had less to do with "banking" and more to do with "banging." Mick gave Monica the names of vendors who could possibly offer less expensive products, and when he was done, he ended up saving over $5,000 from her original budget. Henna also noticed how interested her friend was in Mick's every word. The table wasn't that big; yet she'd often lean over to hear him better. Plus, she was being very coy with his every response. Monica was surely flirting with him. Who could blame her? Mick had a presence that almost forced the body to react favorably. Henna took notes, but she would reserve her comments until the end of the night.

After the main course Henna had warmed up to make conversation, but the evening was almost over by then. Since none of the group wanted dessert, they wrapped up dinner and walked out. Henna felt bad about being so irritable. She decided if Alphonzo asked her out, she would go. She didn't really have an agenda while she was in Atlanta, and Monica was right: spending time with a man could be good. As they were waiting for the valet, Alphonzo asked Henna to a movie later that week. She obliged and they exchanged numbers. She gave him a hug as his car was being pulled around and he left. However, Mick was still lingering, although he hadn't valet parked his ride. He and Monica said their pleasant good-byes, which consisted of a handshake. The grasp, though, lasted a few seconds longer than a cordial grip.

When Monica hopped into the car, she immediately started gabbing about Alphonzo. Henna was quiet as she listened to Monica's nervous chatter.

"Why are you so edgy?"

"What?" Monica asked innocently.

"You heard me."

Monica ignored her question and kept chatting about Alphonzo, but when Henna said nothing, Monica changed her direction.

"If you don't like Alphonzo, I could hook you up with Mick. I know he's your type."

Finally Henna had her segue. "Why would I go out with a man whom you clearly like?" Monica gave her a look of bewilderment. "Don't even try it. You like him. It was all over your face."

"No, it wasn't."

"You couldn't see your face. I could."

Monica was quiet for a couple of blocks, and Henna let her remain silent so that her friend could ponder her actions from the evening. "I have Julian," Monica finally commented.

"Yes, you do, baby doll," Henna replied in a pacifying tone while tapping Monica's leg.

"Stop doing that," Monica said. But after that, the remainder of the car ride was quiet.

That evening when they returned home, Henna asked to see the sketches for Craig's club. Monica glowed when she spoke about her baby brother. He'd played professional guitar since he was eighteen, and the summer after graduation, he got a gig touring with the European group InkBlots. Craig had made good money, but he was young and pretty much lived right at his means, and ruined his credit. From that tour he came back to the states and did a few gigs with Mariah Carey's last project.

Henna didn't have the guts to tell Monica she'd already been briefed about Craig's history; she just let her ramble on. Yet, the more Monica bragged about him, the more she exposed. To Henna's ears Craig sounded like a child. Since Henna was an only child, she didn't understand sibling bonds. She felt Monica was enabling his irresponsible behavior. Monica insisted that he was becoming more mature, but Henna reminded her of the water bottle episode, and that was the end of the Craig conversation. Henna did like the idea of opening a bar, though. That was something she'd always considered doing, but she wouldn't dare try in New York, a city with too many clubs, bars, and lounges. She wanted her place to stand out, and it would take so much money to market a club in New York, she'd rather not be bothered.

Henna looked at the sketches again and smiled. "I applaud him for opening up a spot."

"Yeah, he's got great ideas. He just needs a little guidance."

"We all do," Henna added. "Thanks for making me go out tonight." Henna hugged Monica and went up to her room.

Monica prepared for her next day before going to bed. She was a preparation fanatic who ironed and laid everything out, days ahead. When she was going out of town, she'd pack sometimes two weeks in advance. The Weather Channel predicted overcast skies for the following day, so Monica placed her umbrella by her bedroom door, just for good measure.

Sure enough that next day was cloudy, which was the type of weather Henna loved. She wrote best on gloomy days. She'd often find a spot to squat for hours and do nothing but create. She had her regular venues in New York and had a few hangouts in designated boroughs, depending on the mood. However, she knew nothing about the atmospheric places to create in Atlanta, so she was excited about embarking on new territory. A creative space is essential to any artist, especially those individuals who leaned on the temperamental side. Henna didn't lean; she resided there. She anxiously tossed on a wife beater, an oversize Tshirt and leggings, and went downstairs to have eggs and toast. Monica had already left the house before eight, but she left a note on the refrigerator suggesting that they do lunch. Henna searched the phone books for a rental-car place, and within thirty minutes a nice young man from Enterprise was ringing the doorbell. Henna only booked a car for seven days, although she still hadn't purchased her return ticket, as of yet. With a map of the city in hand, Henna started on her quest. She passed a couple of coffee shops, but longed for something a little more original, something unique with lots of windows. She settled for a spot downtown called Octane. It was near Monica's office, and though it didn't have windows, it had a great atmosphere and served wine. The wine sealed the deal. Henna took out her laptop, opened up Reason, and stared at the program. She'd dabbled a bit with creating music on the computer, but she was still a novice who preferred writing notes to scale, sitting down with a group of musicians and simply hammering out the whole thing. It was more authentic to her. However, she was searching for a new sound; so she attempted to create by using new techniques. But after close to an hour of experimenting, Henna broke out the music sheets and began drawing half and quarter notes to a melody she desperately needed to liberate from within the walls of her head. Close to one, Alphonzo called and invited her to lunch, which she declined, but she made tentative plans with him that evening. Soon after that, Monica called to see what time Henna would be showing up at the office. She wrote down the directions to Monica's job and went to lunch.

Henna was especially gabby that day. She talked about new music, new imaging, and a basic new overhaul. Monica was pleasantly surprised.

"What's with the new burst of energy? Not that I'm complaining," she asked Henna.

"I was thinking that I could essentially reinvent myself, and create an entirely new fan base. I don't really know how to do that, but wouldn't it be cool?"

"I guess so, that is if you want new fans. What about your old fans?"

"That's the mystery. I can't go too new, that I completely lose the old, but I have to put a new spin to an old sound."

Monica listened intently, but Henna could tell that her mind was elsewhere.

"So, are you okay? You seem distracted," inquired Henna.

Monica gave a nod, a half-frown/half-smile combination, that made Henna convinced that all was not well. Henna remained quiet for a few seconds, and just when she had figured out her next words, Monica blurted out an odd question.

"You knew you wanted to marry Ahmad, right?"

Henna stuck her neck out, much like a chicken in midcluck, and raised her eyebrows. Monica continued, "I mean, what made you know he was the one?"

"He wasn't the one," stated Henna.

"We know that now, but there was a time when we didn't know. There was a time when you were so convinced that he was the one, that you converted me into thinking he was the one, even when I had my doubts."

Henna became slightly flustered. "Why are we talking about Ahmad? I am really having a good day. A good day without thinking about him."

Monica apologized, but it didn't stop her annoying conversation. "But really, when did you know? And was there something that made you know, a special moment?"

Henna grimaced and let out a couple of disgusting, grunting noises. Finally she answered. "I don't know if I ever really knew. Ahmad was comfortable. I just knew that my relationship with him was the closest I'd ever been to being happy, and maybe as close as I would ever be, so it seemed right. I didn't really have much to compare it to."

Monica studied her reply as if it were the highest-point question on a final exam. She even repeated parts of it as she pondered its true meaning, but Henna interrupted her deliberation.

"If you are wondering if Julian is the one, I can answer that for you. He's not."

Monica immediately took offense. "You don't know that."

"Babe, I may not be able to pick 'the one,' but I can definitely pick the ones who are not 'the one.'"

"You're a bitch."

"I'm bitter! I'm sorry. I shouldn't have said that."

Monica distorted her lips into a crinkly pucker and let out a disagreeable smirk. She stopped her questions just as lunch was arriving. The two ate most of the lunch in silence as they reflected over their past and failed attempts at securing happiness. Toward the end Monica began talking about Craig.

"You know Craig wants to record with you. I told him you weren't interested."

"Why would you tell him that?"

"You said that you wanted to take a break from music. I told him that you didn't want to be bothered and to leave you alone."

"Did you tell him I said that?" Henna quickly interjected. "I don't want him to think I'm being mean."

"No. But since when do you care if people think you're being mean?"

"I don't really, but he's your brother, and you're family, so he's like family."

"Oh, that's sweet. Well, Craig can be very persistent, so I was trying to spare you. I think it's more a crush than anything else, but I went ahead and texted you his number."

Henna nodded and brushed it off, as though she could care less, but as soon as they parted, she gave Craig a ring.

"So you wanted me to call you. What is it that you want?" she asked with a flirtatious tone.

"Henna James, you know exactly what I want." Just as Henna started to smile, Monica rushed back to the car and tapped on the window. It frightened Henna, and she dropped the phone.

Rolling down the window, she said, "You scared me."

"That means you were doing something you had no business. I forgot my scarf. It's in the seat."

Henna handed her the scarf and Monica trotted off. Henna quickly reached for the phone and told Craig she'd call him back. She drove back to her new writing spot, but as soon as she pulled into the parking lot, Craig called again.

"I told you I was going to call back," Monica stated.

"And I'm supposed to trust that," he said.

"What do you want, young man?"

"I got your young man," he countered, laughing. "Meet me at Monica's house."

"I'm not. I have work to do."

"I have work to do too, which is why you need to meet me at the house."

"Good-bye Craig."

"I'll see you in fifteen minutes." Craig hung up.

Henna was not fond of people telling her what to do, but in this instance she was really feeling it. If she gave in, Craig would think he had her. In the same instance, she could really turn him out and then leave him wanting more. However, if she didn't go, she'd have him questioning whether it was really good or not the first time, which was always a great position to be in, because he would definitely feel the need to come back a second time just to seal the deal. But then again, it could turn him off completely. After two puffs of her cigarette, Henna knew exactly how she'd play this hand.

Chapter 6

"Respect" (Aretha Franklin, 1967)

Henna was becoming familiar with the city, even though it had only been a week. That weekend on her journey through a new set of unfamiliar streets, she passed an obscure building with nothing but an address on the front door. She knew it was a music studio. She'd been in so many, she could detect them in a second. Studios in the South were always some ambiguous building usually made of concrete or stucco. They had little to no windows, and normally a gated parking lot. Studios in the North were normally underneath the ground. Unless, they were studios owned by labels; in that case they were located above the twentieth floor in tall buildings in Manhattan. Henna hit the security buzzer and gave them her name, trying to sound like she was there to record. She walked in and greeted the receptionist. He was about twenty-two years old, and very colorful. He sported a high-top fade, a lime green cardigan, and bright royal blue skinny jeans. He had no inkling as to who she was, and she wasn't getting past his station without an appointment.

"I want to schedule some time here, but I want to see the facilities first."

"You have to make an appointment to see the facility. You can't just wander through here, boo-boo," he said, with the tip of his pen stuck in the corner of his mouth. Henna could detect a sense of attitude, and she knew his "boo-boo" was condescending, not endearing. Apparently, he thought he was somebody just because he was the keeper of studio equipment and wannabe producers.

"I don't want to wander. I want to use the facility."

He pulled out a calendar and slowly skimmed the dates. "How much time are you looking for?"

"That. Depends. On. Your. Facility." Henna's emphasis grew as she pronounced each word.

He huffed, and she puffed, and Henna became increasingly more frustrated with his inflated sense of faux power.

"You're not booked up. I see all kinds of blank boxes on there," she said while pointing to the calendar.

"This is our calendar for regulars. Just because there's no name on here doesn't mean the space isn't being used. A lot of people who've already made it in the industry come here to record. We have a separate calendar for the 'somebodies.'"

"So, basically, you think I'm a nobody," she quickly responded.

He took the pen, tapped it on the table, and delivered an expression that boasted an unmistakable decree of "hell yeah, that's what I'm saying." Just then, one of the studio producers walked by. The front-desk man wiped the scowl off and painted on a big ass-kissing grin.

"What's up, Bobby-B?" he said.

Bobby-B acknowledged his greeting with a brotherly head nod, but he kept his stride moving forward. He glanced at Henna, gave a smile, and then swiped his security pass to open the door. Suddenly his pace halted as he looked at Henna again. He lifted his oversize Gucci shades and spoke.

"Henna James?"

Henna quickly perked up as though she'd been the first pick to play on the cool kids' dodgeball team.

"Yes," she answered, with a gleam in her eye.

Bobby-B rushed over to introduce himself. Though he was a hip-hop producer, he was an ardent fan of Henna's work. He was nearly gushing with excitement. The moment couldn't have been sweeter. He reeled off six or seven questions, stared her up and down, and quickly ushered her behind the security doors. As she walked by, she leaned over and spoke to the studio gatekeeper. "You might want to pull out your other calendar when I come back to make my appointment, boo-boo."

Henna gloated as she was escorted through the tan walls covered with dozens upon dozens of gold and platinum records. The entire time Bobby-B chatted about how inspirational her last two projects were for him. She looked at Bobby with his flashy T-shirt covered in shiny gold Ed Hardy scribble, and checked out his sagging pants, and tacky jewelry. He wasn't one of her typical fans, who were mostly women between the ages of thirty-five and fifty. She liked to think her music reached a variety of people, but his appearance had her puzzled. It didn't matter, though. He gave her access, so she indulged his excitement.

"I've been trying to work with Reason. But I'm so used to doing it the old-fashioned way, I think I'm going to lose something if I use computers to make music," Henna stated.

Bobby-B quickly offered a Reason tutorial, and Henna rushed to the car to get her computer. She wanted to go through it herself while he explained. This is how she learned best. An hour passed, and Henna was well into her lesson, when Lil Wayne walked in the studio. Henna knew of him, and knew his name contained some sort of adolescent prefix—like "young," "baby," or "little"—but she couldn't quite get his name right. Bobby-B rapidly made introductions. Lil Wayne didn't know Henna James, but Bobby insisted that he had to know her.

"I know I've seen you, but I'm sorry, I don't think I've heard your stuff," Wayne apologized.

"It's okay, I don't really listen to your stuff either."

Bobby-B popped in one of Henna's songs.

"Oh yeah, he listens to that shit all the time," Wayne said immediately.

By "that shit," she was hoping he meant "that brilliance," but she made no comment. It was then Henna realized that she was out of touch.

"You should do something on my new song," Lil Wayne said.

"Okay," Henna said, eager to participate in any other world besides her own. "What should I do?"

"She can sing the hook on 'I'd Bust Your Guts,'" suggested Bobby.

Henna was like a kid in a candy store. She was anxious, but she had no idea what she was asking for. She only hoped it'd be sweet.

Bobby-B continued his planning. "We can lay it down, but we better do one without her because of the label shit."

"Who you signed with?" asked Wayne.

"Columbia," Henna replied.

"I know some folk over there," he said. "Cool, let's do this."

Henna's eyes widened. "We're about to do it now?" she asked, filled with some fear and anticipation.

Both the producer and the rapper nodded. "Listen to the track," Bobby said before cranking up the tune.

Henna bobbed her head back and forth. She pretended to dig the song, but she honestly had no idea what Wayne was talking about, nor could she even think of what to say during this so-called "hook." Yet, Henna grabbed a piece of paper and started jotting down some lyrics.

"What exactly are you talking about?" she asked innocently.

Wayne handed Henna a piece of paper with scribbles and scratched out words. She read it and tried to make sense of the words, but nothing was legible. Finally she stopped trying and attempted to grab onto the last word of each one of his sentences. When it was time for the hook, Wayne stopped. He and Bobby looked at Henna and waited for a hip tune to come pouring from her mouth. She gave them a fretful smile and started humming. The hums turned into a word, and eventually a few words. Her hook was finally revealed.

"They only respect the wrong, so why try to do right" was the hook Henna belted out.

Wayne stopped rhyming and looked at Henna. She didn't know if it was a good stare or one of disapproval. She always felt comfortable when it came to her music, but she was far away from the adult contemporary lane.

"I'm feeling what you're doing. Sing it twice, back-to-back, and hold the note on that last word."

Henna smiled proudly. It's not that she had wanted to do a hook on a hip-hop song, it was just that she'd opened herself to try something new, and she had done it well. This gave her a new sense of boldness, and so she sang the hook again.

"More pain," Wayne yelled over the music.

Pain was something Henna could relate to. She'd never been shot or had her guts busted, but the outcry of pain was the same no matter its cause. Henna thought about Ahmad and her career. She crooned the words once again. This time the pain in her song was evident. She canceled her evening plans with Alphonzo and turned off her phone. Henna stayed at the studio and laid down her track, creating with Bobby-B and Wayne for another five hours.

Henna left the session, feeling refreshed and revitalized. Who knew hip-hop could have such a rejuvenating effect? she thought. When Henna returned to the house that night, she felt like she could conquer all her challenges ahead. Outside of her afternoon with Craig, it had been one of her best days in months. And since she'd turned down Craig's last offer, she didn't know if she'd have any more days with him, so she relished that recording moment.

Monica was staying at Julian's place, but Henna gave her a call immediately after walking into the house. She told her about her day. Monica couldn't stop laughing as she pictured Henna in the studio with Lil Wayne.

"You know who Lil Wayne is?" Henna asked.

"Yes, he's a part of Cash Money. Everyone knows Lil Wayne. Was Drake with him?"

"He was by himself. He's going to see if I can be on his CD."

"Maybe you can be in the video too?" Monica sarcastically suggested.

"Really? You think?" Henna said with excitement.

"I was joking," Monica commented.

Henna didn't care; she was flying high. She prepared for bed, not only singing her hook but also rhyming parts of "I'd Bust Your Guts." Henna stuck out her booty, arched her back, and gyrated back and forth a few times. With her lips puckered out, she commented, "I can be a video ho." Henna then gave an oversexed expression and released several giggles.

That night she went to sleep feeling inspired. If her music career failed, she had at least opened the doors to a new profession as a video vixen. Surprisingly, this thought gave her a peaceful night's sleep.

Chapter 7

"I Put a Spell on You"
(Screamin' Jay Hawkins, 1956)

Monica loved dinner parties, but since she didn't like to cook, every other month she convinced Julian to have one at his house. Though they just had one, Monica wanted to have one while Henna was in town, and so she requested that Julian host. It was Monica, Julian, Henna, Alphonzo, Craig, and his date. Therefore, two hours before dinner, the ever-prepared Monica pulled out her sexy red dress and laid it across her bed. Henna walked into the room, carrying two Q-tips.

"I knew you were going to dress up." Henna pointed to the dress.

"This is dinner party attire," Monica said, holding the dress up to her body.

"Well, I'm wearing jeans and a blouse." Henna shook her head and walked back to the bathroom, wiggling the swab in her ear. As she jiggled it, Henna moaned and groaned. Her whines became sensual, and soon it sounded like she was having sex. Monica came rushing to the bathroom door. She watched from the threshold.

"Somebody needs to get laid," she voiced.

"Please, this is much less complicated," Henna replied before she handed Monica a swab. "Try one."

Monica stuck the Q-tip in her ear. "I'm not getting anything," she said, referring to the ear swab.

"You have to wiggle it," Henna said.

Monica moved the Q-tip back and forth and mocked Henna. "Ooh, that's it, yeah, right there."

Henna attempted to shut the door in Monica's face, but Monica held her hand out while laughing. "Hey! Be nice to Alphonzo tonight. He told me you've stood him up twice."

"The first time I was in the studio. The second time . . . I just didn't feel like going."

"That's what I'm talking about. Be nice." Monica gave a stern glare before leaving the bathroom. Henna finished dressing, walked downstairs, and entered the kitchen. She dug into a bowl of cherries sitting by the sink, and then the doorbell rang.

"Could you get that?" Monica called from upstairs.

Henna slowly walked to the door while eating her cherries. However, as soon as she got to the door, she heard keys jingling and saw the door opening.

Henna halted her steps and watched as Craig walked into the house. He was wearing a crisp white cotton shirt and jeans. Craig smiled when he saw Henna, and she returned his pleasantries with a coy grin. Craig and Henna continued to glance and smile at each other, but they said nothing. Craig walked over to Henna's side, dug in the bowl of cherries, and pulled out two. He slowly placed them in his mouth.

"Stop it," Henna requested.

"Stop what?" he said.

"Look, we have to get through this evening, and I don't want you messing with me."

"Really? I think you are begging me to mess with you."

Henna walked away from Craig, grabbed a glass, and retrieved water from the fridge. She drank her water as she ate a few more cherries. Craig kept his eyes on her, but she refused to pay him attention. Monica came into the kitchen.

"Why are you eating? We're about to go to dinner."

Henna and Craig replied in unison, "It's just cherries." Henna turned to see Craig putting the last cherry in his mouth. She frowned, he smiled, and they headed for the door.

"Where's your date?" Monica asked.

"Didn't feel like dealing with her this evening. I just wanted to come hang out with my big sister, and her singer friend," Craig said while glancing at Henna.

"I'm going to follow you, though, in case I make plans for afterward."

They hopped in the car and Craig trailed them to Julian's home. Julian lived downtown in Bass Lofts. It was a small, trendy development with unique home layouts. Julian was on the top floor of the building. His lofty condo held two large bedrooms, a living room, a study, a spacious kitchen, and a dining area. It was as large as most freestanding homes, and it looked like an old antiques shop. He had a chaise from the 1930s, and pieces of furniture from the 1940s and '50s. It was put together nicely, but nowhere near Monica's taste. She was a modern gal. If it wasn't sleek and low to the ground, she didn't care for it. Henna was the opposite; she loved antiques. Julian's place was perfect. She immediately inquired about his distinctive picture frames and rare sculptures. Julian indulged Henna's excitement for his collection, while Monica poured herself a glass of wine. Moments later, Julian was ready to serve appetizers. Alphonzo called Henna and told her he would be a few minutes late, and so she and the others sat down and started with calamari and crab cakes.

"Please tell me you fixed pecan pie for dessert," asked Henna.

"We're just on appetizers and you're already asking about dessert," Craig mentioned.

Henna gave him a displeased look. "If I'd had my slice, then maybe I wouldn't still be asking," she commented.

"Your slice, huh?"

"Stop it, you two!" Monica refereed as if she were chastising her two children. They quieted down and continued to eat. Suddenly Julian rose to play some dinner music.

"Baby, please, none of that Enya, crying with the wolves while walking through the hills . . . Celtic sound," Monica begged. "I can't take that tonight."

"That's good dinner music," claimed Henna.

"Thank you," Julian said.

"Henna doesn't count. Anything slow and depressing sounds good to her," Monica added.

"Got any blues?" asked Craig.

"What you know about the blues, baby boy?" questioned Henna, smirking.

Craig chuckled and then murmured, "I got your baby boy."

Her smirk quickly morphed into a tight-lipped wrinkle. Just then, the doorbell rang.

"That should be Alphonzo!" Monica called out.

"Who's Alphonzo?" asked Craig.

"My date," Henna answered proudly.

Craig grinned. "Oh, you have a date? That's cute." Monica answered the door as Julian continued to talk about music.

"I really liked your last CD. 'Frozen Tears' was my favorite."

"That's my favorite track," Henna commented.

"Mine too," Craig said. Henna doubted he'd ever heard her music, and her apparent expression corresponded with that feeling. Yet, she said nothing as Monica walked Alphonzo over to the table and made introductions.

"Everyone, this is Alphonzo. This is Julian, and my brother, Craig."

Alphonzo took a seat at the table just before he kissed Henna's cheek.

"Hope I haven't missed too much. What's the subject on the table?"

Craig answered, "Music, specifically blues."

"Blues is all right, a little depressing," Alphonzo replied.

"I'm more of a hip-hop head, myself," commented Monica.

"Blues started all of that," Henna replied.

"Here she goes," mumbled Monica.

"Nah, she's right," added Craig.

"C'mon, Mo, you know it. That's why they call it 'rhythm and blues.' Country ain't nothing but blues. Blues artists talk to the music . . . tell stories . . . sometimes rhyme stories. . . . That's hip-hop! Blues is the origin of it all," said Henna. She rose and removed her iPod from her purse. "Julian, may I?" she said, approaching his speakers. Henna hooked into his system and played a song.

"Let's take a listen," she suggested. The group listened to the track for a minute. "Blues is . . . life. It's all how you view it. It's the truth set to music."

Henna strolled over to the table and paced back and forth, as though she were giving a lecture on the blues. Craig remained seated, but he became an eager participant. "Blues is straight up, no ice, no chaser. If a man loves a woman, he says it. If his heart is broken, he says it," Henna started.

"If he wants to sleep with her, he says it. If he thinks she's the finest woman he's seen, he says it," Craig added as he stared at Henna.

She noticed his lingering eye contact, but she continued describing. This time her words held a certain symbolic tone. "If he's an uncontrollable womanizer, he admits it."

Craig joined in. "If she can't keep him off her mind, so does she."

The two were now staring at each other, and everyone else at the table was silent. Monica instantly saw the chemistry between them. Therefore, she jumped up and stood in front of Henna to break the eye line.

"Okay, the blues is not depressing!" Monica yelled.

But Monica's antics weren't enough to stop Craig. He stood and looked beyond his sister to catch Henna's eye once more before speaking. "It's actually quite beautiful, almost intoxicating." Craig locked in on Henna, and for a second she was becoming entranced. However, Monica glanced at Henna, pulled her arm, and shoved a drink in her hand, all in one quick swoop. She needed to break up the obvious sexual tension.

"We should toast," Monica said very cheerfully, yet with a nervous chuckle.

The group raised the 1930s vintage wineglasses, with sterling silver stems, and everyone took a sip. Henna glanced at Craig once more, and he honed in on her lips as they wrapped around the brim, which was also trimmed in sterling silver. Henna hastily looked the other way and said, "I love these glasses, Julian. Your taste is impeccable."

"It certainly is," he said, placing his hand around Monica's waist, and kissing her forehead. Henna smiled at the beautiful couple. Julian really loved Monica, and it was evident. Though Henna didn't totally approve of the age difference, she loved the way he looked at her friend. He was so supportive, a definite keeper. Julian walked into the kitchen to bring out the next dish, and Monica went to change the music. He returned and placed a large wooden salad bowl on the table.

"I hope balsamic is okay. I already added it," he said.

The group dug into the spinach salad that was deliciously decorated with cherry tomatoes, Gorgonzola cheese, and candied walnuts. The table was silent as everyone enjoyed the scrumptious greens. However, after a few minutes, Monica felt the need to strike up a conversation about Alphonzo. She desperately wanted Henna to see how interesting he was, and she felt it was her responsibility to initiate it.

"You know Alphonzo is our head graphic designer. He's heading up the national delivery campaign for Sweet J's. They are going to start national distribution. And tell them about the national tire campaign you just landed."

"That's boring. Craig, tell me about Europe. Monica said you just recently got back," said Alphonzo.

Monica didn't want the conversation going to Craig, but she didn't want to be too noticeable, so she let it go.

"I got back about six months ago. It was cool. I loved playing. There's nothing like it. But touring, that's another story. Right, Henna?"

"Yeah, touring can be hell," she stated with little enthusiasm. It was obvious she was uneasy, and so her conversation was limited.

"So what are you doing next?" asked Alphonzo.

"I just recently purchased this building, gonna turn it into a jazz club," he said proudly. "Hopefully, we can get it up and running by late summer."

"You know, I looked into buying the Attic a few years after I first moved here," added Julian. "It's a great location, but I wanted natural light. It's perfect for what you are doing."

"Oh, I remember the Attic. It used to be the spot back in the day," Alphonzo said.

"You don't look like you used to hang at the Attic," Monica voiced.

"Don't be fooled," he said, smiling.

Henna gave a timid look in Alphonzo's direction. "I like your dimples," she said, placing her pinkie finger in the indentation in his right cheek.

Alphonzo leaned over and whispered, "They like you too." Henna blushed, Monica smiled wide, and Craig loudly cleared his throat.

The group continued to eat their meal as they chatted about careers, family, and music. While Monica was slicing dessert, and the conversation was dying down, Julian invited Henna to see another antique he had in the other room. Henna quickly followed with anticipation. However, she had no idea that the antique he was about to show her was so personal. Julian opened up his top drawer and pulled out a tiny navy blue box. He handed her the velvet casing, and Henna's hand shook as she opened it. She took one look at the ring inside and quickly closed the box.

"Is this for . . ." She was so anxious, she couldn't finish the sentence. Julian simply nodded. Henna began to suspire; at first, it was slow, and then her breathing became more rapid, as though she were having an asthma attack.

"Are you okay?" Julian asked. Henna nodded slowly and opened the case again. Her eyes were fixated on the jewels that set off the beautiful design.

"Is this an engagement ring?"

"I hope so. It's a floral filigree design, circa 1920s. The center stone is a round-cut diamond, but in each of the six floral centers is a garnet," he explained.

"Her birthstone," Henna murmured as she stared at the amazing piece of jewelry. "Are you sure you don't have a handsome brother stashed away somewhere?"

Julian let out a hearty laugh. Just then, Monica walked into the room. "Babe, where is the whipped cream?" Nervous, Henna quickly placed the box down the front of her blouse and didn't turn to face Monica, although she continued walking into the room.

"What are you two up to?" Monica curiously asked. Julian hastily approached, to play interference, as Henna moved closer to the drawer.

"I don't have any cream. I wanted to use a raspberry drizzle, instead."

Monica noticed Henna who still hadn't turned around. "You okay, girl?"

Henna whipped her head around with a huge, fake smile. "Just admiring this chest of drawers. Isn't it nice?" she asked, rubbing her hand across the top. "I mean, the details in the etchings are wonderful. Have you seen it?"

Monica looked at the drawer. "Yes, it's okay. Good thing you're not into old men, I'd think you were trying to steal mine."

Julian quickly frowned. "'Old'?"

Monica was quick to recover. "Old for Henna. She heard your age and automatically called you an old man. I don't care about your age."

"Do you think of me as an old man?" Julian asked Monica. Henna stood back and watched her friend shuffle her way out of the mess of words she'd just created.

"No. I was being facetious. Henna knows what I'm talking about. You give me just what I need." Monica sealed her compelling statement with a kiss, just in case she wasn't as convincing as she'd hoped. Whether or not Julian bought it, he quickly ushered her out of the room, showing her to the raspberry glaze for their chocolate mousse cake. Henna made sure the coast was clear; then she pulled the box from within her bosom and tucked it back in the drawer. She took a deep breath and then started to walk out of the room. However, Monica obstructed her exit, gently forced her back into the bedroom, and closed the door. Henna was praying that Monica wasn't planning to question her about the weird behavior, but she would have no such luck.

"Why are you acting funny?" Monica blurted out.

"Me? I'm acting normal."

"You're different, and I think I know what's going on, so why don't you just tell me," Monica continued.

Henna took a couple of deep inhales, and some deeper exhales, and then prepared herself to tell Monica about the possible proposal. But before she could utter the words, Monica beat her to the punch.

"I saw you and Craig looking at each other, so you might as well confess."

Henna was thrown by her comment, but she was also relieved that Monica had no idea about the ring. Thank God, she hadn't prematurely spilled the beans. Yet, she didn't know how to address the comment on Craig either. Therefore, Henna gave a screwy look and uttered, "Huh?"

"You and Craig have been flirting all night."

"No, I'm with Alphonzo," Henna bantered.

"Your conversation has been with Alphonzo, but your everything else has been with Craig."

"So I flirted a little with Craig. It's only for entertainment. You know how I love to chump down boys who think they can have any woman they lay eyes on."

"Yes, I know," Monica said with a very suspicious tone.

"Well, Craig is one of those guys. He's been flirting with me since the other day, but trust me, I'm not paying any attention to him." Monica smirked while staring into Henna's eyes. "Seriously," she insisted.

"I just want to make sure your head is screwed on straight. I love my brother, but trust me, he is not the guy you want to get wrapped up with."

"First of all, he's a child. Secondly, I'm not getting wrapped up with anyone, including Alphonzo. I'm going back home soon."

"I know you, Henna. Don't lie to me."

"Craig couldn't hit this if my vajayjay had the flu and his penis was a tube of penicillin. Got it!"

"Okay, just checking." Monica paused and then looked at the chest of drawers. "What were you and Julian up to, for real?"

"I was looking at this chest of drawers. It came from Brazil."

"He told you that?" Monica asked.

Immediately Henna knew she'd said too much, but she had to continue with the story. "I think he said Brazil," she hinted with uncertainty.

"Well, he must really want to impress you, because he got that piece from Pier 1. I was with him."

Henna was speechless.

Monica strolled over to the drawer and rubbed her hands across it. "It is nice, though. And you don't have to tell me what you two were talking about, but I know it was something." Monica walked to the bedroom door and then turned around. "Come get some mousse." Henna quickly followed behind her.

While the singer ate dessert, she was conscious of her eye games with the musician; yet they still made quiet music. Though she was enjoying the power trip of flirting with a younger man, she didn't want to draw any more unwanted attention from Monica, and she didn't want to be rude to Alphonzo. Nonetheless, the few times she did glance Craig's way, he was zeroed in like a missile. She noticed the diminutive nuances he displayed as he slid the fork of mousse from his mouth and played with the raspberry drizzle. She knew it was all for her, and though she was careful not to show any signs of enjoyment, she was deeply flattered inside.

At the end of the evening, Alphonzo, Henna, Julian, and Monica walked outside to say his and her good-byes. Monica snuggled tightly under Julian's arm, for the night air was quite cool on top of the parking deck. Henna noticed that Monica didn't have her purse; therefore she was prompted to ask, "Are you staying here?"

Monica looked at Julian and then nodded yes.

"But I rode with you. How am I going to get home?"

Just then, Craig walked out with a plate wrapped in foil.

"You're not supposed to take home plates from a dinner party," Monica uttered.

Craig quickly dismissed her comment and answered Henna, "I'll take you."

Henna looked at Alphonzo, who then felt the pressure to also volunteer. But then, Craig stepped up once more.

"I'm going back to the house, anyway, man. Don't go out of your way."

Alphonzo then glanced at Henna to get a final verdict. She didn't want to ride with Craig, but the fact that Alphonzo didn't jump at the chance to take her home made her no longer want to ride with him either.

Henna finally responded. "If you need to get home, I guess I can ride with Craig," she answered, directing her remark toward Alphonzo.

As soon as Henna got into the car, Craig let out an interesting smirk. "You couldn't wait to get into my truck, just admit it."

"I'm not admitting a damn thing."

They drove off in silence.

Chapter 8

"Then He Kissed Me" (The Crystals, 1963)

The first few miles down the road were as quiet as a bad blind date. But then, Craig put in a CD. Henna grooved to it for a few minutes before inquiring about the singer.

"That's my boy, Travis. Pretty dope, huh?"

"I like it. Ooh, listen to this." Henna anxiously dug in her purse and pulled out her track from the studio session with Lil Wayne. She popped out his CD and quickly replaced the disc with hers.

"Hold on, who said you could touch my system?"

Henna gave a blithe expression and continued with her task. "I did this the other day."

Craig began listening to the track. "This ain't you. This is Weezy."

"Lil Wayne?"

"Yeah, Weezy, like I said."

"Keep listening," she said, turning up the volume a couple of notches. Her hook came blaring through the speakers. A youthful smile spread across Henna's face.

"You're doing hip-hop hooks?" Craig asked, showing unmistakable confusion and possible disappointment.

"No. I mean, maybe," Henna said before she removed the CD. "I'm trying new things."

Craig's expression lifted. "Oh yeah," he said, ogling her.

"Keep your eyes on the road." It was then Henna actually looked out the window and realized that they were heading downtown. "Where are we going?"

"I'm taking you to the spot."

"I don't want to go to the spot. I don't even know what the spot is. I want to go to the house."

"We will afterward."

"I knew I should have gone with Alphonzo," she whispered.

"He didn't want to take you home. He's not your type, anyway."

Henna purposely ignored Craig's comment. She was sure it was strategically thrown to the wind, to bait a response. But she also knew if she didn't counter, that it would eat at him. The games had once again begun. The two pulled up into a vacant parking lot, beside an old two-story brick building. Although the block where they parked seemed safe, the other blocks surrounding it were a bit dicey. Henna cautiously looked out her window, and Craig noticed her uneasiness.

"You live in New York. I know you're not scared."

"I'm wary, not scared," she said, opening her door.

"I got you," Craig replied across the top of the truck as he shut his door. They walked into the building and he flipped on the lights. Downstairs was a large, open space, with a few stools pushed against the wall.

"We are going to use this space as a lounge area, and I'm thinking we might serve desserts. I'm talking to Julian about it now." Henna walked throughout the rectangular room as she ran her fingers across the exposed brick walls.

"This would be a great place for a photo shoot," she said. Her heels gave off a rhythmic tap as she walked across the concrete floor. She slowed her pace, paying detailed attention to the cracks and crevices of the old building.

"I hope you keep most of this wear and tear. It gives this place character. I like it."

"You haven't seen the gem yet," Craig mentioned, motioning for Henna to head upstairs.

Henna looked up the wooden stairs, but the dim lights only lit part of the stairway. "I can't see," she said.

"Just walk, I'm behind you." Craig placed his hand in the small of her back and guided her up the twenty-two stairs. At the top there was an exposed lightbulb, with a metal chain. The chain grazed across Henna's face, and she mistook it for a spider. She quickly scooted up the last two steps and smacked herself in the face, attempting to remove the eight-legged insect. Craig laughed at her reaction, which looked like a silly, new dance craze. She quickly realized that it was only the chain.

"It's not funny," she said as he slowly approached her. Craig flipped on another light, and the room, known as "the Attic," appeared. Henna was in awe. The room looked like an old juke joint from the 1930s. It had old hardwood flooring, exposed brick walls, and exposed lightbulbs. In the corner was an old mahogany piano, and there was a partially built bar in the back, but the place held no furniture. However, on the walls were old sepia-toned photographs of black folk cutting a rug. The pictures were dated before the 1950s. Henna gazed at the photos and ran her hands across the handmade wooden frames.

"Where did you get these?"

"I found this book when I was in London. It had these great old pictures. One day when I needed a little motivation, I copied these and put them in frames. I know it's premature, but I like looking at them. That's the feel I'm going for." Craig began to illustrate just how he wanted them to hang. "Imagine a nail hanging just about here. And a chain or heavy rope with a wooden frame attached. We can hang the frames from the nail."

"I see it. It's going to be nice," Henna commented as she continued to walk across the room. She ran her hands across the top of the piano. "Where did this come from?"

"It was already here. They said I could keep it," Craig answered.

Henna sat down and hit a few keys. "It's in tune," she said, surprised. She started playing Schubert and humming a tune.

Immediately Craig was mesmerized. "See, someone who plays classical music shouldn't be doing hooks on a Lil Wayne song."

"I was trying something new!" Henna forcefully reiterated as she placed a heavy bang on the keys.

Craig walked to the back of the bar, pulled out his guitar, and a bar stool from a back room. He tuned his strings and began playing a song. After a few bars he stopped, looked at Henna, and said a few lines from an old B.B. King tune. He changed a few of the words to chronicle his introduction to Henna. She couldn't help but laugh. Craig suddenly stopped playing, and then stared at her.

"What?" she said. "What's wrong?"

"Nothing," he replied. "It's just . . ." Craig stopped.

"Just what?" Henna urged.

"It's just . . . I hadn't really noticed your smile . . . till just now."

Henna quickly closed her mouth and lowered her head.

"I know you are not shy. What's up?"

With her head still lowered, Henna shook it from side to side.

"Why don't you smile more often?"

"Sometimes you never get over your childhood issues. Life's funny that way."

"I dig." Craig strummed on his guitar and then asked, "What did you think of me when you first saw me?"

"Didn't you ask me that already? I swear, you are determined to get your compliment, one way or another, aren't you?" Henna mocked him and finally gave in. "At first, I thought you were cute, until you pissed me off."

"Well, I thought you were beautiful," he said as Henna slightly blushed, "but then I thought you were a freak."

"What!" she yelped.

"Yeah, look how you dress. You're superconservative, and you wear black and gray all of the time. Either you are very boring, a Goth fanatic, or you're a freak. I gave you the benefit of the doubt."

"So you'd rather have a freak than a bore?" she questioned.

"Who wouldn't?"

Henna didn't respond; she only lowered her face and dabbled with the piano keys. Craig came closer, sat next to her, took his hand and lifted her face. They locked eyes and Craig moved in to kiss her, but Henna quickly rose and walked toward the bar.

"I'm thirsty. Do you have any water in here?"

"I believe there are some bottles in the back room." Craig went to retrieve the water. Henna quickly gathered her emotions and tucked them deep into the pit of her stomach. Craig handed her a bottle of water and placed his bottle of beer on the bar.

"You didn't ask if I wanted beer," Henna said.

"You can have mine. I'll take the water."

"Oh, now you want to share?" Henna spoke. "That's fine. I'll drink my water."

"If you're trying to start some trouble, just say so. I'm here to please." Craig licked his bottom lip and winked.

Henna smirked and walked toward the steps. Craig strummed his strings and spoke a couple of lines. This time his lyrics mimicked her current actions.

"She's trying to leave me, y'all. But she doesn't really wanna go," he said.

"Stop playing, take me home."

Craig continued: "She says she wants to go home, but her heart says she wants to stay."

"For real, Craig, let's go."

"She says she's for real, but I know the deal," he continued to rhyme.

Henna snapped around and joined in on the song. However, she sang with the force of Etta James and the soul of Bessie Smith.

"This man thinks he's gonna get to me. He has no idea who he's fooling with . . ." was her start. Henna remained positioned by the stairs as she crooned four more lines, which ended with "He wrecks my nerves fo' sho, now I told him I'm ready to go. I'm not lying, and I'm not buying his bullshit no mo'. " She placed her hands on her hips and gave him a stern stare. Craig didn't know if she was truly upset or playing along, but he knew there was one way to find out. With his guitar in his right hand, he walked toward her. She felt her heart begin to pulsate as he approached, so she took a few steps backward until she slammed against the wall. Craig was only a breath away from her lips as he placed his left hand firmly on the wall, sandwiching her body between the brick and his chest. Henna took a tiny breath, which ended in a loud swallow. She was suddenly very nervous. Craig stared her square between the eyes, but Henna didn't flinch. He didn't make another move, and neither did she, and the two stayed in this position for at least forty-five seconds. Craig wanted to make a move, but his pride wouldn't let him do any more than he'd already done. Henna didn't know what to do. She knew the games were up, and it was time to make a move, but she didn't truly want to deal with the consequences—her feelings or his. It was only supposed to be one time. It was simpler just to continue with the game, but all games eventually came to an end. Then suddenly she thought about Ahmad, so much so that Craig's face transformed into his, and she wanted to smack him. Instead, Henna quickly closed her lids and opened them again, scooted away from the wall, and moved back toward the stairs. However, once she hit the top step, she realized Craig wasn't following her. It was then, her pride kicked in. She didn't know what possessed her to say it, but she was sure that the words would quickly advance the game into high gear.

"So you're just going to let me walk out of here?" Henna didn't even bother to turn to see his expression as she spoke. Craig walked behind her, pulled keys from his pocket, and dangled them over her left shoulder.

"You weren't going to get far."

Henna turned around, and before she could inhale, Craig was stealing her breath. The kiss was so forceful, it pushed her body against the other wall, and the two stood at the top of the stairs in the dimly lit Attic and kissed for over a minute. Henna placed her hands around the nape of Craig's neck and gripped tightly. Just then, Henna's purse began to vibrate, and this pulsing pulled her back into reality as she withdrew her lips and wiped away the excess moisture with her hand. With her nerves aflutter, she rifled through her purse to find the phone, but she didn't catch it in time. Seconds later, Craig's phone rang.

"It's Monica," they said in harmony. Craig reached in his pocket and answered.

"Don't tell her I'm here with you," Henna whispered loudly in the background. Craig paid her no attention.

"Henna and I stopped by the Attic. I wanted to show her the spot."

Henna slapped him on the shoulders for deliberately snubbing her request. Craig handed Henna the phone. She backed away from it, as though it were a hot potato, and started walking down the steps. Craig chuckled and continued talking to Monica as Henna waited anxiously at the front door. As soon as he hung up, she lit into him.

"Why did you tell her I was here?" she yelled.

"Because you are," he said, approaching the front door.

"Just let me out," Henna stated, rushing him to free her from this emotional quandary.

Craig unlocked the door and Henna quickly stepped outside, taking in a gulp of night air. She was overwhelmed by an assortment of feelings.

"I don't want to hear Monica mouth off about you," she said as Craig continued to chuckle. "It's not funny."

"What is she? Your mom?" he said with a louder guffaw.

As they walked to the truck, Henna attempted to explain, but Craig wasn't listening. His mind was still on the kiss. Amazingly, that intimate lip encounter was arousing more emotions than the sexual one had the other day. The two rode home in silence.

When Craig pulled up in the driveway, he finally spoke. "I apologize."

"You should. You had no business kissing me."

"Oh no. I'm not apologizing for the kiss. I'm sorry for telling Monica we were still together. I didn't realize that you were such a private person."

"I told you," she snapped.

"Now I know," he responded back in a mimicking tone.

Henna carefully thought about her next words. She was somewhat over the flirting game. The kiss had come and gone, and though it was a nice kiss, the anticipation was certainly better than the act itself.

As she mutely tossed her thoughts around, Craig spoke. "Alphonzo didn't call to make sure you made it home okay. I don't like him."

Henna turned to Craig and grinned. "That's not why you don't like him." And with those words, the game was back in play.

"Maybe you're right, but I still think he should have called."

Just then, Craig's phone rang again.

"If it's Monica, tell her I'm in the house," Henna said before he answered. Yet, Craig looked at the ID, ignored the call, and put it back in his pocket. Henna couldn't help but taunt. "I know what that was," she teased.

"Oh yeah. What was it?"

"It was a booty call, and you know it."

"No one says 'booty call' anymore."

Henna noticed that he still had his keys in the ignition.

"You should stop smoking."

"That was random," Henna said. "I haven't smoked all day."

"It was on my mind."

Henna nodded and, for once, didn't get defensive. "I thought you had to get something from the house."

"I lied."

Henna shook her head. "Men," she murmured.

"Don't shake your head at me! You knew I was lying when I said it. You wanted me to take you home. I don't know why you keep playing."

Henna extended her hand, as if to give Craig a handshake. He obliged her formal departure. "Thank you for the ride, and I really liked your place."

"You are welcome," Craig replied.

Henna exited his truck and walked into the house. She didn't turn to wave, but pulled out her keys and walked in.

Craig sat in the driveway for a few seconds and contemplated going inside, but figured he'd be patient. He'd melted some of the ice tonight, and he was satisfied with the evening's outcome. He knew that if the kiss was still lasting with him, it was surely still lingering with her, and that was enough. So he pulled out of the driveway and went home.

Henna opened the back patio, walked out, and took a smoke. She found herself smiling in between the puffs. She would never admit it, but it was the kiss. She didn't even finish her cigarette. Maybe he was making his impression.

"He certainly is cute," she said softly into the evening air. "But . . ." Henna simply shook her head instead of ending her sentence with words. She knew Craig was not the answer, but only a container filled with worms that were waiting to burst from their tin can. It was wrong to use him as bait so that she could get back into the sea. Henna ran her hand across her lips. She could smell Craig on her fingers. He wore the same scent as Ahmad—Dolce & Gabbana Light Blue Pour Homme.

"I should have known," Henna groaned. Thus was the end of all lovely thoughts. She brushed her teeth and went to bed.

Chapter 9

"Follow Your Heart" (The Manhattans, 1966)

Craig and his partner, Travis, had put in twelve-hour days for the last week at the Attic, and progress still seemed to be creeping by. Because renovations had become so costly, they were down to a crew of three—the extra man was Travis's cousin Paul. Paul knew how to lay hardwood floors, so that was his task that week. Meanwhile, Craig worked on finishing the bar, and Travis worked on building the stage. Both Craig and Travis wanted the place to have an old feel, but, of course, the materials they purchased were all new. So they had to build everything from scratch and then give all the wood antique finishes. Problem was, their skill as laborers was limited.

Monica's loan wasn't approved yet, but she wanted to keep Mick updated on the progress. She and Mick stopped by the Attic to see how things were going. Although the floors were partially done, Mick could see the vision. Paul had pulled up the old wood and placed several planks of Red Oak Galliano, which gave the floor a light wood/dark wood combination. After it was complete, he would put a burnt umber finish on top to give it a worn feel. They still had a long way to go. It was April, and the club was supposed to open by July. Although Craig and Travis had all of their food and liquor permits, the physical state of the club was nowhere near ready. The electrical system still needed some work, and until that was running properly and approved by the city, nothing could open. Between the electrical work, final renovations, purchasing of furnishings, initial stock, and hiring staff, the bill was climbing toward $50,000. This didn't include any marketing or advertising.

"This is going to be hot, once everything is done," voiced Mick as he looked around.

"It will be," concurred Monica as she pulled out her phone and called Henna, who was still in town.

Craig eavesdropped on the call, though he pretended to be into his work. It'd been five days since the infamous kiss, and he had not seen or talked to Henna. He only knew she was still in town, because Monica had mentioned her desire to stay a few extra weeks possibly to record. She'd spent a couple of days with Bobby-B in the studio and he'd convinced her to let him produce some tracks for her next CD. Henna liked Bobby, and since she wasn't ready to go back to New York, this gave her the perfect excuse. Due to the relaxing visit, Henna's spirits had been high, but for some reason this morning she woke up feeling kind of blue. It didn't help that she put in the 1959 Miles CD bearing the same title (Kind of Blue), one of her favorites. Those five songs, though beautiful, always put her in a melancholy frame of mind. It didn't help that she'd had three calls from Ahmad, none of which she'd returned. His tone sounded urgent, but he'd only left the message "It's me, call back." So Henna figured if it was really important, he'd say what he wanted. Therefore, she ignored them.

She did agree to meet Monica for lunch, though, and she was looking forward to it. With Henna's recent studio schedule, and Monica staying at Julian's, they hadn't seen each other in four days. When Henna arrived, they greeted one another with huge smiles and open arms. Henna welcomed the embrace, but as she looked over Monica's shoulder, she saw Craig. He hadn't looked up to even acknowledge her presence. He was sanding the corner of the bar. Once he did see her, however, he gave a slight nod and continued working. Henna was a little perturbed by his nonchalant greeting, but she knew this maneuver was very intentional. By now, she was a bit perturbed with the cat-and-mouse game. Travis, however, stopped working and rushed over to say hello.

"I love your music. Craig mentioned you were staying with Monica. How long will you be in town?" He was very effusive, but still no true acknowledgment from Craig.

"I found a studio here, so at least for a few more weeks."

"Cool, maybe we can jam together while you're here."

"I'd like that," Henna replied.

Monica already had the restaurant picked out. They were going to the Tenth for Thai. Henna was hungry, but was more eager to talk. Though she was extremely private, and kept most of her thoughts, ideas, and concerns to herself, she felt comfortable sharing them with Monica. There was a backlog of discussion waiting to be divulged. Monica, however, wasn't aware of her friend's issues, and eagerly invited Mick to join them. Henna quickly became disgruntled. So much so, she rapidly made up an excuse to decline lunch.

"I just got a call from Bobby, and I'm going into the studio," she told Monica.

"No. I wanted us to eat."

"Tonight, what are your plans?" Henna asked.

"I was going to be with Julian, but I can cancel."

"Well, I do miss you, so see what he says."

Monica gave Henna another hug while whispering in her ear, "You okay?"

Henna nodded with a partial grin and returned the whisper with a more provocative question. "What are you doing with him?" she asked, pointing to Mick.

Monica brushed off the significance of the question and simply replied, "Going to lunch." She rushed off to join Mick at the bottom of the steps. Henna knew trouble was brewing, but she felt there was nothing she could do to save her friend. Craig was still at the bar, sanding away, ignoring her. She let him be, said good-bye from where she stood, and left the club.

Disappointed that her lunch date flaked, and Craig had given her absolutely no interest, Henna decided to spend the day at the spa. She had a facial, a massage, and a pedicure, which left her toes polished brightly pink. Henna stopped by Blockbuster, rented a few movies, and then drove home. When she got to the house, she noticed Craig's truck in the driveway. Checking her reflection in the side of the car window before she walked in, Henna gathered her thoughts and silently asked, What am I do-ing? Ironically, she knew the answer, but she refused to listen to it. She walked in the house and looked for Craig in the kitchen, but he wasn't there. She went in the living room, and upstairs, but there was no sign of him.

"Craig," Henna yelled. She soon gave up, went up-stairs, and got her journal. She happened to look out her window and saw Craig in the backyard trimming the weeds around Monica's flowers. Henna watched him for at least four minutes. Craig's actions reminded Henna of her grandfather who used to work in his garden every Sunday, back in Mississippi. Before she realized it, she'd zoned out, and Craig had left the yard and walked in the house. She heard him rustling in the kitchen, and so she tiptoed down the stairs and stood at the kitchen door. Craig was at the fridge, drinking a glass of water. He noticed her and smiled. Craig turned, and in his hand was a tulip. He'd picked it from the backyard. He placed his water down, slowly walked toward the door, and handed her the golden perennial flower. She took it in her hand and smelled the center. Before she could breathe out from her inhale, Craig leaned over and kissed her. Taking her by surprise was his MO, and the kiss was once again so passionate, it forced her body back against the wall. Henna dropped the tulip on the floor; as it was falling, Craig was lifting her into his arms. He walked upstairs, with Henna hanging on like a baby koala bear, and as they approached the door's threshold, Craig was removing Henna's black satin panties. He placed her on the bed, and with their lips still locked, she wiggled her way out of the remainder of her clothes. Craig's pants remained around his ankles as he pulled the lower half of her body off the bed, and it was there on the edge that they became one. About twenty minutes later, the kinkiness set in again, on the bathroom floor, and forty minutes after that, under the sheets. Amazingly, no words were spoken—not during, after, or before each session. They only giggled, smirked, smiled, and spoke with their eyes.

Henna and Craig were so enraptured with the moment that they didn't hear Monica walking in the front door. She paused and listened in the foyer. At first, she heard high screams, and then low moans. Her mouth nearly hit the floor. She knew it couldn't be Craig and Henna, but then she thought, who else would it be? Maybe it's Henna and Alphonzo, she considered. Just then, Henna called out her brother's name, and Monica nearly fainted. The thought of her brother and her friend having sex was sickening. Monica covered her ears with both hands, but they seemed to get louder by the second. She ran down the hall, grabbed a pair of earmuffs, still in her closet from a ski trip, and rushed upstairs to her room. Unfortunately, she had to pass Henna's room en route to hers, and the door was wide open. Monica couldn't hurry from that house fast enough. She ran out, still wearing the earmuffs.

Appalled, and at the same time intrigued, she sat in the car, trying to digest the sex act that was currently taking place in her home. She was like a mother to Craig, and often a mother to Henna, and this act of defiance made her want nothing more than to walk in and whip both her children for their wrongdoings. She'd given both ample warning, and yet they hadn't listened. As she sulked into her palms, she realized she was still wearing earmuffs. She took another look at the house, sighed, and removed the furry objects from her ears. Monica was positive this lewd act was compensating for something neither of them could provide for one another. It was a train wreck bound to happen, and she had no time in her schedule to clean up after the crash. She gave one more disappointed look toward the house, cranked up her car, and drove off.

Craig and Henna continued to lay in bed after Act Three, and this time conversation actually took place. Henna, however, stuck with her tough exterior and pretended as though she had nothing to say, and so Craig started.

"You all right?"

Henna nodded and smiled. She kissed his forehead and walked into the bathroom to shower. Craig followed, but Henna pushed him away.

"This water is not an invitation. Calm down, we can do it again in a few," she said, leering.

"'Calm down'?" Craig replied. "I just want to shower."

***

"Can't you do it at home? Get out of here before Monica comes home."

He ignored her with a blasé hand gesture, grabbed a towel, and went to Monica's bathroom. He took a quick shower and put on his things. When he was leaving, Henna was placing lotion on her heels. Craig stood at the door and watched her.

"What?" she said, watching him as he ogled her.

"Nothing," Craig replied. "I'm gonna go."

It was awkward, and they both knew it, but nothing else was said. Henna remained on the edge of the bed as Craig slowly turned and left the house. She didn't want him to leave, and considering he sat in the driveway four minutes before pulling off, he also didn't want to go. But pride was having its moment of glory. Neither party wanted to admit just how much they'd enjoyed the intimacy that was supposed to happen only that one time. So what was there to say: "Thanks again for the sex. It was just what I needed." Was that it? One time could be explained, but twice? It was best to say nothing and keep it moving. By the time they saw each other again, they could both pretend like it didn't happen, and so that became the plan.

Henna put on her clothes and went downstairs to get some water. She noticed the tulip on the floor, and this brought a huge, uncontrollable smile over her face. She checked her phone for messages, but there were none. She figured Monica was with Julian for the remainder of the evening, so she sent Monica a text telling her she'd be at Cat's Corner. She suddenly had the urge to perform, a desire she hadn't had since three weeks into the tour. But, tonight she wanted to get dressed, grab her guitar, and sing an acoustic set. Every bone in her body wanted to perform, and she knew that if she went to Cat's Corner, it shouldn't be a problem. So she placed on a long A-line black skirt and a heather gray T-shirt with a peace sign logo in black velvet. Henna slicked her hair back and adorned her ponytail with the yellow tulip. She arrived at Cat's Corner an hour later. Monday was open-mic night, and by the time she arrived, there were already fifteen people on the list. Cat's brother, Gerald, who was also a managing partner, was extremely glad to see her.

"My sister told me you were in town," he said, greeting Henna at the bar. "I thought you might have been gone by now."

"I'm recording here over the next few weeks."

Gerald gave a wide flirtatious smile. "You look good," he said.

"You look good too," she responded.

"Please tell me you are going to sing."

Henna, of course, came with the sole purpose of singing, but thought it would be nice to give Gerald the credit. "Because you asked so nicely. I will sing for you."

"Cat is going to be so jealous. If you are not pressed for time, I will let about ten people go first, let the crowd gather, and then we'll bring you up. We have a band, you know."

"I'm good. I may do an acoustic set. My guitar is in the trunk."

Gerald was beaming from ear to ear. He purchased Henna a drink and she sat near the bar and conversed with him for close to thirty minutes. She was actually enjoying herself. The talent that came to the stage was actually very good. Henna was reminded that the world was not short of talented individuals, and that only a one-fourth of those people got any type of recognition. This evening was again a reminder of how fortunate she was to be in that percentile. She looked up and saw Bobby-B walking in, and following him was Mick, Monica's friend. She instantly felt acclimated to the city. She was at a bar with at least three people she knew. This was different from New York, where she could go out every night for months and never see a familiar face, a Big Apple perk she loved. But even New Yorkers have a Cheers moment, and like the theme song said, Henna wanted to go where everybody knew her name. Thus, she strolled over to Bobby-B who was heading toward the bar. She smiled wide and he gave her a friendly embrace. Bobby ordered an Amstel and offered her a drink, but she quickly held up her glass of wine. They stood there talking, since there were no seats available, and he quickly mentioned that Wayne had asked about her.

"I don't think I'm good with those hooks," she replied.

"Are you kidding? Hip-hop is constantly reinventing itself. You could be the next biggest thing. Everyone who's anyone could start requesting you."

Henna laughed as she sipped her wine. Just then, Mick came over to speak, and he introduced her to the young woman he was with. He said it was his neighbor, but she had stars in her eyes that suggested otherwise. Yet, after the introduction he continued conversing as though she weren't there at all. Henna hated the way he ignored her. This was often a heated debate with her and Ahmad. Many men in the music industry looked at their women as token arm pieces. Thus, when conversation commenced, the women were expected to stand by the man's side and simply look cute. Though Henna was in the business, Ahmad often expected her to do the same, but Henna never played her position. Mick's actions and mannerisms were similar to those

men, which automatically put him on her dislike list.
Even if he weren't a complete asshole, he was guilty
by comparison. She was glad when Gerald came over
to inform her that she was next onstage, because she
abhorred making small talk with people she didn't like.

Henna excused herself, rushed to the car to retrieve
her guitar, and quickly tuned it outside by the front
entrance. She was going to play two songs, an original
that she'd only played a few times and "Maybe" by Janis Joplin. Henna was a huge fan and loved taking the
soulful rage of Janis and converging it with the vulnerability of Sade. She didn't have a name for it, but she
had a bit of both of these ladies inside her, and on this
evening they were both going to show.

Gerald took over the MC job to bring on Henna and
he gave her a glowing introduction. Many of the people
had heard her name, but had never purchased any
of her music, but tonight Henna's goal was to make
everyone in that room a fan. She walked onstage and
took a seat. Just as she sat, the tulip fell from her hair.
Henna grinned, picked it up, and spoke soulfully into
the microphone.

"Because of this one yellow tulip, I had about three
orgasms today. You ladies know how that is, right?"

"I'd given you four!" yelled Bobby from the back of
the club.

Henna giggled, while the audience, comprised mostly of women, jeered and whistled. "It's the little things,
fellas. It's the little things," Henna said seductively into
the microphone.

She stuck the tulip back in her ponytail while refer-
encing it. "I thought I'd keep it near, just for a little inspiration. I'm Henna James, everyone, and I'm so glad
to be playing for you tonight. This first song is called 'If
He Weren't Your Man.'"

Henna strummed her maroon-colored guitar and sang. The song started in a low tone, but its crescendo was steady. By the last chorus Henna was belting out the tune and the audience could hear the power in her voice. They were mesmerized, as most people were when they heard Henna in an intimate setting. The audience gave a big round of applause as Henna humbly bowed her head and wrapped her hands around the microphone stand. She pulled the stand closer and spoke. "Thank you. How many in here like Janis Joplin?" There were a few cheers, but for the most part it was quiet. "Well, I am a huge fan. If for no other reason than the fact that she was gravely misunderstood. But she sang with so much passion and craze in her voice that fans wondered if she was going to make it through whatever it was that she was singing about. Um, she moved people, and I think that's what music should do. So the next song is one of hers. I give you 'Maybe.'"

Henna sang her rendition, and it was apparent that her sultry, alto voice was wooing not only the men, but also a few of the women. She put her heart and soul into the two-song performance and left the audience wanting more.

"I hope you all enjoyed this as much as I did. I'm Henna James. Peace and blessings to you. Thanks and good night."

When she left the stage, groups of folks rushed to her. Gerald insisted the crowd give her another ovation, and told everyone to go buy her latest project. Henna felt like a new artist just stepping onto the scene. It was a welcomed emotion. She then joined Bobby-B, who had found a tiny table near the rear exit. Naturally, he gave her glowing reviews about her performance, and she soaked up each word of acclaim. Henna often criticized the big fish in the little ponds and vilified those who remained in smaller cities to avoid the competition that larger cities attracted. However, tonight she understood the metaphor's magic. It just felt good to be praised for her talent on domestic soil. Henna looked up and saw Monica quickly approaching her. She had a scowl across her face. Henna immediately thought Monica had gotten into it with Julian. Henna had no idea that she was the cause of the grimace.

Chapter 10

"Stop" (Howard Tate, 1968)

Monica wanted to strangle Henna for messing around with her little brother. But she knew it took two to tango, which made her want to choke both her and Craig. She whisked through the crowd and stood over Henna.

Henna smiled, but Monica only sneered before taking both her hands and cupping them around Henna's neck.

"What are you doing?" asked Henna.

"Checking for loose screws," Monica replied with an admonishing glare.

"What is wrong with you?"

"I heard you," Monica answered.

"You heard me perform?" Henna said with excitement.

"I guess you could call it that."

Henna tried to comprehend, but she was still confused. Monica leaned over and whispered her secret in her ear. "I heard you this afternoon, you and Craig. I heard both of you."

Though she was partially embarrassed, Henna could only grin at the fact that she was busted. "I just performed, I hate you missed it," Henna stated, avoiding the obvious.

"Who's your friend? I need him to excuse himself so that we can talk."

"Oh, Bobby, this is Monica. This is Bobby-B, the producer I've been working with." The two shook hands formally.

"I need to speak with Henna," reiterated Monica.

"Either of you want a drink?" he asked before excusing himself.

As soon as Bobby stood, Monica sat and started the interrogation. "What in the world were you thinking? I told you not to mess with him," Monica said.

"I'm not messing with him. We slept together, so what? We are grown."

"That's not the point. You aren't over Ahmad, and Craig is not ready to settle down."

"I'm not trying to settle with Craig. He's a baby. It was just sex. You remember what casual sex is, right?"

"Yeah, it went out in the early 1990s, along with smoking cigarettes."

"Ha-ha," replied Henna.

"Once we get to a certain age, casual sex isn't casual. It comes with ties, unsaid expectations, baggage, and other stuff."

"Stop badgering me, it was what I needed. I have been inspired. The performance I gave tonight was the best in over a year. Please just let me enjoy this moment."

Monica was quiet. Maybe her friend really needed whatever it was that her baby brother had given, and she didn't want to ruin the experience. However, she did give a warning. "Y'all better not do it again." Henna gave the okay sign with her right hand and winked with her left eye. Monica motioned to the flower in Henna's hair. "You've been picking flowers from my yard?"

Henna thought about telling her it was from Craig, but figured it was best not to mention his name, so she responded, "Nice touch, right?"

Monica shrugged her shoulders and looked at Henna's empty wineglass. "Merlot?"

"You know it," Henna replied.

Monica went to the bar, but she quickly returned without the wine. She knelt down and whispered to Henna. "Mick is here."

"I know. I don't like him," replied Henna.

"What? Why not? He's a sweetheart." Henna made a face, but didn't respond verbally. Monica continued talking. "Did you talk to him? Who is he here with?"

"Some girl. She's cute. I forgot her name."

Monica then looked his way and strutted off to the bar, deliberately walking in the vicinity of his table, but intentionally not speaking. Henna watched this silly diversion and decided it was time for her to do some of her own stern speaking. As soon as Monica returned to the table, Henna lit into her.

"Why are you playing games with this man, when you already have a man?"

Monica held on to her innocence. "What games?"

"The 'I want him to see me, but I'm not going to speak so that he will be forced to come say something to me later' game. I taught you that game, sophomore year, when you liked that Sigma boy."

"Oooh, Tyson Walker," Monica reminisced. "He was some kind of fine."

"Stop deviating. Please tell me you don't like Mick."

"I don't like Mick," Monica said, loud and clear, but Henna saw through the charade. Ironically, Monica saw what Henna saw, and so she caved in, just seconds later. "I don't know why I'm acting this way," Monica whined.

"Finally I get some truth."

"I love Julian. He is kind and sweet. He's so good to me, and he's been faithful, and everything about him is perfect."

"So what's the problem?" Henna questioned. She had a sarcastic look that read she already knew the answer.

"I don't know," bellyached Monica.

"I do. There is no 'ooh la la.' It is what sustains a relationship. He's perfect on paper, but he's not a credit score, so that doesn't matter."

Monica quickly interjected. "Oh, and he has great credit too. His score is something like seven hundred seventy."

"Damn, that is good. But who cares?" she said, quickly redirecting. "You're a hypocrite. You have to break up with him."

"I am not! Julian is the best thing that has ever happened to me."

"Fine. Stop playing games with tall, dark, and handsome then. Who, by the way, probably has bad credit."

"No, he can't. He's a banker."

"And that means what? Never mind, he's coming over. Don't look," Henna whispered.

Mick appeared behind Monica and tapped her on the shoulder. She pretended that she hadn't noticed him all night. Though it was a silly game, she played it perfectly. Of course he left his date at the table. They spoke casually; he complimented Henna on her performance and walked back to his table. As soon as he got out of ear's reach, Henna spoke.

"I still don't like him. He seems sneaky."

"Yeah, but he is fine," Monica expressed.

"No doubt about that," Henna promptly replied. The two giggled, watched one more act, and decided to leave. Henna said good-bye to Bobby and Gerald, but not before promising to perform a full set one night before she left town. As they walked to the parking lot, Monica commented, "She wasn't that cute."

With no preface, Henna still knew Monica was referring to the woman with Mick.

"Stop it."

"No, really, her weave needed a touch up and her skin was oily."

"You saw all of that in that dark-ass club?" Monica nodded. "You need some help. You headed home, or are you going to see Julian?"

"I told him that I was hanging with you this evening, which were my plans until I came home to the dreadful sounds of you bumping uglies with my brother. So I'll see you at the house."

"Oh, I'm not going home. I have more uglies to bump."

Monica gasped as her face fell to the pavement, and Henna burst into loud laughter.

"I'm joking," she said.

However, when she got into the car and headed in the direction of Monica's house, she got the urge to see Craig. As she recalled how he felt, it took every bit of self-control not to call him. Therefore, she turned up her radio and continued to trail Monica home.

Craig must have been doing some recanting himself, because as soon as Henna pulled into the driveway, her cell phone rang. Craig was on the other end, and she told him that she'd call back once she got to her room. She didn't say why, but it was Monica's scolding voice she couldn't bear to hear. Henna said a few words to Monica once they got in the house, and then she scooted upstairs. However, it was now Monica who needed a friend and wanted to talk, so she soon followed. Just as Henna was about to return Craig's call, Monica knocked on her door. She came in and plopped on the edge of the bed.

"We have to be more responsible," stated Monica.

Henna didn't know where she was going with this statement, so she remained quiet and listened. "You and I are attractive, successful women, and so it's pretty much assumed that we can have most guys that we go after. But there comes a time when we need to go for the guys that we need, instead of the ones we want."

"I guess," Henna commented softly.

"We aren't in our twenties, and we have to start looking at men for the future. We've had our fun."

"But I'm not done having fun. I want to have fun and have a future," noted Henna.

"It doesn't happen like that."

"It can," Henna quickly disagreed. "You can't just settle, because you feel like you're getting old."

"I'm not settling!" Monica loudly defended. "Julian is a great catch."

"I was speaking in general, not necessarily pertaining to your situation."

"Oh," Monica said, quieting down.

Just then, Henna's phone rang. She ignored it and kept talking. "Whoever it is we pick, we just need to know that it is someone we can commit to, and someone who is going to treat us with respect and take care of our needs. That's all we can hope for," Henna firmly stated.

"Julian does all of that."

"Good. Can you commit to him?"

"I can," Monica answered.

"Then you have your future."

Henna's phone beeped to indicate a voice mail was being left. Monica looked in that direction. "Who's calling you this late?"

Henna was quick with a response. "Probably Ahmad. He's been calling a lot lately."

"He wants you back?"

"Don't know. I haven't talked to him."

"Why don't you change your number?"

"I was going to before I left New York, but I didn't want to update everyone with my new number, so I just left it."

Monica drifted into quiet thought as Henna lay down across the bed. However, Monica snapped out of her daze, and rolled Henna off the edge of the bed as she began undressing the sheets.

"What are you doing?" Henna shrieked.

Monica continued removing the sheets before she answered. "These must be burned," she declared. Henna exploded into laughter.

"I was going to wash them, first thing in the morning."

"There isn't enough Tide to wash away the residue skankiness left on these sheets. These five-hundred-thread count sheets, I might add."

"Yes, my delicate skin appreciates your good taste," Henna added while softly grazing her own arms.

"Yeah, well, see if I continue to give you my good sheets," Monica said, balling them into a pile and tossing them on the floor.

Still chuckling, Henna replied, "You're not seriously burning these, are you?"

Monica nodded.

"Well, I will wash them and take them back to New York with me. We are not wasting good sheets, and they're navy blue. I love navy blue."

"You better not be basking in these sheets, thinking about your nasty activities," Monica said.

Henna gave a shifty grin. "It was skanky, wasn't it?"

"Exactly."

"But it was goooooood," Henna grinned.

Monica gagged and left the room. Henna quickly stepped over the sheets and reached for her phone. As she was dialing Craig's number, Monica returned with folded sheets. She tossed the new ones on the bed, said good night, and retired for the evening. Finally it was safe to talk. Henna felt like a sneaky teenager as she closed her door and once again dialed Craig's number. He answered on the second ring and they talked for two hours before hanging up. They covered normal topics, like family and music, to rare subjects, such as favorite mammals and Converse versus Adidas. The dialogue was sweet, not tainted with sexual innuendos alluding to the day's past events. It was though they hadn't had sex yet, which made the exchange precious and refreshing.

It was often difficult to have those types of conversations once the doors of intimacy had been opened. For Henna, it was very rare. If she let a man in sexually, she closed down everywhere else. It was her protection mechanism, but not with Craig. For some reason she was extremely comfortable around him, and on the phone they managed to unveil layers. The tough exteriors melted and they talked as two eager people who couldn't wait to see each other again. Neither asked when that would be, but it was understood that it was going to happen. Henna got off the phone with an incandescent smile stuck on her face. She sensed that across town Craig was bearing a similar grin. She knew the affair wasn't over. Henna buried her face in the Snuggle fresh pillowcase and dreamed of nothing but hot, nasty sex. If her thoughts were any indication of things to come, Monica was soon to be on a first-name basis with the local fire department.

Chapter 11

"Love Is Strange" (Mickey & Sylvia, 1957)

"I have the perfect swatch for your interiors," Monica yelled as she walked into Sweet J's.

Julian's assistant, Cola, looked up from the counter but didn't bat an eyelash. Cola didn't care for Monica, and she wasn't one to conceal her feelings.

"He's in the back," she said, with a quick glance. Monica slowed her roll as she strolled by the pastries.

"I think I want a slice of apple pie," she mentioned to Cola as she continued to walk toward the back. Cola didn't break her stride to pay Monica a bit of attention.

"I have the perfect swatch for your interiors," she repeated this time a tad bit louder as she burst into the office.

"Well, how are you today?" asked Julian as he reached for his girl and gave her a big embrace.

"Look!" Monica shouted, slamming the tiny square of jacquard textile in his face.

Julian removed it from her hand and tried to give her a kiss. Monica finally realized that he wasn't going to look at the swatch until he got some loving attention, so she obliged his kiss. Then, like a magician, she produced another swatch from thin air and demanded he look at them both.

"Look how the gold in the jacquard picks up the gold flecks in the floral satin."

Julian looked at the fabrics, but he wasn't as excited as she'd hoped.

"You don't like it?" Monica questioned.

"I didn't think we were going with flowers."

"They're subtle."

"Where is this fabric going?" he asked.

Monica took Julian by the hand and pulled him out into the café. She pointed to the top of the window. "The jacquard is for the small valance at the top, which will be canvased around a board, not hanging." Monica then pulled Julian over to the counter. "This is the drape for the counter."

"The counter will have a drape? That's not necessary."

"If you want to upgrade, it is necessary," she demanded.

Julian shrugged his shoulders and finally replied. "Whatever you think is best. Now, as I said earlier, how are you today?"

"I'm good, and you?"

"Better, now that I'm looking at you." He reached down for another kiss. "Did you want something?" Julian asked, pointing to the desserts.

"I asked for an apple pie."

Julian looked at Cola and motioned for her to cut the pie. As soon as he turned his back, though, she rolled her eyes, got out the knife, and flicked it in Monica's direction, who continued to gawk as she cut the slice.

"We have tickets to Cat on a Hot Tin Roof tomorrow night."

"That's here?"

"No, it's on Broadway. We fly out in the morning."

Julian perked up, but Monica's excitement died down. "But I have things to do this weekend. How could you make plans without telling me? I don't know if I can change my itinerary."

"Well, as I said, we fly out tomorrow." Julian gave an assertive nod, then walked back into the office.

Monica waited at the counter for her slice. As Cola slid it across the counter, Monica inquired, "What is your problem?"

Cola quickly answered, "Taxes are high. My bank account is low. My son wants to skip college and become a rapper. My blood pressure is rising. I have a bunion on my foot—"

"With me! What is your problem with me?"

Cola replied just as nastily. "You're wading in my dating pool."

"Come again?" Monica said.

"There are plenty of young single men in their thirties. Ones that I can't get, but you can. But no, you want to go fishing in my pond. And to top it off, you're ungrateful. I wish someone would offer me half of what he offers you. I would gladly accept it all, but not you. His gifts are always followed by a complaint, never a thank-you. Do I need to continue, because I have more," Cola earnestly replied.

Monica stood there and took in the insults. She didn't know how to respond. Cola, who had to be around fifty, was her elder, and Monica's mother had taught her to be respectful of her elders, especially the women. Therefore, she bit her tongue as she and Cola continued to stare squarely at each other. After close to twenty seconds of silence, Monica spoke. "Could you warm up my pie?"

Cola peered down at the pie and then up to Monica's eyes, and replied, "No." With that, she walked away to help the next couple. Monica was dumbfounded. She quickly rushed to Julian's office.

"You need to have a microwave available for customers to use." Julian nodded as he went over a few invoice reports. Monica placed her hand on top of his paper-work to gain his attention. "And you need to get rid of any disgruntled employees."

Julian began laughing. "You talking about Cola?"

"You know I am."

Julian laughed harder. "Cola has been with me since the beginning. I can't get rid of her."

"But she's mean."

"Only to you."

"So you noticed? She hates me."

"Yes, she's mentioned it a few times. I told her that I didn't care if she didn't like you, especially in the begin-ning. But I did tell her that if you became my wife, she had to respect you."

"Well, you should have heard what she just said . . . . Hold up, did you say if I became your wife?" Monica had a peculiar look on her face.

Julian pulled her close. "That is where we are headed, right?" Monica was quiet and she digested his words. "I love you, Monica Cole."

Monica looked deep in Julian's eyes and she saw it. Her heart began to race, and then flutter. She saw her-self as his other half, his wife. "I love you too, Julian." She leaned in and kissed him. However, just in time to ruin the romantic moment, Cola came bursting into the office.

"Julian, make sure you order more candied walnuts. We are low and you know it takes four weeks some-times for them to come in."

"Don't you knock?" Monica challenged, but it didn't matter. Cola completely ignored her. As far as Cola was concerned, Monica was a child, and she was not going to be bothered by someone she could have birthed.

"I will place a double order," Julian replied.

"Okay," Cola said as Monica eyed Julian. He knew the cause of her caustic glare.

"And make sure you knock before entering next time," he added.

Cola nodded and shut the door.

"Women are funny," Julian commented.

"Did you guys ever date?" Monica asked.

"Define dating."

"Never mind, that answers my question," Monica smirked. "I still don't like her."

"You just don't like her, because she doesn't like you."

"Wrong. I don't like her, because she likes you. She's going to try to break us up."

Julian wrapped his arms around Monica and pulled her waist into his. "If I wanted to be with Cola, I would be. I want to be with you. You're getting yourself aggravated over nothing."

Sucking her teeth, in classic sista-girl fashion, Monica looked toward the door. "She better watch herself."

Again, Julian grinned. "I like this side of you. It's feisty, saucy."

Monica laughed. "So what time does our flight leave tomorrow?"

"What about your plans?"

"You are my plans," she said, her smile beaming.

"I like the sound of that." Julian reached in his desk drawer and handed her the printed-out itinerary. Monica checked the schedule and put it in her purse. She handed the last morsel of her pie to Julian, who gladly took it from her fork, and then kissed him good-bye.

"Call me tonight," she said, leaving the office. "I'm ordering the fabric." Monica held up the swatches and Julian nodded as he watched his lady turn to walk away.

"I hope you don't think I take you for granted," Monica said before she left.

"I don't. But you could be a little more attentive and thankful."

Monica turned back around and gave Julian another big kiss. "I love you. I just get swept up in my work sometimes." Julian displayed an endearing smile and Monica walked out.

She placed her empty plate on the counter by Cola. She didn't say one word as they passed intense stares across the glass. Monica strolled out of the shop and went back to her office.

Monica immediately called Henna once she got to the car, but Henna didn't have long to speak because she was waiting in the park for Craig and wanted to be off the phone by the time he got there. As she finished her cigarette, Henna answered Monica with a slew of one-word responses.

"Do you think it's unfair to date outside my age range?"

"No," Henna answered.

"Would you curse out an older woman?"

"Depends."

"Julian and I are going to New York this weekend."

"Good," Henna replied.

"What are you doing? Why aren't you talking to me?" Monica asked.

"I am," Henna said as she sat on the bench and continued to look out for Craig.

"You sound busy," Monica said.

"I'm writing." Just then Craig approached from behind. His peck on the neck startled her. "Hold on," Henna said as she held the phone away from her ear.

Henna jokingly pushed Craig away from her face as she grappled with the phone, and tossed down her cigarette butt. "Look, Mo, I have to go. I will talk to you tonight. When do you leave?"

"Tomorrow," Monica replied.

"Okay, so tonight we'll have a talk over a glass of wine."

Henna quickly hung up as Craig swept her up from the bench and spun her around. He continued to hold her in his arms and gave her six gently placed pecks on her face.

"Put me down," Henna said, poking him in the chest.

"No," Craig stated.

"Put me down!" she insisted.

Craig placed her on the bench and sat next to her. The two stared at each other like goofy teenage lovers. And just like most times, Henna caught herself acting bubbly and looked away. She enjoyed it, but at the same time, she feared it. "Have you eaten?" she said, looking across the park.

"No, let's go." Craig stood and held out his hand.

"I don't hold hands," Henna said.

"Me either. I was helping you up," he responded. "How many times do I have to tell you? I'm not sweating you."

Henna gave a very girlish simper, and rose from the bench without his help. "I need to get some new clothes. Wanna go shopping with me later?"

"I don't have time to play with you all day, Henna James. I'm not a superstar like you. Lil Wayne hasn't asked me to do shit for any of his albums."

Henna burst into laughter. She loved his sarcastic sense of humor, and she had a year's worth of cheer to make up for, so he needed to keep it up. "Well, maybe I could hook you up, considering I have Wayne on speed dial and all."

Henna pulled out her phone, acting like she was about to call. Craig stopped walking, which, in turn, halted her steps. "What?" she asked.

"I'm enjoying this."

Henna smiled, and gave in to her first response without thinking. "I'm enjoying you."

The two walked off to eat lunch. They didn't hold hands, but they were close enough for their elbows to graze as they walked. It was just enough contact to say "we're together, but not together." After lunch Craig took Henna to Virginia Highlands, which he tried to liken to SoHo. She sneered at the lame comparison. Sure, there were some great shops, but it certainly was nothing like the neighborhood South of Houston Street. However, Craig did manage to sway her normal shopping pattern. Henna didn't buy one black piece of clothing. In fact, when she grabbed any item in the dark hue, he already had its identical in a brighter color. Henna ended her shopping spree with four pastel-colored shirts, two bright skirts, and two sundresses, one pink, one yellow. Craig was definitely taking her far away from her comfort zone, but she was handling it well. They'd spent the entire afternoon together, and Craig realized he hadn't put but one hour into the bar that day, something he hadn't done in weeks. This was a welcome break for them both.

That evening, when Henna returned home, the tables had turned. It was now Monica sitting around and waiting to spend time with Henna. Monica had already prepared a spring salad with chicken and had cracked open a bottle of wine. Henna didn't even bother taking her things upstairs. She parked them by the kitchen door and poured herself a glass.

"What's in the bags?" Monica asked while grabbing two of them and peeking in.

"Clothes. It was cheaper for me to shop than fly home and get things."

Monica pulled out the pastel pieces and looked at Henna. "You bought these?" she questioned with doubt. "I've never seen you in pink. You don't like pink."

"Yes, I do," Henna said, swiping the items from Monica's grip. "I own a couple of pink things."

"You don't even own pink nail polish."

"Lies." Henna removed her shoes and showed off her pink toe polish.

Monica was taken aback. She took another shirt from the bag and held it up to Henna's body. "The colors suit you, though. This is good. I like the change. Maybe you did need to get some."

"Told you," Henna said, grinning tightly.

Monica had no idea Craig and Henna were spending time together, and since she was dealing with her own can of worms, she had no time to investigate the root of her friend's sudden fashion adjustment.

"You know Cola, at Julian's place."

"Yeah, I actually talked to her the other day. She has the prettiest eyes," Henna commented.

"What?"

"Her eyes are kinda gray-green."

"Fuck her eyes. We don't like her."

"Such language, we who?" questioned Henna.

"We, you and me, and anyone else in our crew."

"Oh, we have a crew now? So, are we planning some type of mutiny against her? I could have Lil Wayne say something bad about her in a song. That's called beef." Henna chuckled.

"Beef? What in the hell is wrong with you? I'm serious," said Monica as she explained the situation and details of her so-called beef. Henna understood completely.

"You know, my mom is single, and she has issues with younger women dating older men. She said that most men her age are either bitter, or have so much baggage they could move to China and not pack a thing. So she doesn't like younger women taking the good men who are left."

"Why doesn't she date younger men?"

"Young men prefer young women, and old men prefer young women, especially if they aren't trying to get married. So the older woman is left to spend her wiser years alone. It isn't fair. People should date in their age range."

"That's not what you said earlier."

"I make the exception for you."

Monica wanted to debate, but her only quick retort was "Craig is ten years younger than you."

"I said people should date in their age range. They can sleep with anyone they want," Henna countered.

"That's stupid. I don't want to talk about it anymore. So how's the recording going? You've been spending quite a bit of time in the studio."

"It's going well," Henna replied, hoping Monica wouldn't want to hear anything. Her last week of "studio time" was an excuse to hang out with Craig, so Henna quickly redirected the conversation. "So, do you want to marry Julian?"

Monica shrugged her shoulders before answering, "I think so. But I don't want to talk about it anymore."

"I'm not going to say anything bad. I like Julian for you. He's a good boyfriend."

Monica smiled. "He's taking me to see Cat on a Hot Tin Roof in New York."

"Damn, correction, he's a great boyfriend."

Monica nodded. "I could marry him."

"You could or you would? There's a big difference there," said Henna.

"I would, if he asked me."

"What if he asks you this weekend?"

"Is he going to ask me this weekend? Do you know something?" Monica asked anxiously.

"No, I'm just saying. Could you take care of him when he gets old and sick?"

"He's not going to be sick."

"You know what I mean. You have to think about that. You may have to feed him and change him."

"That could happen in any relationship."

"Yeah, but it could happen sooner for you. I've seen you really in love, and I think right now, you're in like. Just give it some more time. Don't let him pressure you to rush into anything."

The two sat in silence as Monica contemplated changing Julian's diaper, and Henna tried to think of more conversation.

"What are you wearing to the play?" Henna asked. "Let's go put your outfit together."

"Have some salad first," Monica told her.

"I'm so full. I went to Artuzzi's today."

Monica made a disappointed face. "Craig loves that spot."

Henna froze. Had she said too much? She prayed the conversation ended there, and it did, thankfully. Monica had too many other things on her mind to put two and two together.

"Actually, I will have a little salad." Henna said, rising. They ate and then spent an hour putting together the perfect Broadway ensemble. Just before bed Henna spoke with Alphonzo and made plans to have lunch with him tomorrow. She was back in the swing of dating, and enjoying every moment. Plus, she didn't want her time to be totally consumed with Craig. Alphonzo was the perfect diversion. Although she still wanted to speak with Craig just before bed, they'd spent enough hours together already, and talking just before bed

seemed too much like a real relationship. She decided
against it.

Monica couldn't seem to get her conversation with
Cola off her mind. She was over the age difference, but
Monica couldn't stand people talking about her. It was
a problem she'd had all her life. She was a pleaser, and
she hated the thought of her actions making others
upset. That evening she went to sleep with a nervous
feeling gnawing at her tummy. She was determined
to show Cola that she was a good girlfriend. Her mo-
tive was completely wrong, but in Monica's warped
purpose, she was hoping she would indeed become
that loving, appreciative girlfriend, and eventually that
wonderful wife.

"Fake it 'till you make it," she whispered to herself.

In this case she would fake it until she became it.
Monica, now filled with insecurity, called Julian, de-
spite the late hour. As he was answering, she asked,
"Am I a good girlfriend?"

A half-asleep Julian replied, "If I had a problem, I'd
tell you."

That's not the answer she wanted, but she knew not
to press it. "I love you," she said, and hung up.

She tossed in her bed for another hour before her
eyes became heavy. Just before Monica drifted, she
thought about Mick. Her conscience had her second-
guessing her value, and rightfully so. She turned on
her television and watched Law & Order. It took three
back-to-back episodes to silence her thoughts. She finally closed her eyes around 4:00 A.M.

Chapter 12

"Honey Hush" (Big Joe Turner, 1953)

Henna's cell phone was her alarm the next morning. She answered without paying much attention to the ID. It was Ahmad.

"Where have you been?" he asked, sounding tense.

"What do you want, Ahmad?"

"I've been trying to reach you. I thought something happened to you."

"Again, what do you want?"

"Where are you?" he persisted.

"I'm hanging up."

"Please don't. Just tell me that you are safe."

"I'm safe. I'm on vacation. Don't call me anymore."

Henna hung up the phone. Her disconnection from him was both physical and mental. She didn't think about Ahmad the rest of the day. His effect was waning.

Henna prepared for lunch with Alphonzo. They spoke around 11:00 A.M., and planned to meet in Grant Park at noon. When Henna arrived, she was surprised to see that Alphonzo had planned a picnic in the park. She felt like a woman who was being wooed. She sat next to a bowl of strawberries, and as soon as she bit into the first one, her cell phone rang. This time it was Craig. She ignored the first call, but when he phoned right back, she excused herself from the picnic and answered.

"Hey, let's meet for lunch," he suggested.

"I can't."

"You in the studio?"

Henna wasn't good at lying. She didn't even know why she was considering telling a fib. She owed him nothing; still, she felt guilty about being on a date with Alphonzo.

"I will be in a few," she answered.

"So later?" he asked.

"I will call you."

"Are you trying to be coy, Ms. James? If you must hear it, I want to see you," Craig said.

"I want to see you too. So, yeah, I'll call you later, okay? Bye." Henna felt Alphonzo looking her way, so she quickly hung up. She walked back to the blanket. The couple had a wonderful lunch, which lasted two hours. Although Alphonzo admitted that he'd purchased the panninis, instead of making them, the lunch was just as romantic. When he leaned over and kissed Henna, she let the pucker land on her lips, instead of her cheek. She then laughed, before responding, "I guess this is your trick. You take a woman to the park to show her your quixotic side."

"I'm not sure what that means, but if it's working in a good way, then yes."

Henna laughed. She liked Alphonzo. He didn't provide the va va voom, but it was enough to keep her interested. If she used him to balance out her time with Craig, was that so bad? She looked at him again and smiled.

"'Quixotic' means romantic, dreamy . . . you know."

"Actually, it's no act. I am romantic. At least my ex used to say that I was."

"Then why is she your ex?"

"She had a teenager, and I wanted another kid, but she was done. She said she'd been a mother all her adult life and wanted to start living. She didn't want to compromise, so it wasn't going to work."

"That's sad."

"You want kids?" asked Alphonzo.

"Maybe. I used to, but as I get older, I get less and less enthused about it."

"But if you got married, you would have at least one?"

"Maybe," Henna reiterated. Alphonzo stopped pursuing the line of questioning and hand-fed Henna another strawberry. They packed up the basket and decided to take a stroll down to the lake. In the two hours they'd discussed everything there was to say. The conversation didn't keep flowing, as it did with her and Craig, or with Ahmad for that matter. It was forced, and Henna had to concentrate on what she should say next. Basically, she was bored out of her mind. She tried to enjoy the moment, but she was ready to go moments after eating. When he talked, she drifted off into song verses. Several times he noticed her far-off stare and questioned if she was all right. Henna replied with a genuine nod and smile, until she couldn't take it anymore.

"I have to go to the studio." Lately that had become the excuse for everything. Eventually she was going to have to produce a CD, seeing that she was always in this supposed studio. Maybe she would actually go today.

Henna thanked Alphonzo for the lunch, promised to see him later this week, and got in her car. She drove by the studio and saw Bobby's black Hummer parked out front, so she went in. This time the receptionist, industry wannabe, recognized her and began kissing up.

"Oh, how things have changed," Henna whispered underneath her breath.

"Ms. James," he called out, "I listened to your last project, girl. It was absolutely fabulous, just like those shoes you're wearing."

She returned his fake smile with one even more spurious and walked to Bobby-B's office, but he wasn't in. Then she walked into studio A, but he wasn't there either. Finally she walked into the mixing studio in the back and pushed the door open. Bobby-B was in there, but he wasn't mixing, at least not music. He was having an intimate moment with a friend, a gentleman friend. Henna was shocked. She ran out of the room and down the hallway. Bobby-B ran after her. "Henna," he called out. She slowed down as he approached.

"I'm sorry, I shouldn't have barged in." Henna was very embarrassed.

"It's okay," he responded. "Let's go in here." Bobby and Henna stepped into his office and he closed the door behind her.

Henna stared at him speechlessly; it was as if he were a ghost. Finally she spoke. "I didn't know."

"Didn't know what?" Bobby said, playing innocent.

"You know . . . that you were gay," she said.

"Oh, I'm not gay. I just like to kiss boys from time to time."

Henna didn't know how to respond, so she held her breath until Bobby cracked a smile. "I'm joking. I'm a hip-hop producer. I can't be open about my sexuality. I may not get work."

Henna lowered her head and gave a heavy sigh. "That's sad."

"It is what it is. There are lots of homosexual people in my industry, but it's such a genre of rough and tough, testosterone-driven music, no one wants to admit that their banging track was created by a gay producer."

"That's stupid."

"But it's true."

"Well, your secret is safe with me," Henna promised. Though they were alone, she whispered her next question, concerned that others would hear. "Is Lil Wayne gay too?"

"Oh, hell nah. He'd probably shoot you in the face if he heard you ask. Wayne is cool. He tried to hook me up with his cousin LaRhonda. When she said I didn't try to hit it, he asked if I was gay."

"What did you say?" Henna said, greatly intrigued.

"I said, 'Man, I was trying to respect you.'"

"And what did he say?" Henna continued with more curiosity.

"He said, 'Oh, word? Appreciate that, but she's my third cousin. She ain't my sister or nothing,' then laughed, and that was that."

"Well, again, your secret is safe with me."

"Hey, my son is having career day. It would be cool if you came and spoke to his class," Bobby mentioned.

"Your son?" inquired Henna.

"Prom night, that was the last time I was with a woman."

"That bad, huh?"

"Just not my thing," he responded.

"But you said you would have given me four orgasms. You were joking?"

"No, you're the incredible Henna James. I'd make an exception for you." Bobby winked, and Henna blushed.

"Well, I was wondering if you'd like to help me with my next project. Officially, I need your rates and ideas," Henna stated.

Bobby smiled like a young boy with a crush; then he kissed the top of Henna's hand. "Why, Ms. James, I would be honored."

"Great. Let me know about career day. Of course I will participate, but for now, I'll let you get back to your session," Henna said, smiling.

Henna hugged Bobby and left the studio. On the way to the house, she called to check on Monica, who was having a great time in New York. She and Julian had been shopping and eating all day. They hadn't made it over to Brooklyn yet, but Monica promised that she would get Henna's mail from Haydu, and grab those few requested items before she left. Henna insisted that Monica have a great time, relax, and enjoy the moment, and Monica swore to do just that. They disconnected as Henna pulled in the driveway.

She hadn't called Craig back and knew that if she made that call now, he'd come over, and she couldn't be responsible for what would happen. Though her hormones were screaming to be satisfied, she decided against calling him. Instead, she went in, ate the remainder of the salad from the day before, and turned on the television. Henna rarely watched TV but was quickly sucked into its world of reality programming. Hours passed as she watched one show after another. She couldn't believe the mess that her mind was taking in, but she couldn't stop watching. She was so engrossed, she didn't realize that she'd left her phone in the room, and it wasn't until she heard a knock on the door that she jumped up and broke the tube's trance.

"Who is it?" she called out, but there was no answer.

Henna went to the door and peeped out, but she saw no one. She turned and took two steps, and then the doorbell rang once more. She ran to the dining room and peered out the window and saw Craig's truck in the driveway. Henna sauntered back to the door and swung it open. But Craig wasn't at the door. As soon as she closed it, however, he was walking up behind her.

Craig scared the crap out of Henna, and she didn't take it well. She turned and whopped him upside his head with the television remote.

"I hate surprises! How many times do I have to tell you that!" Craig was starting to get the picture as a lump started to form just above his left brow.

"I'm in pain," he said, holding his head.

"Good!" Henna exclaimed as she walked into the kitchen to grab some ice. She came back with the ice cubes wrapped in a towel and handed it to him.

"You could at least put it on my head," he requested. "You're a baby."

"I am, so baby me." He handed the cubes back to her, took a seat on the couch, and laid his head back. Henna acted as though she was being tortured, but she enjoyed every minute of it. The faux tension between the two of them quickly melted the ice cubes, and before long, neither of them was thinking about the lump on his head. Henna straddled Craig, and somehow her sweatpants were on the floor seconds later.

"The couch! Monica would kill us if we did it here."

"Monica is in New York," Craig said, but then he remembered how anal his sister was. At the same time they both said, "What if she has cameras?"

They quickly rushed upstairs to the bedroom. It was just as great as before, if not better, for they were quick studies of each other's body movements. Close to an hour later, Craig and Henna lay in bed, staring at the ceiling. They both fought the cliché of staring into each other's eyes. While they looked at the plaster, those inevitable after-sex words were finally spoken.

"I don't expect anything from you, just because we are having sex now," said Henna.

"Same here. I mean, what we have is cool, but—"

"I don't live here," she interrupted. "And I don't have any plans to move here, so this is what it is. . . ."

"And nothing more," Craig finished the sentence.

Both still staring at the ceiling, the couple listened to the words they'd just released into the universe. The expressions were spoken simply to conceal his and her true feelings, and they continued speaking to convince not only one another but also themselves.

"I do have fun with you, though. I don't want you to think it's just sex," Henna commented.

"I know. I have fun with you too."

"But this couldn't work, though. You know that, right?" she added.

Craig finally turned to face Henna, and though she didn't want to look at him, she felt obligated. She slowly turned and looked into the eyes of the man she'd let in, both literally and figuratively. Nonetheless, she felt exposed, and so she placed her attention downward toward his bare chest.

"No pressure. You don't have to worry about me falling all in love and chasing you all over the country. My focus is my club. I don't have time for a relationship."

"And I don't want one," she quickly responded.

"So, are we good?" Craig asked, lowering his face to force eye contact.

"We're good," Henna said.

Even as the words were being said, the falling had begun. Just how long they could fight love's gravity was the question.

Chapter 13

"Who Do You Love?" (Bo Diddley, 1956)

When Monica returned from New York, her ring finger was adorned with an exquisite piece of antique jewelry. Henna had a difficult time mustering up fake excitement when Monica showed off her diamond and garnet ring, and it was then that Monica realized Henna had seen it already. All she could say was "Why didn't you tell me?"

Henna smiled and replied, "I don't like surprises, but you do."

Henna noticed Monica gazing at the ring whenever a quiet moment arose, but Monica never mentioned the particulars of the proposal. She wondered if Julian had proposed, or if he simply gave her the ring as a token of love. Finally, after two days, Henna had to ask.

"Did he ask you to marry him?"

Monica nodded yes and gave a perky smile, just before running out the door to work. That was it. She gave no specifics. Henna could only assume she said yes, since she was wearing the ring, but it seemed odd. When a woman received a ring from the man she loved, she'd give details in the vein of a movie scene, complete with backdrop, actions, transitions, and dialogue. No one shows the ring, nods, and keeps going—unless the woman had been engaged multiple times or was hiding something. Henna knew her friend was in over her head. Unfortunately, she had no time to harp on Monica's uncertain decisions, she had her own to deal with. She and Craig had seen each other at least two hours every day for the past two weeks. Either she would meet him at his place, or he'd come there while Monica was at work. She was going to have to admit it to Monica, because as private as Henna was, she didn't like lying to her close friend.

Today she and Craig were going to meet up after her career day presentation. For that reason Henna put on her pastel pink dress; then she did a very unusual act. She didn't place her hair in a bun or a ponytail. She wore it down. Ponytails were her trademark. It started when she was a teenager, embarrassed by her hair's texture.

Henna's hair was very thick, and wiry, and she didn't need a relaxer for her hair to be straight, it was naturally that way. Though her mother still called it "good hair," Henna despised that expression. It was that description that had gotten her beaten up in the seventh grade. She was "that tall, light-skinned girl, with the good hair, who thought she was better than everyone else."

She remembered it like it was yesterday. Henna never understood why her childhood friends suddenly turned on her once they got to middle school, and then gave her that false title. She still lived in the same deprived neighborhood in Columbus, Mississippi. She still wore used clothes from the thrift store and was the daughter of a hardworking single parent. But for some reason the boy Theresa Hines liked had a thing for "good hair," and this follicle war would haunt her through high school. Because of this one incident, the young girls of Marion County became the Hatfields and the McCoys, forever divided into the good-haired girls and their nappy-haired foes. Every time she would question her mom about it, she gave the same vague response.

"Child, it goes way back to slavery days."

This was not the explanation Henna desired, but it became the reason Henna originally felt she wasn't "black enough" to be a soul singer. When they moved to New York her junior year, she carried that same stigma, and felt she'd only be accepted by the Puerto Rican girls. Therefore, she assimilated in the Latin community, and the so-called nappy chicks figured she was one of them and left her alone. It was then Henna began sporting her infamous ponytail, and it carried over to her singing career. Her face was beautiful and there was nothing she could do about that, but wearing her hair down added to the glamour, which she felt took away from her talent. She didn't want to be just another pretty-faced singer, and she felt empowered and more assertive when she slicked her hair back into a bun. It eventually became her signature look.

Today, with her hair swaying from side to side, Henna walked into the school and instantly she began turning heads. The women gawked and the men eagerly introduced themselves. With her three-inch wedge heels, Henna was right at five feet eleven inches, and she stood out like a beauty queen at a hoedown. Bobby-B spotted her and quickly escorted her to the office to retrieve her name tag and then took her to his son's room. Though Henna looked heavenly, she equated the music industry with being evil. The first five minutes were great. She spoke about the process of creating music, and learning to take care of the instrument, known as the voice. However, when one of the kids asked her about getting a record deal, Henna unknowingly went into her tirade. She compared the executives to vampires who wanted to suck every inch they could out of artists.

"It's hard not to sell your soul in order to make the charts, so an artist has to decide from the start whether she or he will be commercial or independent. But beware if you do go commercial, vampires will be at your door ready to bite." The young kids looked horrified. Henna then realized her speech had taken a course down the wrong path. She quickly tried to change up, by mentioning her latest surprise adventure. They all perked up when she told them she recorded a hook on a Lil Wayne song. Hands flew up. The boys wanted her to freestyle and the girls wanted to know how many tattoos he had. The joy in their eyes took Henna back down memory lane, to when she first became curious about singing. She realized that her presentation was less uplifting than she would have liked, so she made sure she ended on a positive note.

"When you're given a gift such as singing, dancing, writing, whatever, there is nothing more rewarding than sharing your talent with others. It's difficult to be an artist and a businessperson. But surround yourself with a good team of people, and put in the hard work, and it will pay off. It may take ten months or ten years, but don't give up, especially if that's what you were put here to do."

The classroom gave her a standing ovation. Afterward, she took a few pictures with the class for their wall of fame and left. Once in the car, she went straight to the Attic, where she was supposed to meet Craig. However, when she got there, Craig had just left to go get wood. Henna talked to Travis for a while, and then she sat at the piano and played around with a song. She made up a couple of verses and came up with a melody. Travis joined in. He sat at the piano and played along.

"How's the project coming along?"

"It's not!" Henna said, making a ridiculous expression. "I'm trying to come up with something fresh, but not so different that I lose my fans or the essence of my sound."

"Well, maybe Atlanta will provide some new inspiration," Craig said, walking in.

Henna looked up and smiled. "I think it will," she responded, suggesting there was much more to the statement. Craig and another gentleman placed the wood down by the bar, and then Craig waltzed over to Henna. He was beaming.

"Your hair! I can't believe you are wearing it down."

"I went and spoke at the school today."

"Oh, so the kids can get you to wear your hair down, but not me?"

"I didn't wear it down for anyone. I just thought I would try something different."

Craig pulled her up from the bench and spun her around. "You look amazing," he observed.

"You ready for lunch?"

"I can't," he answered.

Henna, in a juvenile manner, poked out her bottom lip. "But I'm dressed for lunch on someone's patio."

"But I have to help put the siding on this bar."

"That's right," Travis interjected. "You've had my boy missing in action."

Henna pouted and sat back down at the piano. Craig sat beside her. "I'll come over tonight."

"Monica will be there," Henna whined.

"So it's about time she knew about us, anyway."

"'Us'? We're an us, now?"

Craig answered with a smirk, and then rose to work on the bar. Henna only hung around a few more minutes.

She was officially bored. She'd been in Atlanta close to
a month. She'd eaten at the best restaurants, been to all
the good shops, and had figured out all the backstreets
to Monica's house. Yet, she wasn't ready to leave. She
pulled out her phone and called Haydu. However, once
she spoke to him and caught up on the latest gossip,
she realized that she wasn't missing anything in New
York either. All she could do was find some sort of ac-
tivity, stay in Atlanta, and finish working on her latest
project. Consequently Henna called and scheduled her
studio time throughout the next two weeks, and then
she stopped by Cat's Corner. Luckily, Cat was in, and
once Henna told her she'd be there for at least two more
weeks, Cat scheduled a full show. Then she told Henna
about an after-school program looking for volunteers.
She was sure they needed someone to teach music.
Henna enjoyed working with kids, but her patience ran
on the short side when it came to excess talking and
playing. She'd done programs like this before, but this
one sounded more like babysitting than actual teaching.

"Is it bad that I don't want to help the kids?" Henna
asked, bothered by her guilty conscience.

"If it's not for you, it's not for you. But here's the address in case you change your mind." Henna took the
business card from Cat, who was preparing to leave
town for a couple of days. She told Henna that she was
welcome to hang around, but Henna left and spent the
remainder of the afternoon at the bookstore. She purchased a new cookbook, went to the grocery store, and
decided to make a new dish for dinner.

Henna was chopping up yellow peppers at around
six that evening, when Monica's doorbell rang. She
was expecting Monica home around eight o'clock and
figured it had to be Craig. She didn't know why he
insisted on ringing the doorbell, when he had a key,

but she walked into the foyer and opened the door. To her surprise it was Ahmad. Henna nearly dropped the four-inch knife on her foot.

"What are you doing here?" she questioned; shock stretched from her, ear to ear.

"I needed to speak with you, and since you won't take my calls, I came here."

"How did you know I was here?"

"Phillip said you were recording in Atlanta. Then I called Haydu and tricked him into telling me you were staying with Monica."

"But how did you know where to find me?"

"We stayed here a couple of days when you were on tour two years ago. I know my way around Atlanta, and her address was still in my phone. I don't erase shit, you know that."

With a manner as cold as freezing steel, Henna stayed positioned at the door.

"Can I come in?" he asked.

Henna didn't budge. She continued to pierce through him.

"Why are you doing hooks for Lil Wayne?"

"What? How do you know about that?" Henna asked.

"Either come out here on the porch or let me in—this is ridiculous." Henna grabbed her cigarettes and stepped onto the porch. She took a defensive stand by the door.

"Wayne's manager called to find out if you could appear on his CD and what it would cost. Phillip said you weren't returning his calls, and so he called me. So what's that about?"

Henna blew out a puff and answered casually. "I was at the studio, he asked me to do the hook, and so I said yes."

"Well, it's a bad move. I'm not approving it."

"You're not my manager, so you can't approve or dis-approve anything that has to do with me." Henna blew smoke into his face.

He stared at her through the cloud of nicotine as she looked off into the distance.

"I've missed you," Ahmad said.

Henna gave him an ill-tempered grunt.

She turned to walk into the house, but he grabbed her hand. "Please," he said. "Hear me out."

"You better let go of my arm," she demanded.

Ahmad released her hand but moved to block her entrance back into the house. "I was wrong. I was just—"

"Just what?"

"I'm going to be honest. I met someone, and I thought it was what I wanted, but I was wrong. I want you. I want what we had. We have too much history to just let it go." Just then, Craig pulled up. Henna began to fidget. Ahmad noticed the difference but continued to speak. "Come back home. Let's at least talk about it. I'm ready to make a commitment." Henna's eyes followed Craig as he got out of his truck and approached the porch. Finally Ahmad turned around and acknowledged him.

"What's up, man?" said Ahmad.

"Not much. What's up?" responded Craig, who then made eye contact with Henna. "You okay?" he asked.

"I'm good," Henna answered while keeping her body in a firm stance. Craig sensed that something was off, but he wasn't sure. He looked at Henna once again and spoke. "I'm going in, let me know if you need me." He didn't try to kiss her, but he took his hand and gently brushed it across her stomach as he walked inside. It was just enough contact to show their closeness, but nothing too forward. As intended, Ahmad noticed it all.

As soon as Craig crossed the door's threshold, Ahmad commented, "You hanging with baby boy?"

"What?" Henna said, pretending she didn't under-stand his statement.

"I see. I ain't mad. Do your thing. When you get bored, which you will, holla at me."

"Good-bye, Ahmad," Henna scorned.

"I'll be in town for a few days. You've got my cell, and I will be back over so we can finish this conversa-tion when you're not babysitting." Ahmad grinned and walked off the steps. "Oh, you need to call Phillip," he called out. "He's pissed about this Lil Wayne thing."

Ahmad got in his rental and drove off. He wasn't the least bit intimidated by Craig. Ahmad was a forty-year-old New Yorker, born and bred. He had been in the music industry for eighteen years and had so much swagger pouring from his body, it could be seen all the way in the Bronx even though he was standing on a corner in downtown Brooklyn. He was that confident, to the point of conceit, but that's the way Henna liked them. He partied with Jay-Z and did business with Tommy Mottola. He wasn't going to be unnerved about a twenty-four-year-old drummer from Atlanta, no mat-ter how many times the young buck might have banged his ex-girlfriend. Henna was a sucker for his smug atti-tude, but she didn't trust one ounce of it. Therefore, she brushed off the conversation, put out her cigarette, and walked in.

Craig was at the bar, drinking a glass of water. Henna quickly bounced back into normal conversa-tion without missing a beat. "So how was your day?" she asked, leaning over to kiss Craig. He obliged her kiss, but he immediately asked the identity of the porch visitor. Henna decided against lying. After all, she and Craig were just friends. "It was Ahmad, my ex-manag-er." Fortunately, she'd never mentioned that Ahmad was also her ex-boyfriend, and she didn't disclose it at that moment either. "He was letting me know how pissed the label is that I did that hook for Lil Wayne. The whole thing is so stupid. Dinner should be ready in about twenty minutes." Henna walked over to the oven and checked on her minestrone pasta delight.

However, Craig wasn't done with the conversation. "He came all the way here to let you know? Why didn't he call?"

"He did," Henna answered. "But I stopped taking his calls."

"So, if he's your ex-manager, why is he concerned at all?"

"If we are just kicking it, why are you asking so many questions?" stated Henna.

Craig had nothing to say. He grinned and drank his water. Henna pulled her dish from the oven and checked to see if it was ready. "It's almost done. It's a new dish. I hope it's good." Henna placed it back in the oven.

Craig walked over to Henna, pinning her body between his and the counter. With her lanky arms draped over his shoulders, she kissed him.

"I think someone is a little jealous?" hinted Henna.

"'Jealous'? Is that the new word for 'horny'? Because if so, yeah, I'm jealous as hell," Craig joked.

They continued to kiss, until Monica walked in and busted them in the middle of their spit swap.

"What in the hell are you doing!" she yelled.

Craig and Henna simply laughed. The jig was up.

"Have you two been seeing each other the whole time?"

Craig and Henna both nodded as Monica collapsed onto the bar stool. "You bastards," she murmured. Again, Craig and Henna laughed.

"It's not funny," Monica continued.

"I'm sorry, Mo." Henna hopped down from the counter and walked over to console her friend. "I wanted to tell you, but I knew how you felt."

"So you've been sneaking around the past couple of weeks?"

"Yep. But if it makes you feel any better, it would have been so much sweeter if I could have shared the scandal with you," Henna said as she attempted to wrap her arms around Monica's shoulders.

"Don't touch me," Monica jokingly barked. "There's no telling what kind of dungeons he's had you in. I have to go upstairs to process this." Monica marched upstairs as Henna and Craig continued to giggle.

About three minutes later, her processing was done, and she returned to the kitchen to poke fun at the couple. They were quick to admit, "We're not together. It's just a physical-attraction type of thing."

"It's still a bad idea. You can only have sex for so long before someone catches feelings," Monica warned.

Henna and Craig looked at one another. Craig asked, "You catching feelings?"

"I'm not catching feelings. You?" Henna responded.

"Nope," he answered.

Then Henna turned to Monica and said, "We're straight."

Monica saw through the sham but played along. She still had a major problem with her baby brother and her friend sleeping together. But that night she held her peace.

Chapter 14

"Sweet Soul Music" (Arthur Conley, 1967)

Now that Monica knew about Craig and Henna, they no longer had to contain their affair to the daytime. The next evening after Monica went to Julian's, Craig and Henna stretched across the sofa with their heads meeting in the middle of the cushion and their legs dangling over each of the ends. They quietly stared at the ceiling as Craig twirled his fingers around the ends of Henna's hair. After seven or so minutes of stillness, Craig spoke.

"Whatcha thinking about?"

"What I'm going to do if I were to stop singing."

Craig maneuvered his body so that he was now facing her instead of the ceiling. "What do you mean 'stop singing'? You're a singer, it's who you are."

"It's what I do. Not who I am."

"Maybe that's the problem. You're looking at it the wrong way. You shouldn't see it as a job."

"Once upon a time, I didn't," Henna said, still staring at the ceiling.

Craig waited a few seconds and then continued with his case. "Why did you choose music?"

Almost with a haunted voice she whispered, "It chose me." Henna paused and then sat up on the couch. She tucked her legs underneath her and looked at Craig. "When I was eleven, my dad left my mom. I was devastated, which is why I have trust issues, according to my therapist, but that's another story. But my mom listened to 'Sugar on the Floor', by Elton John, for a month straight, every day, all day, after they split. The first week she cried, playing the song over and over for hours. Week two she began to smile. By week four she would dance through the whole song. It's like the song healed her. I thought . . . that's what I want to do. . . . I want to heal people with music I create."

"Sugar on the Floor?" asked Craig. "What's the song about?"

"It's about a one-sided relationship, when someone with so many insecurities and baggage just can't love the other person like they should. Can you imagine feeling like sugar on the floor? I wouldn't ever want to feel like that.

"Yeah me either" Craig said as he stared into space. Each reflected for a second before continuing.

"When did you know that you could sing?"

"Remember the girl I told you didn't like me because of my hair?" Craig nodded. "Well, before we were enemies, we used to do talent shows together, and she'd always make me sing lead. She said I sounded like Diana Ross."

"You don't sound anything like Diana."

"It was the 1980s and we were eight. To us, everyone sounded like Diana Ross."

"Who's your favorite singer?" he asked.

"Etta James, something about the power in her voice. I would sing her songs in talent shows too. My friends thought I was crazy. Ooh, Etta did a version of 'Sugar on the Floor' too. I love it, the things she does with her voice. . . ."

Craig continued with the interrogation. "So when did you really know you could sing?"

"When my mom started coming to our shows, she told me I had a really nice voice, and then she stuck me in the choir at church. I started doing solos, and by the time I was sixteen, I was writing my own music."

"Do you remember when you were sixteen?" Craig asked. "Do you remember how it felt to write your first song?" Craig stared her in the eyes, and Henna slowly nodded. "Every time you sit down and write, you need to find that place. Pure creation comes from the soul, not popular demand," Craig encouraged.

"Easier said than done," Henna commented.

"Of course it is. That's why everyone can't do it. Take a hiatus. The break makes people want you more."

"I can't. I have one more project to do."

"By when?"

Henna shrugged her shoulders. "I just want to get it done."

"You need to relax."

"Okay," said Henna as she placed her head in Craig's lap. "I'm relaxing."

"You know what I mean," he said, chuckling. "Have you ever played word-connect with Monica?"

"Of course I have. I even started doing it on the road with my band members." With Henna's head still in his lap, Craig continued to play with her hair as she closed her eyes and tried to relax.

"I see . . ." he started. It took Henna a minute to get into the word-connect routine, but she began.

"My life . . ."

"I see my life in music . . ."

"And when I hear . . ." Henna continued.

"Music . . ." he added.

Henna took a minute to put the whole thing together. "Stop thinking, just let it flow," Craig insisted.

"Okay, I see my life in music and when I hear music . . . I become . . ."

"Vulnerable," Craig stated.

Henna lifted up from his lap. "Really?" she asked.

"Yes! Keep it going."

Henna then jumped back into the sentence. ". . . I become vulnerable, but ironically . . ."

"... ironically, it's my ..."

"Refuge," Henna firmly avowed, ending the sentence.

Craig put the whole thing together. "I see my life in music and when I hear music, I become vulnerable, but ironically, it's my refuge."

"That's a good one," Henna said.

Craig agreed and pointed for her to start the next one. She repositioned herself on his lap and began.

"Silence is ..." Henna started.

"Silence is golden because ..."

"... it makes ..." Henna added.

"... it makes the truth...," he continued.

"... easier to hear," ended Henna. The two were still as they thought about the statement. The longer they sat in the quiet, the more they heard from one another. Henna was fading into slumber, but Craig didn't want the night to end.

"One more," he requested. "People are ..."

Henna didn't answer. Craig gently shook her body.

"You still with me?" he asked.

"Yeah, people are ... mammals."

Craig laughed at her statement and soon realized the meditation technique had worked. Henna drifted in and out of sleep. He gently cradled her body in his arms and took her upstairs. He kissed her forehead goodnight, and left the house.

Early that next morning Henna rose, and she felt refreshed. She thought about her childhood friend, Theresa, and what she loved about those talent shows. It was the process of creating with someone. The collaboration was half the fun. She used to love the studio sessions with the band, but during the last two projects, the band offered less and less input. They basically waited for Henna to come up with the ideas and then they followed along. Maybe it was because she was a control freak, or perhaps they also had started looking at the music as a job. Either way, she wanted this project to be some type of collaboration. Henna rushed downstairs and saw Monica in the kitchen eating a bowl of fruit.

"Ahmad's in town. He came over here yesterday."

"What? You're talking to Ahmad?" Monica asked.

"No. Phillip told him I was in Atlanta, and he put two and two together. Then he talked to Haydu, who confirmed everything. He said he missed me." By now, Henna was slicing a grapefruit and pouring sugar over the half.

Monica was so shocked, she'd stopped eating her fruit and was engrossed in the conversation. "So, do you believe him?"

"I don't know. But after he left yesterday, I didn't think too much about him."

"That's because of Craig. You know you can't replace one for the other. It doesn't work like that."

"Oh, and speaking of Craig, he was here when Ahmad stopped by. Ahmad noticed something between us, and basically told me to have my fun with him, but then get back with him, when I got bored."

Monica quickly got an attitude. "So you're just playing with my brother?"

"No!" Henna was quick to respond. "I like Craig. We have fun, and we have an understanding. The point is, Ahmad didn't seem to care about Craig. If he really loved me, he would care, right? Maybe he was just pretending not to care."

By now, Monica didn't want to discuss the conversation anymore. She placed her fruit in a Ziplock bag and prepared to leave for work.

"Are you mad?"

"Nope," Monica responded while washing her hands.

Henna could see the attitude and knew it had everything to do with Craig. "This is why I didn't want you to know about Craig and me. He is an adult, you know."

Monica stood at the edge of the door and replied, "I know, you both are. So when everything goes sour, which it will, I hope you two adults can handle it on your own, because I'm out of it."

Henna followed Monica out of the kitchen and into the foyer. She didn't want to leave on a bad note, so she asked, "What are you doing today? Maybe you can come to the studio."

"I won't have time. I'm signing the loan papers. It went through," Monica explained. "We'll talk later." She left the house.

Henna knew Monica would have some issues with her and Craig messing around, but this morning's conversation had her riled. Desperate to communicate, Henna called Monica on her cell. Henna immediately began talking.

"I know you just left. But I want you to know that in no way am I playing your brother to get Ahmad back. I hope you don't think that."

"Here's what I think. You are using Craig to get your groove back, not Ahmad. I also think Craig is really starting to like you, but neither one of you has been completely honest. Therefore, when you leave, I'm going to be the go-between, and I don't have time to be the voice of reason for two irresponsible adults. Have a good day." Monica hung up.

"Wow, she's really upset," Henna said aloud after disconnecting. Henna started to call Craig to tell him, but she decided to wait until later when they hooked up. She went upstairs to get dressed, but it really bothered her that Monica was upset. Normally, Henna didn't care about what others thought, but this was her friend, and Monica's opinion mattered greatly. Maybe I should just leave him alone, Henna thought as she prepared to leave the house. She called Craig to get lunch details, but she didn't mention Monica.

Henna was already digging into her Doc Green's salad when Craig arrived, and though Monica had spoiled her morning, she was still eager to share her collaboration idea. He sat and they began to plan. Henna mentioned her surprise at the amount of very talented unsigned artists in Atlanta, and how it would be great to incorporate some of them.

"I just want a clean, pure sound."

"Why don't you do an unplugged set?" suggested Craig.

"An unplugged set of duets!" Henna shouted.

This was just the inspiration she was looking for. Henna wanted to start right away. Just before they finished lunch, Henna mentioned Monica, but Craig nonchalantly brushed it off.

"Don't worry about Monica. I will talk to her," he said before jumping into his truck. He then went to work on his bar, and Henna went to Cat's Corner.

Cat was out of town, but Gerald gave Henna a list of some of the regulars who came to open-mic night. Gerald thought the idea was wonderfully clever.

"This is a chance of a lifetime for some of these artists. Not to mention an unplugged CD is timeless," Henna said.

Gerald grinned. "I love it."

Henna felt like a kid with a new toy. She couldn't wait to crack it open and start to play. She took her list of open-mic artists and made plans to come Monday night. Henna then called Bobby, told him about the concept, and asked would he also join her on Monday. Just as excited, he immediately went online and started looking up some of the names she mentioned. Henna made a call to her lawyer to ask a few questions about her contract with Columbia and made notes. Things were under way, and so Henna made the dreaded call to Phillip, the lead vampire himself.

"If you start fussing, I'm hanging up" were Henna's first words. "I need five minutes to explain," she continued.

Phillip quickly responded, "You've got three."

Henna quickly gave her explanation of where she was, literally and figuratively. She didn't bother talking about the Lil Wayne project, because she couldn't fit it in her three-minute time constraint.

At the end of her spiel, Phillip spoke. "Creatively, I think the unplugged idea works."

"Really?" Henna said, her voice filled with pep.

"But it doesn't do big numbers. So . . . no," he rebuffed. "You can do it in addition to, maybe as a teaser to the project."

"There's nothing in my contract that says you can stipulate the creative direction of my project, as long as I stay in the same genre of music. If I give you a completed project, you have to accept it," Henna defended.

"But we don't have to release it."

"True."

"And why put your sweat into something that might end up being shelved indefinitely?"

"Because I believe in it, and when I put my heart into something I truly believe in, it's always incredible."

Phillip was quiet for a few seconds before speaking. "It's a bad idea."

"Fine," Henna replied, still deciding to move forward with the plan.

"And what is this hip-hop collaboration thing you are doing? You should come back to New York. I don't think the South is providing good inspiration."

"Just the opposite. The Lil Wayne thing was fun, nothing too serious."

"Well, I'm getting calls about it. Certain people here want to approve the collaboration because of the numbers he gets. They don't care about your name, but I do. I think it's not going to go over well with your fan base."

"Most of my fans don't know who Lil Wayne is."

"Hip-hop gets lots of promotion. The fans will see your name, take a listen, and think you're going in a different direction. It's a bad idea."

"'It's a bad idea. It's a bad idea,'" Henna mocked. "Everything is a bad idea to you, Phillip. What if I used another name?"

"An alias? That could work," Phillip said.

"I guess that means I couldn't be in the video, though?"

"What!" Phillip shrieked. "Are you going through some sort of midlife crisis?"

"I'm joking, Phillip."

"Tell you what. I will approve use of your voice on that hip-hop song, if you reconsider doing the unplugged CD."

"No deal. I'm doing the unplugged CD, with a few unsigned artists, and if you approve the Lil Wayne project, I will consider you being my manager."

Phillip was quiet once more. Henna knew she had dangled the perfect bait. "Think about it and get back with me. I have to go." Henna hung up the phone before Phillip could speak. She was proud of herself. Feeling in control and motivated, she began going through her journal and wrote music the remainder of the day.

Monday came around, and Henna was nearly excited out of her mind. In Cat's Corner, she, Bobby, and Craig had front-row seats to the hottest unsigned artist showcase in Atlanta. As Henna looked around the space, she made a suggestion. "We could do a DVD recording right here, and package it with the CD."

Craig also looked around the space. "It's too small, and too cramped."

"Not enough character," Bobby added.

"It's just a thought," Henna said as the first artist stepped to the mic.

Gerald made sure to get all the performers' information, but he didn't want to make them aware of the reason. The three critiqued all seventeen artists who performed that night. Henna was focused until she looked up and saw Ahmad. He was staring right at her. She attempted to pay no attention to him, but it was difficult. Moments after he knew he'd agitated her, he had the waitress give her a note. At first, Henna kept it folded and placed it in her pocket without reading it. But after five minutes, temptation got the best of her. She pulled it out and read it silently. I'm leaving tomorrow. Call me tonight. Henna glanced back in his direction. He mouthed the words "Please, baby." Ahmad never begged. Henna couldn't believe she'd read his lips correctly, but she saw it in his eyes. He was sincere. Yet, it didn't change the fact he'd left her for another woman. So she quickly turned her attention back to the stage and focused on the task at hand. Henna was looking to do the set with at least seven different artists. She'd probably do a ten-song CD, but she would record a minimum of fourteen songs to choose from. They decided not to share comments until after the performances were done, to see if they were on the same page.

Afterward, they ordered a pizza, went to the Attic, and compared notes. All three creators agreed on performers two, six and seventeen. From there, the choices varied tremendously. Henna, Craig, and Bobby discussed, compared, and argued until five that morning. They finally agreed on eight artists. Bobby wanted to hit a few other open-mic places, but Henna wanted to start right away. She did agree, though, to visit another spot that night and finalize her decision after that.

Although the sun was rising in a couple of hours, the trio was nowhere near tired. They were all too anxious to sleep. However, Bobby had to leave town the next day, and Craig had a full day ahead of him. Since the loan had been approved, he was able to hire a full work crew. His plan was to have the bar open in two months, and it looked like he was going to make his schedule. The group parted with high expectations of the future project. Still very excited, Henna couldn't sleep when she got home. She wanted to call each of the performers and inform them of her plans. But it was now six-thirty in the morning, and so she closed her eyes and tried to sleep. Her body quickly overruled her overactive mind and she was asleep within minutes.

When she woke that afternoon, she got directions to the Tavern and convinced Monica to go with her that evening. Monica agreed, but Henna was less than pleased when she showed up with Mick. Their interaction seemed innocent enough, but then Henna thought of her own behavior with Craig. Their public interaction seemed harmless as well, but behind closed doors it was another story. Henna gave Monica a word of warning, and then she focused on the show. She was again blown away by the talent.

The only difference between the performers that evening was ethnicity. The Tavern showcased white artists; Cat's Corner was primarily black. Such was the way of the South, where most of the places she visited were voluntarily segregated. It was a reminder of what she missed about New York. But Henna got the numbers of three more artists and added them to the roster. She arranged a meeting at the studio with Bobby and invited all eleven artists. Henna detailed her plans at this meeting. One singer was just recently signed and wouldn't be able to commit to any other projects, and another just wasn't interested. However, the other nine

were ready and willing to start. Henna recorded everyone's schedule conflicts and set an agenda.

This was the beginning of her new CD. Henna knew
this was her purpose for coming to Atlanta, and she
was so glad she stuck around long enough for it to come
to fruition. The day had passed and she hadn't called
Ahmad. Although it was on her mind, she'd resisted.
Henna was proud of herself. She'd stuck to her guns
with Phillip, resisted Ahmad, and was about to record
possibly her greatest CD to date. It was going to move
people, and it was going to be a classic. Henna smiled,
picked up the phone, and called Craig. As soon as he answered, Henna rolled off two words, "Thank you."

Craig wasn't sure what she was grateful for, but he
replied, "You are most welcome."

"I'll talk to you later," she said before she hung up.

Henna took in a deep breath and reached for her
cigarettes. She looked at the pack and placed it back in
her purse. She rushed to the car, went to Walgreens,
and purchased a pack of Nicoderm patches and three
packs of Nicorette gum. Since she was taking so well
to this fresh start, Henna figured it would be a great
time to quit smoking. She stood outside Walgreens,
pulled out one last cigarette, and smoked it down to
a tiny butt. She then tossed the remaining pack in the
trash can, and whispered, "Here's to a new beginning."
Henna stuck the Nicoderm patch on her arm, walked
away, and embraced the unknown challenges ahead.

Chapter 15

"Don't Make Me Over"
(Dionne Warwick, 1962)

Henna kept trying to think of a perfect time to speak
with Monica about her interaction with Mick. But she
was so involved with recording, and Monica was so
consumed with restructuring Julian's business, that
their schedules hadn't coincided lately. When Henna
had a spare moment, she was with Craig; and when
Monica had a spare moment, Henna was asleep.

Therefore, she decided not to go out of her way to
say anything and continued working. The rehearsal
sessions with the artists had been going exceptionally
well, and so far, Henna liked working with a young girl
named Kathleen Vine the best. She saw Kathleen at
the Tavern, and her voice had a similar tone to Natalie
Merchant's. She and Henna's voices blended well together. Henna loved the fact that she was also a singer/
songwriter who played guitar. Ironically, she'd just recently gone through a breakup too. When Henna told
her about Ahmad, they decided to write about that.
Currently the piece was entitled "I Can't Give You My
Forever."

Henna also thoroughly enjoyed working with a brother
named Zion. Yes, she disliked his one-name pronounce-
ment, but she couldn't deny his talent. He didn't play any
instruments, but his baritone voice was powerful, yet

smooth. He didn't sound like anyone out there, which was just what Henna loved. Unfortunately, that was what the record labels hated. Zion had been through similar woes as Henna had, with the industry insisting he change his sound, something he refused to do. Thus, he relished this opportunity, and Henna insisted that he take lead on their song. She made sure that each of her CD guests were registered with ASCAP, and she and Bobby kept precise records of each artists' input so that everyone got accurate credits for writing and publishing. Henna was becoming the perfect little businesswoman, and she was enjoying every moment.

After a week of nothing but rehearsals, Henna arrived home on a Friday, around four o'clock. Surprised to see Monica's car in the driveway, she rushed in, waving her rehearsal tapes in the air, only to hear Monica on the phone.

Henna wasn't sure to whom Monica was talking, but from the foyer she heard Monica say, "I just don't want to break anyone's heart, but it's not going to work. The situation has gotten way out of control. I feel bad, but I know it's too late to stop it now."

Henna stood in the foyer and eavesdropped. She knew it was just a matter of time before Monica had to admit that she was falling for Mick. Now she was going to break Julian's heart.

"Poor Julian," Henna said. Just then, she heard Monica's footsteps from around the corner. Henna quickly walked into the kitchen and went to the sink to wash her hands. Monica immediately hung up the phone and struck up a conversation. Henna didn't know how to admit she'd been spying, so she asked, "Was that Julian on the phone?"

"Um . . . yeah," Monica said with a squeak in her voice. "He's coming over for dinner. You going to be around?"

"Should I be around?" she asked.

"I don't care. We've just got some important things to talk about. He wants to lock down a date for the wedding."

"And . . ."

"And what?" Monica innocently asked.

"And how does that make you feel?" Henna continued to hint.

Monica gave Henna an odd expression and then answered, "Good."

Henna decided to leave it alone. She could stay, so that Monica could postpone the heartbreak, or she could leave and let it be over. She decided to leave.

"I may go out to dinner," Henna stated.

Monica gave a nonchalant nod, and Henna went upstairs. Monica had been a little distant since she found out about Craig, and Henna didn't know how to make her comfortable with the situation. She, too, skirted around the elephant in the room.

Henna, likewise, had some heartbreaking news to deliver herself. Alphonzo had called several times, and she didn't have the heart to tell him she just wasn't interested. Maybe she would use this night of truth to deliver her own news. She called Alphonzo and asked him to dinner. He eagerly accepted. He offered to pick Henna up, but she knew that wasn't wise, considering the topic of conversation. Therefore, she suggested they meet around 7:00 P.M. Henna got dressed, and though she sported a little color in her wardrobe, she pulled her hair back into a bun. Tonight was not about "flirtatious fun" Henna; it was "get down to business" Henna. She'd played around with Alphonzo long enough, and she was running out of excuses to avoid him.

They met at the restaurant, and as usual he greeted her with a kiss on the cheek. As soon as they sat down,

Alphonzo looked at her and said, "I'm surprised to be eating with you tonight. You haven't returned my calls all week."

"I've been recording. It takes up most of my days and evenings."

"I thought you were avoiding me."

Henna didn't say anything. She only sipped her water and grinned. Minutes later, Alphonzo mentioned it again.

"Henna, I'm into you. If you don't feel the same way, I would appreciate you admitting it."

"I'm not into you," she blurted out. "You're cool, but—"

"No need to expound. I knew it. I was just hoping I was wrong."

"My ex and I just broke up, and I'm not ready."

"Please, I'd rather you just keep it simple. You're not into me."

"Okay," Henna murmured. "Do you want to finish our meal?"

"Of course. If it's okay with you," Alphonzo said.

"I'd like to finish," Henna said, smiling.

The two finished dinner with nice pleasantries and small talk, and Henna was home before nine o'clock.

Henna walked in and found Monica in the kitchen alone. There was no sign of Julian, but she did smell the residue of his cologne. Henna assumed Monica had done her dirty deed and he'd left.

"You okay?" Henna asked as she walked in.

Monica was startled, but before she could answer, a young woman walked in behind Henna and introduced herself. "Hi, I'm Nia."

"Monica's little play sister, I saw your picture on the fridge. I'm Henna. I've heard nice things about you. Nice to meet you finally."

Nia walked over to the bar and sat down beside Monica. Henna wanted to talk about Alphonzo, but she didn't want to discuss her dirty laundry in the company of strangers. Instead, she looked in the freezer for something sweet. Nia was gabbing about looking for employment, and Monica seemed to be very distracted.

Just then, Craig walked in. Henna turned around with a wide smile and began approaching him. However, Nia cut through her beeline, and headed straight into Craig's arms.

"Hi, baby. Surprise!" She clung to his neck as he looked like a deer caught in headlights. Henna braced herself on the counter and watched the spectacle. Craig was frozen.

"What are you doing here?"

"After our last talk, I realized that if we are going to make this work, I needed to be where you are. If you believe in something, you have to follow your heart. Isn't that right, Monica?"

As though she were center stage in an opera house, everyone stared in silence, and waited for her to speak. "Well . . . that's what the Wiz said . . . you know, to Dorothy . . . when—when she was lost . . ." Monica stammered.

"I wasn't going to come, but the other night when you said you still loved me, I packed my things, and I'm here," Nia explained. Henna could tell Craig was completely caught off guard. His eyes jerked, and his knees kept buckling.

"Wait for me in the car," Craig said, pushing Nia out the door. Henna headed up the stairs, and just as Craig went to follow, Monica stopped him.

"Henna!" Craig called out, but Henna kept walking. She didn't even turn to acknowledge his voice.

"Henna!" Craig yelled once more.

This time, now at the top of the stairs, Henna turned around. "Yes, Craig," she said, with an impassive expression.

"I—I . . ." he stuttered.

". . . should go check on your girlfriend." Henna finished the sentence for him, turned, and walked away.

Again, Craig tried to follow.

"Let her go!" Monica insisted.

Craig turned and gave his sister an evil look. "This is all your fault!" he exclaimed.

"Me? I told you not to start anything with Henna, and I thought it was over with Nia. Don't blame me because you can't keep your shit straight."

Craig whipped around and stormed out of the home. Monica went upstairs to check on Henna. She knocked on Henna's door.

"Come in," Henna uttered. Monica opened the door and stood by the frame.

"If you're here to check on me, I'm fine." Henna rose, walked to the bathroom, and brushed her teeth. Monica followed and this time stood by the bathroom door.

"Are you going to follow me from room to room?" Henna said, giggling.

"I just want to make sure you're good."

Henna spit out her toothpaste and asked, "Why didn't you tell me about Nia?"

"I thought you knew. Supposedly, they broke up, but it's been off and on for so many years now, I never know when it's final or not."

"Why would I know? Craig wouldn't tell me that. You should have said something when I asked who that was on the fridge."

"There was no need to say anything. He usually doesn't hide it. He's tacky that way. Plus, you guys are the ones into truth, and blues, so-called truth music.

And you said that you guys were 'just kickin' it,' anyway. Remember?"

Henna gave a smile and said, "You're right, and I'm good. Trust me."

Monica turned slowly and walked back to the door. She turned one more time and gave Henna a look.

"Stop staring at me. I'm okay. By the way, I ended things with Alphonzo tonight. It just wasn't working."

Monica nodded and walked out of the room. Henna fell backward onto the bed and stared at the ceiling.

"That son of a bitch," she whispered. "Hey, I guess it was what it was, and now it's done."

Henna closed her eyes and tried to get some rest.

Across town, Craig wasn't getting any rest, though. He was pacing the room as Nia explained why she'd just packed up and moved across the country to Atlanta.

"I know you think I'm crazy, but it's something still there. I can't just throw that away. I'm always talking about how I feel, but I really don't do anything about it, so I'm here."

Craig replied, "I'm going through a lot right now, Nia. You can't just pack up and expect me to adjust my life."

"Craig, I've been patient with the touring and recording schedule. When you told me you weren't moving back to Cali after the tour, I was angry. I didn't want a long-distance relationship. . . . I knew it wouldn't work."

"I moved here to open the bar, you know that."

"But I'm tired of waiting around to see where you're going to take this relationship. I'm not getting any younger. Do you love me?"

Craig held his head down. Nia stood beside him, grabbed his shoulder, and made him look at her. "Do you love me?" she repeated.

"Nia, you know I do."

"I love you too." Nia kissed Craig. Craig indulged the kiss for a few seconds before pulling his body away.

"We've been together for five years. It was a big step for me to move here. Are you saying you don't want to meet me halfway? Are you saying our relationship isn't worth fighting for?"

Craig shook his head no and spoke. "I'm saying, you should have told me you were coming. This may not work."

"We won't know until we try it." Nia tried to kiss Craig once more.

"Where are you staying?"

"With you," Nia said confidently.

"You need to get your own place."

"That doesn't make sense. We lived together already. It would be taking a step backward." Nia could feel Craig's resistance. "If it doesn't work out after a month, I will move out."

Craig grabbed his wallet. "I'll be back."

"But—" Nia attempted to stop him.

"We'll talk about it when I get back," Craig insisted, and walked out the door.

Craig called Henna as soon as he got to his truck, but, of course, she didn't answer. She'd turned her phone off. Therefore, he got in his truck and drove to Monica's house. Craig let himself in and called her cell again. He boldly walked up the stairs and knocked on her door. Thinking it was Monica, Henna told him to come in. She was half asleep; so by the time she realized it was Craig, he was sitting next to her body on the bed.

"Get out of my room."

"Please let me explain."

Henna sat up and turned to Craig. Her arms were folded and her defenses were higher than when they first met. Craig reached for her hand.

"Don't touch me. Just say what you have to say and get out."

"Nia is not my girlfriend. I mean, she used to be, but we broke up."

"Craig, just admit she's your girl. Lying will only make it worse."

"We've had this on-again, off-again relationship, but I don't want to be with her." Henna sighed heavily and looked away. "I don't. Honestly, I want to be with you." Craig was being as sincere as he knew how, but it was too late. "We have a connection. I know it. You know it too."

"Go home to your girlfriend. We had fun. It was nice, and now it's over."

"I don't want it to be over."

"Too bad." Henna slumped down in the bed and turned her back toward Craig. "Get out of my room, please."

"Why are you mad? You're the one who didn't want a relationship, anyway."

"You're right. So you didn't have to lie, Craig. That's what I'm mad about."

Craig slowly got up and walked to Henna's door. But he wasn't done with his plea. "I know there was something between you and your old manager, from the way he looked at me. But I didn't have an attitude when he came to visit you."

Henna started to fume that he had the nerve to compare Nia to Ahmad. But she knew just how to play Craig. She'd have more power if she said nothing. Henna kept still, acting like she was going to sleep.

"Henna!" She remained still. "I'm telling you right now, I want to be with you. If you don't turn around, I can only assume you never wanted to be with me, and that this was all some game to you."

Henna turned around. "I don't want you to assume anything, so I will tell you, face-to-face. What you and I had was fun, but it was a fling. It wasn't anything to build a relationship on. So good night."

Henna turned back over and closed her eyes, but inside she was hurting.

Craig, still a proud man, wasn't going to combat her any longer. He walked out and went home.

Chapter 16

"Love Don't Love Nobody"
(The Spinners, 1974)

That morning, when Henna woke, Monica was in the kitchen as usual. Henna rifled through the cabinets and spoke. "Is there any pancake mix? I want pancakes."

"Ooh, that sounds good. But I don't have time. I have to be at work in thirty minutes." Monica handed Henna a letter. "I assume Craig came here last night and left it."

Henna took the letter, ripped it in half, and tossed it in the trash. Monica watched Henna's actions, but she didn't say a word.

"I'll be at Julian's tonight. He's cooking. You're welcome to come over after rehearsal."

"I just might do that," Henna said with a grin.

Just then, Monica's phone rang. "What's up, Craig? I gave it to her. Um . . . I don't think she wants to talk, but I will tell her you called." Monica hung up the phone and glanced at Henna.

"I'm not thinking about your brother. I have too many good things going on right now. You know he came to my room late last night and expected me to talk to him."

"He feels bad, Henna. But this is exactly what I was talking about. I knew I'd be in the middle of this. Craig had no idea Nia would move here. None of us did.

She'd been calling me, and asking my advice, but I didn't want to break her heart."

"You were talking about her the other day?"

"What?" Monica questioned.

"I thought you were talking about hurting Julian, but I now see you were talking about hurting Nia. I overheard your conversation."

"Actually, I was talking about hurting you. You can pretend all you want, but you care about Craig."

"But I—"

"But I nothing. I know you, Henna Jameston. I know you well. And I'm not even saying 'I told you so.'"

"Thank you," Henna said, with her head lowered. Then she looked up and asked, "So you're not breaking up with Julian?"

"No. We're talking about the wedding tonight. You should come for real, help put in ideas."

Henna perked up. She'd grown to like Julian, and she was feeling bad about the assumed breakup. "I have plenty of ideas." Henna beamed. "What time should I be there?"

"Around eight."

Monica grabbed her granola bar and walked out. Henna made a few phone calls, got dressed, and headed to the studio.

Monica arrived at Julian's that evening around six-thirty. She had more swatches and menu designs for him to look at. They sat over a glass of wine, and discussed the designs and Craig's drama until dinner was ready.

"I felt so bad for everyone," Monica said. "Henna really cares about Craig. I don't care what she says. I've seen her around plenty of men, but she's never reacted like that before. She had googly eyes and everything."

It was apparent that Julian didn't really want to hear about Craig and Henna. He'd much rather discuss their wedding, but Julian wanted to pacify Monica's concerns. Because of that, he continued to listen.

"He usually tells women about his other woman, just so they don't think it's anything more than sex."

"I'm sure she'll be okay," Julian said.

"I'm sure she will be. She's the amazing rubber girl, who always bounces back. But I still feel bad. I feel bad for both of them."

"Maybe he really likes Henna, and that's why he didn't mention Nia. Maybe it was more than just sex."

"Possibly." Monica deliberated on that statement for a second before she continued. "Or maybe he didn't mention Nia, because he's a cheat. Men cheat. It's in their DNA."

"I don't cheat," Julian firmly announced.

"Yeah, well, most of them cheat. You are the exception."

"So how about I get a kiss for being the exception."

Monica grinned, leaned over, and gave her man a kiss. Julian rose to check on his lamb chops as Monica continued to vent.

"I should have said something. I know Henna is the queen of bounce back, but I can tell she's hurting."

Just then, Henna knocked on the door. "It's open!" yelled Julian. Henna walked in, and instantly she could tell her name had just been spoken.

"You can stop talking about me now." Henna peered at Monica. "Julian, will you tell your girlfriend that I am doing just fine?"

Julian chuckled as he, too, looked at Monica. Henna handed Julian a peach cobbler. "I know I shouldn't bring dessert to a pastry chef, but I didn't want to come empty-handed."

"Where did this come from?"

Henna didn't answer immediately. Instead, she made a quirky face.

Monica looked over at the dessert. "It came from Publix," she said, frowning.

"It's the thought that counts," Henna claimed.

The three sat and ate dinner, and the topic was the pending nuptials. Julian wanted a fall wedding, and Monica wanted spring. Julian preferred outdoors; Monica chose a church. There were lots of compromises to be met. The only thing they narrowed it down to was orchids. Both Monica and Julian loved orchids. It was Henna's favorite flower too. All parties agreed that orchids would be the official wedding flower, but other than that, nothing else was decided. Dinner, however, was great.

Henna left close to ten that evening and drove home. She checked her messages en route and listened to Craig's five calls, all pleading the same thing. "Just talk to me." Henna didn't want to talk, though. She wasn't actually mad at him, but more disappointed in herself for allowing him to get in. If he'd been honest about Nia from the start, she would have known how far to push it. But she actually let her guard down and had begun to care for him. Now she viewed that as a mistake, and it would be a long time before anyone ever got in again.

When Craig finally got his chance to tell Travis what had transpired, Travis couldn't contain his laughter. Craig still didn't see the humor in any of it.

"Monica won't even let me come to the house. She said it makes Henna feel uncomfortable. I'm her brother!"

Travis continued to laugh. "Women stick together, especially in situations like this. You'll be lucky if you ever get back in the house."

Craig mumbled a few words, went to the back, and got a beer. He looked at the time. "I need you to take me somewhere. I let Nia use the car to go to a job interview."

"Man, we've got work to do."

"This will only take an hour. I'll be back. I just need you to drop me off."

Begrudgingly Travis dropped his tools, and he and Craig left. When they got to the dance studio in Buckhead, Travis couldn't believe what Craig was explaining to him. He had to go in and see for himself. Craig was taking tango lessons.

"I'd planned on taking Henna dancing, and I told her I could tango, so—"

"So your ass is here doing a one-two step, when we have work to do."

The dance teacher walked up and spoke. "Good, you brought a partner today." Travis gave her a bewildered expression. "I'm just dropping off," he said.

"Nonsense. He needs to partner up with someone. Both of you, get in there now."

She pushed both men toward the hardwood room surrounded with mirrors. Travis turned and made an attempt to leave as he saw the other Latin beauties filing out of the class. He glanced at Craig, who silently pleaded that he stay. Craig looked so pitiful, Travis agreed, and the two of them danced arm in arm for the next hour. Fortunately, it was a private class, and both men vowed it would never go beyond those doors.

"The things we do for women," Travis said on the way back to the Attic. "Are you sure you just don't want this girl because she is not chasing you?"

"I'm sure. I vibed with her like no other woman."

"So what's up with Nia?"

"We have history, but the passion is gone," Craig responded.

"Sounds like a marriage."

"Before I went on tour, we weren't even having sex."

"Sounds like a marriage," Travis reiterated.

"I love Nia, but I'm telling you, she's not the one," said Craig.

"'The one'? Man, there's no magic one floating around. . . . There is no happenstance moment. Once you commit, she becomes the one," Travis rebutted.

"But I want that like . . . boom, love-at-first-sight type of shit."

"'Love at first sight'? That's easy. Love after thirty years, that's the mystery," said Travis, who'd been married for five years.

Craig envisioned Henna's smile, which made him smile. He finally spoke. "I'm serious. Henna is what I've been missing."

"Well, my brother, you've got some decisions to make."

Craig was mostly silent the remainder of the day as he thought about how he could fix this mess of a situation.

The next week Henna flew to New York to visit Phillip. She took him some tapes from the rehearsal sessions so that he could hear the direction of the CD. She was going to produce it with or without his blessing, but Henna knew it was still smart to have the executives on her side. She also knew she needed a manager outside of the label. She only used the manager idea to bait Phillip. Hopefully, he would simply go for the

project, because she also met with three other independent music executives that week in hopes to find a real
manager. Henna had a busy week. She hung out with
Haydu, and then spent a day doing nothing but dust-
ing her home. On Wednesday she received a call from
Ahmad, and as though he had LoJack on her booty, his
first words were "I heard you were back in New York."

"You've got spies, I see," she said to him. Naturally,
he wanted to go to dinner. Henna figured it was a bad
idea, but she obliged his request, anyway. She hated
to admit it, but she wanted to discuss her new project
with him. He was savvy and she needed his expertise,
so they met in Manhattan and ate at one of her favorite
Cuban bistros, between Thirty-fourth and Thirty-fifth
Street. Henna was so over men, that even Ahmad and
his arrogant charm wasn't going to win her over. But
she felt it was important that they make amends.

Ahmad had been one of the first people to believe in
Henna's talent, and though it felt weird with him not
being in her personal life, it was even stranger with
him not being a part of her career. She figured that they
would never be able to work together again, but for
some reason she still wanted his approval. Henna had
downloaded a few of the sessions onto her iPod, so she
pulled it out and let him hear it. He gave no expression
as he listened to the three songs. Henna knew he liked
it, because Ahmad would have turned it off after the
first song if he didn't like what he heard.

As soon as he was done listening, Henna jumped in.
"Sounds good, right?"

"You're doing an acoustic project?" he questioned.

Henna gave an unsure nod. His expression had given
her doubt in just a matter of seconds. She respected
Ahmad's opinion much more than Phillip's. Phillip was
a numbers guy, but Ahmad knew the streets. He knew

the fans and the trends of the market. He could tell her if this CD was going to sink or swim. Ahmad was quiet as he rolled through Henna's play list.

Finally he looked up and spoke. "It's going to sell," he said, smiling. "It's different and fresh. I really like the idea of using unsigned talent. Who's doing your paperwork?"

"Bloomberg."

Ahmad nodded, with a larger grin. "Proud of you. Who's mixing it?"

"Bobby-B," Henna said proudly.

"I met that nigga at a party once. He tries to floss too much. And I heard he tries to holla at his artists, so watch your back."

Henna smirked. "Bobby's gay." Just as the words were leaving her mouth, Henna tried to swallow them, but it was too late.

Ahmad was shocked. "That nigga's gay?"

"I—I heard he was. I don't know," Henna said as she looked away.

"Nah, you know something. I can tell you're lying."

"Don't say anything, please!"

Ahmad let out a loud chortle. "I can't believe that shit!"

"Ahmad, don't!"

"I'm not going to say anything."

Henna knew it was out. Ahmad was going to say something. He couldn't be trusted with that type of juicy information. She just prayed it didn't spread. She was so used to sharing everything with him, it just came out.

"Damn it," she murmured underneath her breath.

Ahmad continued to chuckle. They caught up on industry gossip while they finished dinner. Amazingly, the evening seemed like old times, but without the intimacy. Henna wasn't sure what had happened over the last couple of months, but her feelings for Ahmad had done a 180. She didn't see him with the same eyes. Maybe they could be friends. It was too soon to tell, but definitely a nice thought. Afterward, he stayed with her until she got her cab, and they didn't talk the remainder of the visit. Henna wondered if this was the beginning of a new friendship phase.

Henna arrived back in Atlanta the following Monday, but she felt guilty about going to the studio. She knew the news had probably traveled down the coast, and that Bobby was just waiting to accuse her of blabbing his secret. But that wasn't the case. He was glad to see her, and he had his own great news.

"I know where we can shoot the DVD," he said as soon as she walked in.

"Where?" Henna asked.

"The Righteous Room."

"Where?" Henna asked.

"Craig's place."

"The Attic? What's the Righteous Room?"

"That's the name of his place now. I guess he changed it. Anyway, I talked with Craig and he said it was cool, and it's cozy and vintage."

Henna frowned and then replied, "No, I don't think so."

"But it's perfect. It will be ready by the time the CD is done. It has character, and Craig said he'll let you do it there for free."

"Why are you talking to Craig?"

"He came by here last week looking for you." Henna grumbled at his response. "Is there something I should know?" Bobby questioned.

"No, I just don't want to have it there, that's all."

"Because you don't like the space, or something else?"

"Something else," Henna uttered while curiously lowering her head.

Bobby's nosiness gave way to an inquisitive stare. Henna finally explained some of the situation. She normally wouldn't have said anything, but her conscience made her feel that she needed to give up something, just to compensate for what she'd done. At the end of his newfound enlightenment, Bobby spoke. "You should talk to him. He's not used to dealing with someone of your caliber, and he messed up."

"I don't want to talk to him."

Bobby smirked and playfully poked Henna in the stomach. "Yes, you do."

"I do not," Henna mumbled, but she had a mischievous grin. "Let's get to work."

On the way home from the studio, Henna checked her messages and noticed Craig had called again. She decided it was time to talk. Henna didn't bother calling. Instead, she drove by the Attic, soon to be the Righteous Room, to see if Craig's truck was in the lot. It was, so she stopped and went in. Travis was in the front; he was laying plastic on top of the newly laid floors.

"Hi, Travis. Craig here?"

Travis was surprised but glad to see Henna. He quickly called out for Craig, who came rushing from the back.

"What's up?" Craig asked before seeing Henna standing by the stairs. "Henna?" He looked as though he'd seen a ghost.

"We need to talk," she said.

Travis looked at his watch and gathered his things. "I'm gonna get out of here."

"No, don't leave because of me," said Henna.

"I need to head home, anyway. My wife's been complaining about the hours I've put in up here. She'll be glad to see me home early."

Henna went to her now-favorite spot in the room, the piano bench. She took a seat and dabbled on the keys, while Travis and Craig talked about plans for tomorrow. Moments later, Craig pulled up a bar stool and leaned toward Henna with his elbows on the piano top. He stared into her eyes. "I'm sorry," Craig said.

"Yes, you are. Sorry and trifling," Henna answered, smiling. "I'm joking. I just wanted to talk and tell you that there were no hard feelings."

"Then why are you not talking to me?"

"I just haven't felt like talking. I needed to gather my thoughts."

"Henna, I'm feeling you. I know we said we were just kicking it, but you're not going to tell me that there was no relationship chemistry to us."

"It was. I wouldn't lie about that. But I'm too old for you."

"You're too old?"

"Let me finish. I have my life. You have yours. I live in New York, and you live here. It was going to be over in a few weeks, anyway."

"But I didn't want it to end like this. I didn't really want it to end. I should have said something."

"You should have. Look, Craig, I think you're wonderful. And, I admit, I did let you in and I was jealous when I found out about Nia. I just wish you'd been honest."

"You're right."

"Honest with both of us. Nia's got to care about you a lot to move here. I'd have to be head over heels, and then some, in order to pack up and move for a man. Go be with her."

"But—"

"We're going to finish this project, and it's going to be brilliant, and we'll have a friendship and a business relationship. That's the best kind, anyway."

Craig was in disbelief over Henna's calm and pleasant nature.

"I don't know," said Craig.

"Well, you can't keep sleeping with me, with your girlfriend here. It's time to start doing the right thing."

Craig was quiet as Henna rose to leave. He reached out for her hand as she passed, but only got a hold of her fingertips. Henna turned and smiled. "This project is going to be da bomb!" Henna displayed an eager grin. "Do people still say 'da bomb'?" she laughingly asked.

"Henna, I don't want to lose you."

"Craig, I was never yours to lose." Henna turned and walked to the stairs. When she got across the room, she turned and spoke once more. "Seriously, why don't you commit to Nia. It's not every day you find a person who truly loves you unconditionally."

Henna walked out of the bar. When she got downstairs, she stood outside her car and lit up a cigarette. She had quit for two weeks in Atlanta, and had cut her usage down considerably, but tonight she needed some nicotine. She was edgy and anxious, but it didn't stop the excellent performance she'd just delivered. She was so convincing, she almost had herself fooled. Henna got in her car and tossed out the last bit of her cigarette. She took in a deep breath, and at the end of its release, a tiny tear fell from the corner of her eye. It had been a long time since she had cried; she knew another meltdown from all of last year's adversities was brewing. Tears were funny that way. They liked to team up and create waterfalls. If she didn't gather her composure, Henna could find herself outside crying until six the next morning. She let the one tear fall, and then she concentrated on the salty wet spot it left on her pants. She thought about today's rehearsal, thought about how she was changing lives, and then imagined performing her songs live. Her eyes quickly dried, and then a smile formed.

"Worst-case scenario, if I get lonely, I could always get back with Ahmad," Henna said, laughing. And with that irrational thought, the queen of bounce back turned up the music and drove home.

Chapter 17

"Ooh Baby Baby"
(Smokey Robinson & the Miracles, 1965)

It was a rare Wednesday evening when Monica and Henna both arrived home at a decent time to eat dinner together. Monica tightly embraced Henna, and said, "I'm enjoying my roommate. I think you should move here."

"I can't leave New York," Henna countered.

"Why? New York is passé."

"Blasphemous! Hush your mouth. Don't ever talk about my home like that."

"Girl, you're from Mississippi. Stop playing."

Both women laughed and browsed through the cabinets, looking for food.

"When was the last time you spoke with Craig?" Monica asked.

"Over a week ago. Why?"

"Just asked. What are we cooking? There's nothing in here. You know I rarely cook."

"Let's go to the store," Henna suggested.

"Good, I need to get some tampons, anyway." The two left. En route to the store, Monica struck up a strange conversation.

"You think I'm settling?" Henna didn't know the origin of this, and thus didn't know how to answer. "I know you do," Monica continued.

"What are you talking about?" Henna asked.

"With Julian. Do you think I'm settling with Julian?"

They rode a few more feet as Henna mulled over her response. She liked Julian, but she did think Monica was settling. Therefore, she placed the question back on her.

"Do you think you're settling?" Henna inquired.

"No fair. I want your opinion."

"I do," Henna quickly responded. "But I think it is what you truly want."

"How can it be what I want, but still be settling?"

"Because you know, and I know, you could find a man your age who gives you that 'ooh-wee' feeling you desire, if that's what you want. He may not come when you want him, but he's out there. But Julian is what you need. He's good for you, and that's what takes priority right now. Maybe it's not called 'settling.' Maybe it's 'prioritizing.'"

"I just don't want to miss out on a good man," Monica stated.

Henna sighed as she thought about Craig and then Ahmad. "I understand, but don't jump into the water because you're tired of hanging out on the beach. Only jump in because you really want to take a swim."

Monica smiled as they pulled into the store's parking lot.

"I need to buy some tampons too," Henna said as they walked in.

"Have we synced up? How cool is that! It's like we're in college again."

Henna laughed and pulled out her calendar. She walked through the aisles as Monica grabbed some pasta, chicken, ground turkey, bread, and other items. Somewhere around aisle eight Monica realized that Henna was no longer with her. Monica rushed over two or three more aisles, looking for Henna, who was standing in the middle of aisle five and staring into space.

"What's wrong with you?" asked Monica.

Henna gave her a peculiar look and responded, "I don't know."

"Well, come on," Monica insisted, and pulled her along. They got in the car and Monica noticed Henna's strange behavior.

When they pulled into the house's driveway, Henna spoke. "My period should have started and ended by now. I was so busy with everything, I just forgot."

Monica stared at Henna's stomach. "What are you saying?"

Henna broke from her daze and chuckled. "Nothing. I'm sure it's just stress." Monica instantly wheeled from the driveway as quickly as she'd pulled in.

"Where are we going?"

"Back to the store," Monica answered.

Thirty minutes later, they were coming back to the house with an additional two items, a First Response kit and, for good measure, e.p.t., just in case the First Response gave an unacceptable response.

Henna paced back and forth before she went to pee on the stick. She truly didn't want to take the test. "This can't be happening."

"Maybe you're going through early menopause?" suggested Monica.

"I hope so. My bones are feeling a little weak."

"Girl, go take this test." Monica tossed the box at Henna. She finally went into the bathroom and waited until she couldn't stand it. Henna rushed out before the results were evident. Monica nervously waited. "What happened?" she asked.

"I left it in there."

Monica went into the bathroom and came out moments later with the stick in her hand. She didn't say anything, but Henna already knew.

"I don't want to see it."

"You don't have to see it, but in about nine months, you're gonna feel it."

Henna slumped to the floor, screaming, "Why? Why? Why me, Lord? Why me?"

"Stop being so dramatic."

"Easy for you to say, you're not the one carrying the seed of a liar."

Monica's face lit up. "Oh my God, that's right. You're carrying my niece or nephew. I'm gonna be an auntie!" she yelled.

"This can't be happening. I'm taking the other test."

Ten minutes later, Henna slumped back into the kitchen with the same somber expression.

"It seems e.p.t. and First Response are conspiring against me."

"What now?" Monica asked.

"I don't know. Give me some time. Whatever you do, don't tell Craig."

"Oh, Henna, please don't put me in that position."

Henna put her hands together and pleaded silently. "Just give me two days to sort things out." Henna turned to leave the kitchen.

"What about dinner?"

"My appetite left as soon as I peed on that stick. I'm going to bed."

Henna went upstairs, and Monica spent the remainder of the evening trying to busy her mind.

The next day Craig visited Monica at work, something he never did. He seemed to have a lot on his mind when he came in the door. At first, Monica thought Henna had already spoken with him. However, when he asked, "Did Henna go back to New York again?" she knew nothing had been said. Craig took a seat by his big sister's desk. She knew he wanted to talk, because he only came to visit when he was going through something or considering a big decision.

"I think I'm going to marry Nia."

Monica's mouth flew open. "Why?" was all she could say. "Why?" she repeated.

"Because she loves me. I love her too. I mean, why not?"

"Cause . . ." Monica so badly wanted to say something about the baby, but she couldn't. She'd promised Henna. "You haven't done it already, have you?" Monica asked.

"No, Nia wants a big old-fashioned wedding."

"Yeah, I forgot."

"Tell me I'm doing the right thing. She's a great girl. She puts up with my bullshit. I may never find another woman like that."

"That's no reason to marry her."

"But she's good for me. Isn't that why you said you were marrying Julian?"

Monica was silenced by her own words. Either she was about to become a hypocrite or a blabbermouth. "You should call Henna."

"Why? Henna and I talked. It's over. I'm going to play on her CD project. That's all she cares about."

"No, I think you should call. I think she misses you."

Craig gave a look of disbelief. "You're just saying stuff to keep me from being with Nia. I thought you liked her."

"I do. I just don't want you making any rash decisions."

"We've been together for years, and I've thought about it. I just wanted to tell you."

Monica looked into her brother's eyes. "You've already asked her, haven't you?"

Craig nodded.

"Damn. You shouldn't have done that."

"Why not?"

Monica was one second from telling him, and then her cell phone rang. It was Julian. She tried to hang up with him quickly, but he was rambling about some location for the wedding. When they hung up, Craig looked at the time and dashed from her office.

"I have to go. I have a meeting in thirty minutes." He leaned over and kissed his sister's forehead. "I really appreciate everything you do for me." Craig smiled. "The club is going to be hot!"

"It better, I put everything on the line for this loan."

"So I heard," he said, smirking suggestively.

She didn't know what he was talking about, but she figured Henna had been running her mouth about Mick.

Monica quickly got Henna on the phone. "Call Craig. Tell him today."

"Not today. I perform my show tomorrow at Cat's Corner. The conversation may ruin my mood, which, in turn, will ruin the show. I'll tell him Sunday."

"Sunday is too late. You need to tell him today," Monica said in a very serious tone.

Henna's phone beeped, and she saw Craig's name on the ID. "This is Craig," she said to Monica. "Did you say something to him?"

"No. But I will if you don't."

"Please give me until Sunday," begged Henna.

"Are you keeping this baby?" Monica asked.

Henna didn't answer. She only said good-bye and hung up.

Then, as though she were the pregnant one, Monica suddenly felt nauseous. She knew she had to say something, and if Henna didn't tell him by Sunday, she'd be the one informing her brother of his new responsibility. She hadn't mentioned it to anyone, but an hour later she reached out to Julian for advice. She walked into Sweet J's, only to be greeted by Cola, who was as ornery as she had been days before. Today, however, Monica wasn't in the mood.

"Where's Julian?"

"Do I have GPS stamped on my forehead?" Cola barked.

Monica leaned in close, as though she were looking. "No, it looks like 'bitch' is stamped on there. Sorry, I'll ask someone else."

Monica continued to walk toward Julian's office. She knocked on the door and walked in. Monica immediately sat on his lap. Something she rarely did. Julian loved being the caretaker, and he wished he saw more of this vulnerable side.

"I don't know what to do. Henna is pregnant by Craig, but she hasn't told him. He proposed to Nia, 'cause he thinks Henna is over him. She's not; though she's managed to convince herself that she is. And they think they can just make music together, and everything will be all right, but it won't." Monica laid her head on Julian's shoulder as he gently patted his girlfriend's back.

"Both Henna and Craig are adults. Don't get yourself too worked up over this. They will work it out."

Monica looked at him and scowled. "No, they won't. If they were adults, they would have used protection and not gotten themselves into this situation."

"Come on, you can't be serious. You can't take care of Craig forever. You have to let go."

Monica wasn't paying attention to Julian. She kept insisting that she was going to have to tell Craig, because she thought Henna might keep it from him. "If she decides to have an abortion, he should know."

"If you got pregnant, would you tell me?" Julian asked.

"Of course! We're getting married, so it's different."

"Well, friends usually come from the same mold. So I'm sure Henna will do the right thing."

Monica took a deep breath and prayed that Julian was right. She finally was able to change the subject, but it still wasn't about the wedding. "Are you going with me to the show tomorrow night?"

"I don't know. My mother's coming into town this weekend, and I need to get some things together. You didn't forget, did you?"

Truthfully, she had, but she knew it was best simply to smile and say, "I've been looking forward to meeting her. We're spending Sunday together, right?" Julian nodded as Monica stood from his lap. "Thanks for listening to me vent. I appreciate you." She gave him a kiss. "Call me later," she said, forgetting about the wedding location question. She left in the same hurry in which she'd come.

Julian was beginning to feel like Monica wasn't as committed as he was. Something needed to be said, so he started preparing for the imminent conversation.

Chapter 18

"Mercy Mercy Me" (Marvin Gaye, 1971)

Henna often stood in front of the mirror and poked her stomach out as far as she could.

"I don't have time for this. Do I?"

Henna turned to the side and poked it out again. When Monica knocked on her door, Henna quickly jumped in her bed and got underneath the covers. She tried to pretend she was asleep. "Come in," she uttered with her "pretend sleep" voice. Monica opened the door and stood at the entrance. "I decided to turn in early," Henna claimed.

"I bet you did." Monica grimaced.

"Don't start," Henna said with a slight attitude.

"I just came to ask what you were wearing Saturday for the show."

"I don't know. I don't want to buy anything. I've spent enough money. I'll probably just wear my long black dress."

"Which one? You have at least seven of them here."

"I don't know. Help me decide in the morning."

Monica lingered. Henna didn't know if she was there to badger her about the pregnancy or if she had some issues of her own. Monica finally spoke. "Julian's mom is coming here this weekend."

"She's still living?"

"Are you still pregnant?" Monica asked in the same manner. Neither was in the mood for jokes. Henna looked away as Monica moved closer to the bed.

"Yes, she is still living, and she's not gonna like me."

"Girl, it doesn't matter. Julian loves you."

Monica gave a few sighs. "Have you been smoking?"

"Once, right after I found out. But none since then."

"Well, you wanted a good reason to quit," Monica observed.

"Not an eighteen-year reason."

"So you're keeping the baby?" Monica asked.

Henna's face contorted to an overexaggerated frown.

"Fine. I will talk to you in the morning," Monica said before walking out.

Henna then hopped out of bed and removed her clothing. She took a shower, but as soon as she got out, she felt ill. She immediately bent to the floor and heaved into the toilet. She was hot and cold at the same time.

"Oh no, I can't go through this." She tried to get up, but not before she threw up once more. Slouching over the sink, she brushed her teeth and then crawled over to the bed. Henna was exhausted. She thought about Craig for a few minutes, but she was soon asleep.

When Saturday night came, Cat's Corner was packed. Monica was backstage helping Henna get dressed.

"I want a ciggy," said Henna.

"Your baby is gonna have lung disease."

"Don't say that," Henna insisted. Monica smirked and continued to zip up Henna's dress.

Henna sat at the table, pulled her hair back into a ponytail, and wrapped it into a bun. Because she was nervous and jittery, it took a little longer than usual. When she stood, she looked like classic Henna. She placed on a few pieces of chunky turquoise jewelry, which complemented the strapless long dress, and smiled. "How do I look?"

Monica beamed. "Like my friend."

Henna did a few last-minute touch-ups and was about to go out, when she suddenly felt light-headed. She braced herself against the wall as Monica rushed to her.

"I need some water," requested Henna.

Monica rushed out of the room and came back with a bottle of Fiji. Gerald trotted in, right behind Monica. "Is the star ready?" he asked. Henna nodded. "I'm about to announce the opening act."

Henna had asked Zion to open for her. He was going to sing at least two songs, so she had a few minutes to get herself together. Henna sat in the back and drank her water. "It's packed," whispered Monica. Henna smiled, but underneath it all, she didn't want to do the show. Her mind was on the pregnancy, and she knew Craig was in the audience. She certainly didn't want to see him, and with the unsettling queasiness in her tummy, she no longer wanted to see anyone.

"Are you going to be okay?" asked Monica.

Henna continued to nod. She grabbed a few crackers from her purse and nibbled on the unsalted wafers. They listened as Zion wrapped up his set. Henna took a deep breath and went to the side of the stage. With a napkin filled with crackers and her bottle of water, Henna was about to walk onstage. Monica pulled on Henna's arm. "You can't go out there with crackers and water. It screams pregnancy." Henna looked at Monica as though she was speaking in an alien language. She walked onstage with her home-made remedy.

Henna's first two songs were from her first CD. She did the singles that were released and got everyone in the mood. She then brought on Zion, and they did one of the duets she was thinking about putting on the newest CD. She'd rehearsed the pieces with the band, so she didn't want to wander too far from what they'd practiced, but she wanted to do a few other songs. Therefore, she asked the band to be patient with her for a minute, and Henna went to the keyboard and took a seat. She sang a song she'd written years ago, but had only performed once. It was called "Blues, My Baby and I."

When Henna walked around to sit at the keyboard, she caught a glimpse of Craig. He was sitting in the back with Nia. Henna felt a knot in the side of her belly. She was glad she saw them before she started the song; this way she could avoid looking that way the remainder of the night. However, she was very surprised when she saw Mick come in and sit next to Monica. Henna figured if she focused on Monica's supposed love triangle she could make it through the evening without stammering or getting sick.

Henna gave a one-hour performance, and it was incredible. Her song repertoire was astounding. Each of the artists participating on her newest project was there. Most of them hadn't ever seen Henna put on a performance. They became more elated after seeing her that evening. Afterward, Henna stuck around to sign a few CDs, but then she scooted out not long after the show had ended. The baby was draining her energy, and she hadn't had a nap that day. Henna was asleep ten minutes after she walked in the house.

That morning, when Henna woke, she went into Monica's room, only to see that her bed hadn't been touched. Henna immediately grabbed her cell phone, but Monica didn't answer. When she left the club last night, Monica was with Mick. Henna was praying that Monica left his side and went straight to Julian's, but she wasn't sure.

Just then, Monica called back. "What's up?"

"Where are you?" Henna asked.

"I'm with Julian. We are getting breakfast before we go to the airport to get his mom."

Henna gave a sigh of relief. "I thought you might be with Mick."

"You are crazy," Monica said, obviously playing off her statement in front of Julian. "So we'll talk later, after you speak to Craig."

"Is it Sunday already?" Henna asked.

"Don't play."

"I'm joking. I'm calling him now," Henna said before hanging up.

She waited another three hours, however, before she called. She was hoping he wouldn't answer. When he did, Henna asked if he would meet her in the park. Of course he obliged, and they agreed to meet in thirty minutes. Henna didn't know how Craig would react, but she was hoping that he wouldn't insist that she have the baby, because she was still partially undecided.

Henna was sitting on the park bench when he arrived. She thought it was best to not beat around the bush, but just to blurt it out. But when she saw him, she couldn't do it.

Craig trotted over to her, all smiles. He gave her a hug and told her how wonderful the performance was. Then Craig looked her up and down, and hugged her again. "I've missed hanging out with you," he said.

Henna noticed his tone was changed. He sounded like a buddy. There was no flirting in his demeanor. This made her feel a little better about telling him.

"I've got something to tell you," Craig said.

"I need to talk to you as well, but you go first."

"No, you go first," Craig insisted.

Henna rose from the bench and walked over to the
swings. "Come over here." Henna didn't have a plan,
but she figured if she was on the swings, she didn't
have to face him. She could just casually blurt out "I'm
pregnant," which is what she did just as he was about
to push her.

Instead, Craig held on to the chains and the force
jerked Henna from the seat. Consequently she fell onto
the dirt patch below. Craig knelt to help her up, and
they locked eyes. Henna thought they were connecting,
but Craig had zoned out. When she leaned over, thinking that they would kiss, Craig pulled away.

"I'm marrying Nia," he said.

"What?"

"I asked her to marry me," Craig repeated.

"But why?"

"It was you who told me to commit."

"So you asked her, because I told you to?" Henna
questioned.

"I asked her because I love her. Hold up! You're
pregnant!" Craig finally came out of his stupor to realize what Henna had said. "Are you saying it's mine?" he
asked with grave reservation.

"No, it's the tooth fairy's! Of course it's yours. What
in the hell is wrong with you?"

Craig slowly stood and then took a seat on the swing
from which Henna had just fallen. Henna dusted herself off as he stared at the ground. She stood in front of
him, and they looked like a couple of Mormon teenag-
ers who had to go home and announce this baby news
to their very strict parents.

"Say something," Henna requested.

"What do you want me to say?"

"Say what you feel."

Craig rose from the seat, looked Henna in the eyes,
and spoke. "I don't want you to have it." Henna was

flabbergasted. With her mouth open she desperately reached for words, but none came out, and so Craig continued. "We don't know each other, and I'm getting married to Nia. I can't tell her that I'm having a baby by another woman."

By now, Henna had her words together and she began rolling them off like water dribbling from an infant's mouth. "First of all, if you were really going to marry Nia, you would have done it already, so don't use that as an excuse. And yes, we don't know each other, but that didn't stop you from screwing me every time you got a thirty-minute break. I didn't come here to ask your opinion on what I should do. I came here to tell you I was pregnant, because I thought you should know. Correction, Monica thought you should know. I was going to tell you after I decided what I wanted to do with my body. So I don't care if you don't want me to have it. I will decide that, not you." Henna stormed away, but Craig quickly caught up with her. She was livid, and she didn't realize how angry she actually was until she replayed her words in her head as she was walking away. Anger was also like tears. It could build up behind the dam, and when the dam broke, hell hath no fury.

"Hold up!" Craig yelled. "Why are you fussing at me? You asked me to tell you what I thought. I was being honest."

"Fine time to be honest now."

"You're still mad about Nia?"

Henna snapped. "I guess I am, Craig. So what?"

"So, are you trying to have this baby to get me back, or something? Are you trying to trap me?"

Henna couldn't believe her ears. "Trap you? Shit, I'm the catch! You have nothing but debt. Yeah, you're cute, but I've had better. Why would I trap a no-good,

broke-ass, lying, twenty-four-year-old guitar player?"
Henna spun back around and walked away.

Again, Craig rushed to catch up with her. By now,
their argument was garnering attention, and Henna
just wanted to get away. She sped up, and didn't turn
as Craig called out, "Henna, why are you doing this to
me?" Henna ignored him, even though he was only a
few steps behind her. "Henna!" he yelled at the top of
his lungs.

She finally acknowledged him. "To you? I'm the one
who got knocked up. You know what, Craig, go ahead
and get married. Hell, I'll sing at your wedding. But
know that this situation is not about you, or something
I'm doing to you. This is a decision I must make, and I
will let you know when I decide!"

Craig grabbed her arm, and Henna could have spit
fire.

"If you don't let go of me, I swear to God, I will punch
you in the face right now!" she spoke in a low voice that
sounded demonic. Craig saw the fury in her eyes, and
let go. He watched Henna stomp across the field and
back to her car. He quickly reached for his cell to ring
Monica, but she ignored his call. She and Julian had
just picked up his mother, and the last thing she wanted her future mother-in-law to hear was baby-mama
drama. Craig would just have to wait. To no avail, Craig
continued to call Monica's phone all day. He knew
there was no need to call Henna, and he didn't want
to alert Nia, so he was forced to go through the next
twenty-four hours in agony.

Henna, on the other hand, was enjoying her time by
rehearsing and setting up dates for a few more performances. She was still undecided about the baby, but
she knew she truly needed to give it serious thought.
Henna was never good with big decisions; she was

much more comfortable with her loved ones making choices for her. But this was a choice she had to make on her own. Henna went to the park near Monica's house just to clear her thoughts. She sat on a bench next to an older woman and watched a few of the children playing in the grass. The elderly woman displayed a friendly smile and began to speak.

"Which one is yours?" asked the woman, motioning toward the playground.

"Oh, I don't have kids."

"Really?"

"They're a lot of responsibility," explained Henna.

"Oh, but it's worth it. My daughter used to say the same thing, until she had that little one out there, the one with those blue shorts on." Henna looked out onto the field and watched the scrappy kid kicking a soccer ball. "It changed her perspective. Kids will do that."

Henna reached for her cigarettes just to hold one in her hand. She'd gotten rid of her matches and her lighter, as not to be too tempted, but she twirled the nicotine stick in her fingers. She thought about what the woman had just said.

"I'm Audrey, by the way," said the woman.

"Hi, Ms. Audrey. I'm Henna."

"Well, Henna, I will say this. You may be unsure about kids now, but when the time is right, you will know. I know you will be a great mother. I have a sense about these things. You take care." Audrey rose from the bench and motioned for her grandson. He kicked the ball in her direction and followed her off the grass and toward the parking lot. Henna sat and deliberated over Audrey's last words.

"Yeah, when the time is right," she whispered to herself. Henna sat on that bench in that same spot for another two hours. She stared at the kids, the parents, and the trees. When her legs finally became stiff, she got up, stretched, and went home.

Henna was in a haze the remainder of the afternoon. Yet, when she awoke from her nap, she'd made her decision. She went downstairs to get a jar of peaches from the refrigerator. She was standing against the counter, eating from the jar, when Monica walked in. The two women looked at one another, and the tension was thick. Monica was torn, and it was evident, for she couldn't even look Henna in the eye.

"How was the mother-in-law meeting?"

"Good," answered Monica, who rarely gave one-answer responses. She was the girl who elaborated on everything, even personal matters.

Henna knew it was simply best to go ahead and tell her. "I'm going to keep the baby," said Henna, with a half-happy and half-worried expression that simply looked like she was constipated.

Monica's odd face contortion equally matched Henna's, which showed she didn't know how to feel either. Monica wasn't sure, but she assumed Craig wouldn't be happy about the decision, but she also wanted to be there for her friend. "I'm glad you came to a decision," Monica commented before leaving the kitchen.

Henna continued eating her peaches as she thought about how she was going to inform Craig. She was still scared about the decision and how this would change her life, but she had no one to turn to now. Her mom would simply tell her to come home, stop singing, and get a job working as a music teacher at some university. Haydu would want he and his lover to raise the baby with Henna as an alternative couple, and Monica . . . Well, she had no idea how Monica really felt. But Henna knew that from this point on, things would ultimately change between them. She prayed that it would be for the best.

Chapter 19

"Going Out of My Head"
(Little Anthony & the Imperials, 1964)

Henna started recording the live acoustic sessions, and she was very pleased with the progress of the project. She was spending many late nights at the studio. Because after deciding to have the child, she wanted to get the project done as soon as possible so that she could get back to New York and start working with a new manager to line up a few tour dates. Henna's plan was to record enough songs for two discs, and to use the tour performances to market the CD. She would give ten songs to Phillip and keep ten to put out as an indie project, just in case he decided to shelve the entire venture. She wasn't sure of the legalities of pushing an independent project, and unless she got a manager who knew the ins and outs of the business, this was going to be difficult. But Henna knew it all started with making this project the best it could be, and so she spent every day over the next two weeks completing her dream CD.

Although Craig was supposed to play on a few of the songs, he told Bobby-B that he would come in and prerecord his part. However, Henna insisted that it be recorded live, and so for good measure, Bobby found a few other musicians to play behind the singers. Henna actually played her guitar on three of the tracks, and she and Bobby-B had to decide which tracks to submit to Columbia and which ones to keep. The more Henna listened to her new music, the more she felt like she'd already given birth. She hadn't communicated much with Craig, but they did speak on the phone a couple of times. Each conversation ended up in an argument. Craig insisted that she not have the baby, and Henna didn't want to hear anything he had to say. The lovers had become enemies, and Craig didn't know how to get through to her, but he continued to try.

Craig eventually decided to talk to Monica, who had remained out of the situation for the last two weeks. Yet, she wasn't going to be so lucky the Friday before Henna's return to New York. Craig called his sister at work and told her he was coming over that evening and to be there, please. Knowing her brother was suffering, Monica obliged his request. She called Henna and gave her a warning, just so she'd know what she was coming home to. Therefore, Henna decided to stay at Bobby's that evening. Unfortunately, things between Monica and Henna were still uneasy. Henna genuinely wanted to salvage their relationship before she left, but her focus was the music, so any other energy expenditure was not a priority.

By the time Monica got home from work, Craig was already perched on the kitchen balcony, sipping a beer. From the crazed look upon his face, Monica knew she was in for an evening of ranting and raving. Monica changed into her sweats before joining her brother. Luckily, she'd picked up a pizza on the way home, so the venting session could be continuous. Monica grabbed her slice of cheese, a beer, kissed her brother's bald head, and took a seat next to him.

He looked at her and grinned. "I appreciate you," he started.

"You're my baby brother. I have no choice but to take care of you," Monica replied, sporting a bigger smile than his.

They sat quietly and sipped their beers, until Craig came up with his opening statement. "I've never gotten a girl pregnant. Did you know that?"

"Nah, I thought you had about ten babies spread all over the world." Monica expressed herself through sardonic humor.

Craig chuckled a bit, and continued to sip. "Why is she doing this to me?"

"She's not doing anything to you, Craig. Henna is looking out for Henna. That's what she's always done."

"It's not fair. It's like I don't have shit to do with it. Does she even want this baby, or does she just want to mess me up?"

Monica laughed. "Yeah, I think Henna would go through labor, and eighteen years of responsibility, just to mess with you. She's a woman, and there's a thing that happens to us when we get pregnant."

Craig looked at his sister, questioning her familiarity with this type of situation.

"Don't ask, just trust that I know," she commented.

"She shouldn't have it, and that's that," he countered.

"It's not a 'that's that' situation. You have no idea what you are asking her to do, and for once, you need to think about what someone else is going through."

Craig grimaced. "I can't tell Nia that I'm having a baby by someone else. It would kill her."

"Once again, it's back on you." Craig was irritating Monica, and so she became more opinionated. "Nia is crazy, but she's not stupid. She knows you mess around. She's probably getting some on the side too." Craig gave her an agitated look as he reached for another beer; Monica continued her lecture. "That's right, I said it. If she's letting you get away with something, it's because she's getting away with something too. Ugh . . . y'all make me so sick."

"Not all men are alike."

"Oh really, Craig? Our dad cheated on my mom. Roger slept with my roommate while we were engaged. I don't think you've ever been faithful. Maybe all men are not alike, but the ones I know are trifling." Monica persisted.

It seemed like Monica also had some venting to do. Craig didn't know how the conversation had jumped from him and Henna to "all men are dogs," but he desperately tried to get it back on track. He took a different approach. "Julian's not trifling."

Monica pursed her lips and replied with aggravation: "Yeah, yeah, Julian is perfect."

Craig was confused by her expression and tone. Was Julian in the doghouse as well? he wondered. Craig simply waited for her next comment, which came a few seconds later.

"Craig, I don't want to take sides. I love you."

"Well, act like it then. I'm already in the hole with the bar, and now this. I can't afford a baby."

Monica wished that she could stomach more of the conversation, but it was giving her a headache. There was no solution that would make everyone happy, and she hated being in the middle. She gave her brother the only advice, she knew. "Look, I'm going to tell you exactly what I told Henna. You slept together under the pretense that neither one of you owed the other anything, which was a bad idea in the first place. Now you've produced a life, and, ironically, you owe each other everything. First on that list is respect." Monica grabbed another slice of pizza from the greasy box and headed back into the kitchen. Craig grabbed her wrist as she passed, and kissed the top of her hand. Monica gave him a nod, a tiny reassuring smile, and walked into the house. With his feet placed on the railing of the patio, Craig sat in the evening air and continued to drink his beer.

The night before she was to head back to New York, Henna and Monica sat in Henna's room and packed her things. This was the most time they'd spent together since she announced that she was keeping the baby. Henna knew Monica was not going to let her leave town without giving her another piece of advice, but when Monica started in, Henna couldn't believe what she was hearing.

"Are you having this baby in hopes that he will leave Nia?"

"I can't believe you are asking me that!" Henna said as her tone shrieked.

"I'm sorry. But you became a lot more pro-life after you found out about the marriage proposal. I know you like him, and I'm just saying—

"What are you saying? Look, I don't care if your trifling brother gets married tomorrow. I'm still having this child." Monica sighed and moved toward the window. Henna continued to talk out loud. "The woman in the park was a sign from God. She said that we have to take the good and bad as blessings. Ride them out and pray for the best. Then she said, when the time is right, I will make a good mother. Now, if that is not an angel, what is?"

Monica glanced in her direction and spoke. "Did she have wings?" Monica was joking, but she got no laugh out of Henna. So she continued in a different vein. "Fine. She said when the time was right, not the time was right now."

"I'm having this baby. I just want Craig to understand. He thinks I'm punishing him."

"Craig has managed to go twenty-four years without
an ounce of responsibility. You having this baby makes
him own up to something. He's never liked anyone to
make decisions for him," Monica explained.

"Well, I wasn't sitting around, waiting for a baby. I
loved my life the way it was. How am I going to tour
nine months pregnant . . . huh? You can't!"

Monica grabbed a few of Henna's shirts and began
folding the pieces and stacking them by the luggage.
She continued arguing her case. "I'll support you either
way. But deep down, I know you want a husband and a
stable family."

"I was raised by a single mom," Henna stated.

"That doesn't mean you have to be one," Monica
added, but Henna had no response. She took the folded
shirts and placed them in the luggage. After they were
done, Monica sat on the bed and reached for Henna's
hand, and so Henna sat beside her. Henna hated the
friction between the two of them, and she knew she had
to breach it. She leaned her head onto Monica's lap and
whispered, "Just tell me that you understand."

Monica rubbed Henna's temples, brushing Henna's
hair from her face. "I do, and I know you really like
my brother, whether you admit it or not. I know you
wished you two could be together."

"No, I—"

Monica silenced Henna. "And I know you will never
admit that either. But, Henna, I have to be honest. I
love my brother, but he may not be there for you. I'm
sorry."

Henna took several deep breaths and remained in
Monica's lap for a few minutes before they each retired
and went to sleep.

***

The next morning before Henna took her vehicle back to the rental-car place, she stopped by the Righteous Room/the Attic to see if Craig was there. She didn't know what she'd say, but she just wanted to see him before she left. Henna rushed in, but only Travis and a few others were inside. Henna told Travis that she was leaving, and she promised to come back to see the place when it was done. When she turned to leave, Henna saw Nia walking up the stairs. Nia gave a pleasant nod, but Henna just couldn't muster up a smile. Nia paused and silently questioned her heavyhearted appearance. Henna paused, and for an instant thought about telling Nia the whole thing. She knew Craig hadn't said a word, and this would be payback for all of the men who had ever done her wrong.

"Do you know where Craig is?" Henna asked as a lead-in.

"No, I'm looking for him too. Why?" Nia asked, showing off her big, innocent doe eyes.

Because I'm his baby's mama, and I should know his whereabouts, Henna thought, as the words started to migrate to the tip of her tongue, but spite was never Henna's game. Therefore, she smiled and said, "I'm going back to New York and I just wanted to say bye."

Nia tightly embraced Henna as though they'd been best friends since the sixth grade. She may not have known the entire story, but women have intuition. True, Nia was the emotional type, but this hug overflowed with good riddance. Henna left the Attic, returned her car, and shuttled to the airport.

As the plane lifted, Henna's weight became heavier by the second. She was about to start her life as a single mother. How had this simple getaway turned into a life-altering state of affairs? Thankfully, she had a project to be ecstatic about, because everything else in her life was in a state of chaos. Just before she left, she'd downloaded her new songs to her iPod, and so Henna put the earplugs in and listened. It eased some of the anxiety, but she knew it was only temporary, for the flight was short. Therefore, she had 110 minutes to pull it together and find the energy to move forward.

Craig and Travis were in the last stages of renovation. It was amazing how the crew had transformed this attic into Craig's vision. The place was starting to look like the Righteous Room he had dreamed of, but Craig couldn't get excited about it. Nia was pressuring him to finalize the wedding date, and he hadn't spoken to Henna in over a week.

Travis didn't know what was going on with his boy, but he was tired of Craig spacing out in the middle of work or random conversation. He'd asked repeatedly about the issue, but Craig would give the vague reply "Just sorting things out." Travis wasn't taking that answer anymore.

After the crew left, and while he and Craig were staining the wood on the walls, he insisted that Craig come clean. Craig finally grumbled and responded, "I'm going to be a dad."

Travis smirked and then let out a garbled laugh before saying, "Nia finally got your ass, huh?"

"Not Nia," he said, his expression disoriented.

"What? Who?"

Craig gazed across the room, and Travis followed his stare, which landed on the piano. "No! Are you serious? Henna?" Craig slowly assented with a nod. Both men were speechless as they continued to stain the next panel.

Seconds passed before Travis spoke. "So what's up? What are you going to do?" Craig shrugged his shoulders and kept working. Travis felt compelled to give his two cents. "At least she has her own money."

"That's supposed to make me feel better?" Craig said, frowning.

"Yeah," Travis stated. "At least you know she's going to hold her weight, and not try to drag you down."

"Money or not, she's not the type of girl who would drag me down. But that's not the point. She's having the baby, she's in New York, and I didn't have anything to do with the decision. She's stubborn, man, and wants everything her way."

"Sounds like somebody I know," Travis said, looking Craig directly in the face. Though Craig instantly knew Travis was referring to him, he let it go and continued to pick apart Henna. "She didn't even consider my feelings or the fact that we barely know each other."

Travis cut through the bull, and got right to the point. "What's the issue? Are you mad because you can't have her? Do you love her?"

"What? Nah, I barely know her. She's so closed . . . doesn't say much. I mean, I like her." His comments were fragmented and random, but he continued to speak. "Something about her eyes. They have this innocence, and at the same time she is wise beyond her years . . . like an old soul of a child. I don't know, man. She's just so sexy, it's hard to be mad at her. But this time she's really pissed me off."

"You're saying a whole lot for someone you barely know."

"I guess I know her. Hell, who knows? If it weren't for this baby, we'd probably still be kicking it."

"Yeah, insemination can ruin a 'kicking-it' relationship. Besides, how you gonna kick it when Nia's at your house?"

"That's another pain in my ass. She means well, but damn. . . ."

Travis figured it was best to stop the conversation there. He felt Craig gearing up to talk for another hour, and he had to get home. Travis placed his stain brush in the can, walked over to the bar, and grabbed his wallet and keys.

"I'm gonna head home. Congratulations?" Travis said; there was a definite question mark at the end.

"Yeah, man, good night," Craig murmured. Craig stayed at the bar that night until morning. He finished staining the entire left wall and crashed in his office.

Henna was feeling a little rejuvenated, and was glad to be back in New York. She enjoyed the break, but she'd missed the hustle and bustle. Henna had forgotten how slow things moved in the South, until she stepped off a curb and was nearly knocked over by a yellow taxi. Thankfully, Haydu was there to pull her back to the curb. She hadn't spilled the beans about the baby yet, for Haydu was a hyper, overanxious neurotic, which was a character trait she normally adored. Unfortunately, his tendency to overplan would mean he'd have the child's "sweet sixteen" party location on hold by her second trimester. She wanted to have the baby, but she wasn't ready to share her news with others who might be more excited than she was. So she kept it to herself.

She and Haydu were on their way to meet Claudia Killroy, a woman whose management firm represented many big industry names. Henna knew from the Fifth Avenue address that Claudia Killroy would be a very opinionated manager, and she wasn't sure she wanted that at this stage of her career. Haydu made her go, anyway. As they crossed Fourth Street, Henna noticed a familiar face on one of the newsstands. She grabbed Haydu's hand, walked over, and picked up the periodical. It was Bobby-B, and next to his picture was the headline: IS ONE OF THE HOTTEST HIP-HOP PRODUCERS GAY?

Haydu looked over her shoulders and silently read the title.

"Of course he is," answered Haydu.

"Why would you say that?" Henna said with panic.

"I have great gaydar."

"But this is a—"

"I'm that good," Haydu butted in, chuckling.

Henna hit him over the head with the paper, gave the newsstand attendant $3.50, opened the article, and read it from start to finish. She peered at the cover once more and grunted one word, once she was done.

"Ahmad!"

Henna immediately called Ahmad and left him an urgent message. She didn't know if Bobby had seen the cover, but she was praying that he couldn't link her to its release. She wasn't sure it was Ahmad, but according to the sources, a high-profile music executive had confirmed its validity. Fuming, Henna went into the meeting with Ms. Killroy, and ten minutes later, she and Haydu were leaving the building. Again, Henna already knew that she would be too uppity for her taste. A woman like Claudia Killroy wouldn't want to take chances, she was a rule player.

Henna needed a risk taker, like Ahmad, whom she had tried calling again. This time he picked up. Henna lit into him but he insisted that he hadn't said a word to anyone. For some reason Henna didn't believe him. He offered to take her out for drinks as a welcome home, and Henna quickly agreed, just so she could look him in the eyes and ask again. In person she could always tell when he was lying.

It wasn't until Henna arrived at the spot that evening, she remembered she couldn't ingest alcohol. She was pregnant. Ahmad questioned her cranberry juice choice, but she ignored his question by interrogating him about Bobby. Ahmad didn't look her in the eye when he answered, which was a giveaway. But after he continued to insist he hadn't spilled the beans, Henna let it go. She knew Ahmad couldn't be trusted, and she just had to accept the fact that she'd possibly ruined the career of her newfound friend. Henna and Ahmad left the bar and walked over to a jazz spot a few doors down. The interaction between them was cordial, a complete turnaround from the years they'd been together, which caused her to ask, "So we're friends now?"

"I guess so," he replied.

She didn't know why she was no longer upset with him. Was it that her current situation had taken precedence, or had she finally come to terms that he was never healthy to begin with? Either way, it felt good, to be in a different emotional place. She waited the entire night for him to make his move, but he never did. Henna was still unsure if she and Ahmad were going to be able to handle this transition, but this night seemed to be working. She desperately wanted him back as a manager, but she didn't know if that was a good idea, until his comment toward the end of the evening.

"I respect the personal decisions you've made. But I feel we've both put too much into your career to hand it over to a stranger. I still want to be your manager."

"I was thinking the same thing," she said. "But can we do this, and not get tangled back into a relationship?"

"I'm a professional. I wouldn't do anything you didn't want me to do, and you've made it clear that you don't want to be with me."

"As long as you know that, then we can try it. You know my voice better than anyone."

"Okay, deal," said Ahmad.

Henna walked a few more blocks and then said a soft, "This is good."

Ahmad drove Henna home that evening, and he walked her to her door. He gave her a nod as she walked in, but that was it.

Later, Henna thought about Ahmad and what he had said. True, he had put lots of time into building her career, but he also managed five other bigger-named artists and wasn't hurting for money. Did he genuinely care, or was this a scheme? She didn't know. Yet, she was sure that she needed him to ink some of the deals she wanted to request. Therefore, if she kept it professional, he had no choice but to do the same.

Henna had to up her game and always be one step ahead of him. She could no longer see Ahmad as her loyal, trusted man. She had to look at him the same way she looked at Phillip, a bloodsucking executive. Ahmad may not be full-blooded vampire, but he was definitely a vampeal, a half-breed. Which meant when times got desperate, he, too, would go after human blood. Henna had to make sure her neck was protected at all times.

Chapter 20

"Teardrops from My Eyes"
(Ruth Brown, 1950)

Henna went to her doctor the next morning. She'd made the appointment while she was in Atlanta; luckily, they'd had a cancellation. Normally, it took four months to book, and she didn't want to find a new gynecologist, especially since hers also practiced obstetrics. So she arrived at ten in the morning and sat in the waiting room with several others. Next to her was a woman who looked like she could give birth any second. Henna looked down at her own stomach and then looked at the woman's protruding belly. "I don't want to get that big," she whispered to herself. It looked painful, and just when Henna was about to ask the woman her due date, the lady was called into the back. Henna watched her struggle to rise from the chair; then she realized she should help her. Hell, this might be her in a few months. She took the lady by the arm, lifted her gently, and then watched her wobble to the back area. Henna frowned at the thought of wobbling onstage to perform. There was nothing graceful about it, and she'd have to get new gowns, and she couldn't wear her heels, and . . .

"Ms. Henna James," called the receptionist just in time. Henna went to the back for her first OB appointment.

An hour later, she was eating at a pizza parlor and staring at her medical paperwork. According to Dr. Lisa Polzcheck, Henna was five and a half weeks pregnant. She stared at the paper, still somewhat shocked, and then looked out the window at the thousands of people passing by. Suddenly she felt lonely—much different from alone. Henna wanted the company of someone, anyone. She didn't know if this was hormonal or based on the fact that for the first time, in a long time, she was truly alone. She didn't have a man, her relationship with Monica was strained because of the baby, and she'd isolated herself from her fake industry buds, because she'd needed a break. There was Haydu, but he was very self-absorbed, had a loving partner, and didn't have lots of time to give her. It was supposed to be one of the happiest moments in her life, but she was depressed.

Henna went home and listened to her music, and this time it didn't even help. She'd critiqued the new music so much that when it played, she only heard the mistakes. Furthermore, thinking about Phillip possibly shelving the project only made it worse. Henna checked her e-mail and decided to go to bed early, but as she was preparing, her phone rang. Ahmad was inviting her to a P. Diddy "Black Party." Supposedly, the soirée, two days from that evening, was a launch for one of his new groups, and all media was going to be there. Though Henna wasn't in the mood to party, she knew it was good networking, and so she agreed to go, as long as Ahmad understood that they wouldn't be going as a couple. He did, and they agreed to meet there.

Henna brushed her teeth and got into bed. As she was going to sleep, she thought about the publicity Diddy's parties normally got. It sparked an idea. Henna hopped up from the bed and called Bobby-B. They hadn't talked since she saw the article, and she hoped he didn't mention it. As soon as he answered, she invited him to be her date to the party. At first, he turned down the request, due to his session schedule, but after Henna begged and pleaded, he finally caved. Henna didn't tell him her overall plan, but she knew that if he made it to New York, next week's headlines would tell a different story.

The "Black Party" was held at a private penthouse in upper Manhattan, and Ahmad was right. It was a who's who of industry professionals. Henna and Bobby-B made their appearance close to eleven that night, and as soon as they stepped into the spot, all heads turned. By now, Henna had made Bobby aware of her plan to change his tainted image overnight. They were the hot new couple on the scene. Many were surprised, for they assumed Henna and Ahmad were still together. Plus, with the recent tabloid outing, others were surprised to see Henna and Bobby canoodling all night. If Henna wasn't holding his hand or sitting on his lap, she was gazing fondly into his eyes. He returned the affection, and the two of them had a blast. Every photographer wanted a picture.

Ahmad watched from across the room, and when he saw Henna part from her date, he cornered her in the back by the bathrooms. He didn't have to speak; she knew from his expression that he wanted to know the deal. Henna couldn't tell him the truth, for he might just blab that as well. Therefore, she just gave him a wily smile and replied, "Bobby and I became very close while working on the project." Henna knew that was just enough fodder for the tabloids to go wild with exaggeration. Henna then turned and walked into the bathroom. Ahmad went back to his networking and her plan went off without a hitch.

Neither was a big enough star to warrant tons of paparazzi, but just to be on the safe side, Bobby stayed at Henna's place that night. Therefore, if anyone captured any additional photos, it would be shots of them cuddling that night, or walking into her place, or leaving the next morning to eat breakfast.

Over their eggs and bacon, the two laughed about the silly, pretentious people in the business. As Henna gazed into Bobby's eyes, she thought, *if only he liked women*. Just as quickly she remembered her current dilemma, and she decided it was time for a tell-all.

"I'm pregnant," she whispered across the table.

Bobby's mouth fell open and he actually gasped. "I knew something was up. Craig?" he murmured.

Henna nodded her head.

"Does he know?"

She nodded again.

Bobby reached across the table and squeezed her hand. His eyes were lit with joy. "How excited are you?" he said.

"Not very," she replied, and then she explained the entire story.

When she was done, Bobby just sat and shook his head. "We've got to get you back to Atlanta. I miss you."

"You actually want me to leave New York. Are you crazy?"

Bobby looked outside at the city. "It's dirty, and it's smelly."

"But it's New York."

"Well, we can't carry on this long-distance relationship. What would they say?" Bobby said with laughter.

Henna giggled, but then a sharp pain hit the right side of her stomach. "I don't think the baby likes waffles." The pain got stronger. "I need to go home."

Bobby helped Henna home and he tended to her as she got in the bed. They spent the rest of the evening at the house; however, later that night Henna began spotting, so Bobby-B took her to the emergency room and sat in the waiting area until the sun came up. When the doctors came to get Bobby, he walked in the room to find Henna resting. He sat by her bed and gently rubbed her hand. Henna opened her eyes and glanced over at Bobby.

She gave a tiny smile and whispered, "It's like you really are my boyfriend."

"The doctor said—"

"I know," she interrupted. "All of this baby hullaballoo, and now what?" Henna murmured sarcastically.

Bobby continued to hold her hand as she took several deep breaths.

"You okay?"

"Yeah, I was ready for a drink, anyway," Henna said, with a peculiar faux smile behind her words.

Bobby let out one short breath of laughter, but he quickly followed it with an endearing look of concern.

Henna had never expressed it, but she had become excited about becoming a mother. She'd wished it had been under better circumstances, but still, she was looking forward to having a little one. Before now, Henna hadn't given kids much thought. Although she cared about Ahmad, she knew he was too selfish to be a dad, and she was too involved with her career to raise a child. However, because she was in a new season of her life, the idea of being a mother was giving her a new perspective. She would now be leaving a legacy, outside of her music. At night, when she placed her hand on her stomach, this thought made her feel significant in the grand scheme of nature. She was thinking of names, wondering what the baby would look like, and even speculating about his or her musical talent. She didn't give much thought about her lack of communication or torn relationship with Craig, because Henna was strong and used to dealing with things on her own.

In her mind this was just another one of life's upsets that she'd have to deal with alone. This was the first time, in a long time, that she had to deal with such a great loss, and she likened the pain to what she felt when her father walked out. She didn't know how to deal with that pain then, and she didn't know how to deal with it now, and so she closed herself off and buried the pain.

Bobby didn't know Henna as well as her friends did, so he wasn't sure how to approach her. Though she was determined not to show it, Bobby could see her grief underneath the shallow veneer. Therefore, he thought it best to say nothing but simply place his head on her chest.

True to her nature, Henna tried more lighthearted humor as an attempt to ease and mask the hurt, but it wasn't working. Inside, her heart was breaking. Henna insisted that Bobby go out and grab some food—really, it was to give her a moment alone.

When he left, Henna was free to grieve. She closed her eyes and softly lamented the loss, throughout the night and into the early morning. She finally drifted off to sleep, and when she woke, she looked over and saw Bobby in the chair next to her bed.

Henna closed her eyes and whispered, "Thank you, thank you."

The first thank-you was to Bobby for being a good friend; the second one was to God for not letting her go through this disappointment alone.

Chapter 21

"Breaking Up Is Hard to Do"
(Neil Sedaka, 1962)

Nia was eagerly planning her wedding to Craig, but she was growing impatient with the tedious details, especially since Craig wasn't helping. He was busy with planning the club opening, and he made it clear to Nia that it was his priority. He would be more involved with the wedding after the opening date in four weeks. However, Nia made a change of plans. She decided that she'd rather go to the justice of the peace and have a reception, instead. Craig preferred the idea, as opposed to a wedding, for cost reasons; however, he knew that a date at the courthouse would happen much quicker than a date before family and friends. He was right, because Nia was ready to go that Friday. Craig rushed from the house while Nia was getting dressed for work, and he wiggled his way out of an answer. He knew that before he went to sleep that night, she was going to need a response. It was the first item of discussion on the agenda when he arrived at the club. Travis, being a married man, told Craig that he needed to be sure.

"It's not a whimsical decision to be taken lightly," he insisted. "I know you say you love her, but can you commit to her for life?" Travis questioned.

Craig slowly nodded but the far-off gaze in his eye was as uncertain as a lottery ticket. Travis caught wind of his stare and commented: "You're not ready." Yet. Craig was determined to prove them all wrong. He could commit, and he could be a great husband. He knew Nia would stick by him, and he felt like he wouldn't find another who would do the same. Sure, he cared about Henna, but she was off doing God knows what. She hadn't called, she didn't respect his opinion, nor did she consider him as a viable mate. Nia, on the other hand, worshipped the ground he walked on. It sounded like a no-brainer. However, Craig didn't want to start their relationship off with a lie. He was going to have to tell Nia about the baby. He knew that it might damage their bond, but if they could get through it, then he knew she was the one.

By two o'clock that afternoon, Travis officially left his friend to his own demise by using a large set of Bose earphones to block out the remainder of Craig's statements and random rhetorical questions. Travis was sick of talking to a man who wasn't listening to anyone but himself.

In New York, Henna had been resting for twenty-four hours since she'd been home from the hospital. When she woke up about six that evening, she decided to call Craig. Bobby had gotten on a plane early that afternoon, but not before making Henna a bowl of tuna salad. She got herself a big serving, with a roll of crackers, and stretched across her living-room couch. And while Craig was on his way home to tell Nia about creating a life, Henna was 850 miles north of him, contemplating how she was going to tell him about losing it. It wasn't that she thought he'd be upset; it was more that she didn't want to hear him say, "I told you it wasn't supposed to be." Though the words might have been true, Henna was in no mood to hear anyone gloat about her misfortune. Henna called Monica first. They talked for a minute, but Monica seemed to be acting strangely. She wasn't saying much and she was antsy. Henna spent more time questioning Monica's behavior than talking about her own issue. At the very end of the conversation, Henna finally told her. Monica was quiet, so silent that Henna thought the line had disconnected.

"Are you okay? Do I need to come up there?" Monica asked.

"I'm good. I just wanted to tell you," Henna replied.

"Have you talked to Craig?" asked Monica.

"I'm calling him next. I know he's going to say, 'I told you so.'"

"He wouldn't do that. Craig can be an asshole, but he's not that insensitive." Henna nodded quietly, as though Monica could see her actions.

"Hello?" Monica called out.

"Yeah, I'm gonna call him now," Henna repeated.

"I love you, and if you need me, call me."

"I will," promised Henna.

They hung up and Henna went to the bathroom.

Craig was walking in the door of his home, where Nia awaited him. She was anxious to finish the conversation that had begun that morning. Although Nia had planned a romantic dinner, complete with candles, Craig walked in, knowing he was about to break her heart. She greeted him with a kiss, and then he went to the bedroom to change. After washing up, Nia had the table set, and before he could initiate conversation, she handed him the scheduling at the justice of the peace.

"We can't do it this Friday. We have to do it Wednesday or Thursday. If that's cool, then I can go to the courthouse tomorrow and get all of the paperwork."

"Um . . . it's Monday. Maybe we should wait until next week."

"Why? Next week is no different from this week."

"It's seven more days to get everything together."

"There's nothing to get together," said Nia.

"I need to talk to you about something important," Craig urged.

Nia became aggravated. She assumed this talk was to distract her from the marriage conversation, and so she didn't want to hear it. "What?" Nia was vexed.

Just then, Craig's phone rang, and they both looked at the cell.

"This is important, Craig." Nia demanded his attention; thus, Craig ignored the ring. "Now, what is it that's more important than us getting married?"

"There are some things I need to clear up beforehand. We'd been apart for a year and . . ." His cell rang again. This time Craig rose to see who was calling him. Nia grunted as he left the table.

"Your food is going to get cold!" she called out.

Craig ignored her comment and rushed to catch the phone on the last ring. "Hey, what's up?" he said to Henna as she was identified on ID. Henna was silent. She didn't know what to say. "Henna, you okay?" Craig continued.

"I'm good," she whispered. "I just needed to talk to you."

"I need to talk to you too, but can I call you back?"

Henna knew that she needed to talk to Craig immediately, prolonging this conversation was only going to make it more difficult.

"It won't take long," Henna said, but Craig heard Nia walking toward him.

"I promise I'll call you back," he assured. "In a couple of hours." By now, Nia was standing, akimbo, at the door. She was quiet, but she was giving off much attitude. Craig quickly hung up.

Henna listened to the dial tone a few seconds and then released a long, agonized groan.

Craig gave Nia a remorseful stare and tried his best to form the needed words: I have to say, "I have a baby coming."

Nia didn't give him time to speak. "Craig, what is wrong with you? Why are you acting weird?"

"I have to tell you something, and you're not going to like it."

Nia's heart began to race.

Just then, Craig's phone buzzed with a text message. He glanced down and read it silently. He looked up at Nia and spoke. "Please forgive me, I have to step out."

"What!" Nia shrieked as Craig grabbed his keys.

"Sorry," he said, closing the door behind him. He rushed to the truck, took off, and called Henna.

"I got your text. What's the emergency?"

Henna gave a quick but soft response. "I lost the baby, Craig."

"Oh God," he said.

"I know you're busy. I'll let you go. I just wanted to tell you."

"No," Craig insisted. "How are you holding up?"

"I'm good. A little sore, but I'm okay."

"I'm coming to see you," Craig stated.

"No, that's only going to cause trouble."

"Let me worry about mine," said Craig.

"Look, I'll let you go. I'm okay, I promise. Besides, I will be booking a few dates, and I'm busy working to get this project mixed and to the label."

"How's that going?" he asked.

"Good. I think it's the best one I've ever done. Of course Phillip doesn't think so."

"Phillip?" Craig questioned.

"The label rep I was telling you about."

"The vampire?"

"Yeah," Henna agreed with a chuckle.

They were extremely uncomfortable speaking to one another. Yet, neither wanted to hang up.

"I should come see you," Craig said once more.

"No, I'm fine," Henna insisted.

"I'll call you tomorrow. Call me if you need me, for anything," Craig volunteered just before hanging up. He took a few minutes to gather his thoughts before driving back around the block. He was having mixed emotions about everything. No, he didn't want Henna to have the baby; yet he didn't want her to miscarry either. Now that she had, should he tell his bride-to-be about a baby that no longer existed? Craig needed a drink. He wasn't going to deal with any of it at the moment. He went back to the house, but before Nia could start, he silenced her with a stopping hand gesture.

"A friend of mine is going through something terrible, and I just can't talk about this right now. I want to marry you. That's all that matters. We can do it next week, or the week after. This week is not good. I will be leaving town in a couple of days—"

"What?" Nia interrupted.

"That's what I was trying to tell you when I sat down," Craig conveniently lied.

"Why?" she questioned.

"I'm going to New York for some music stuff." Craig wolfed down his dinner, while Nia sat in her bundle of confusion. When he was done, Craig rose, washed the plates, and grabbed his keys.

"Now, where are you going?" Nia asked, more aggravated.

"To Monica's house." Craig kissed Nia's forehead and left her drowning in a pool of uncertainty.

Craig rushed to Monica's, and though he called her several times without an answer, it didn't stop him from continuing. Luckily, her car was outside, and so he rushed in.

"Monica!" he yelled as he walked in. "Monica!" he continued.

Monica came rushing downstairs. "What in the world is wrong with you?" she yelled.

"Henna lost the baby."

"I know," Monica said, wrapped in her robe.

"Why are you asleep?" Craig asked, pointing to her lounging attire.

"I'm tired," she answered.

Craig placed his head on his sister's shoulders. Monica softly rubbed the back of his bald scalp.

"I'm tired too. Can I stay here tonight?"

Monica didn't answer immediately; in fact, she tried to convince Craig otherwise, but she could tell that her brother couldn't bear going home.

"You can stay in Henna's room. I mean, the guest room."

Craig heard noises upstairs. "Julian up there?"

"Yeah," Monica answered. "But it's okay, he was going to sleep."

Monica and Craig went into the kitchen to talk.

"Now that she's not having the baby, we don't have any ties to each other."

"Is that a question?" Monica asked.

"A statement, I guess," Craig replied.

"So I guess you are free and clear to marry Nia," Monica stated.

"Is that a question?" Craig asked.

"Is it?" Monica posed.

They sat and looked at each other, until Monica asked, "Why are you marrying this girl?"

"I know you don't think I love her, but I do."

"I never questioned whether or not you loved Nia, but loving someone doesn't mean you should marry them."

"I'm marrying her for the same reason you're marrying Julian."

"I doubt it," Monica said.

"I know you a lot better than you think," said Craig, "and we are a lot more alike than you know."

"Maybe, but I think you're marrying Nia out of guilt. You feel like you owe her something for the years that she's been faithful to you. You know that she'll be a good wife, and you know if you do mess up, she'll probably forgive you and take you back."

"Not true."

Monica looked on with doubt.

"Not entirely true," he admitted before asking, "So you are marrying Julian because . . ."

"Because I'm tired of dating. There, I said it. Julian loves me unconditionally, and he's good for me."

"Nia's good for me."

"No, she's not. She's not strong enough for you."

"How could you say that?"

"You will run over Nia, like you always have."

"Just because I can do something doesn't mean I will," said Craig.

"Yes, it does. If you have a Porsche that you know can go one hundred thirty miles per hour, you will try it once. Even if you shouldn't."

"That's not a good analogy. We're talking about human emotion. I'm becoming a better person. I'm growing up. I wouldn't cut Nia just because I know she'll heal. I wouldn't hurt her."

"Not on purpose," Monica said directly. "You always have good intentions, just misguided ones."

"I think marrying her will make me stronger."

Monica sighed and replied, "Then you have my blessing." Monica, mentally exhausted, rose and went upstairs.

Craig booked his ticket to New York, and then sat on the couch and watched television until he went to sleep.

The next morning, around five o'clock, Craig woke up when he heard footsteps coming down the stairs. He looked up and saw a tall figure passing by.

"Julian?" he said, still in a slumber. Craig wiped his eyes just as the man was walking out. He then realized it wasn't his sister's fiancé leaving, but her skeletons, instead. It was Mick. He couldn't believe it. Craig could follow behind him, and never let Monica know he was in on her dirty little secret, or he could play his role as her bratty baby brother and make her feel like crap. Naturally, he chose the latter.

Craig had been so wrapped up in the bar and Henna, he had no idea what was going on with Monica. He suspected she wasn't going to go through with the wedding, but he never thought she had another man on the side.

He didn't hear Monica tinkering upstairs, but he knew that she'd be heading downstairs in an hour or so for her morning java. So Craig walked into the kitchen to start the percolator.

When Monica came trotting into the kitchen, she was startled to see him. "How long have you been up?" she questioned, an apprehensive look stretched upon her face. However, Craig didn't have to say a word. She already knew from the curious smirk on his lips. Her dirt had been exposed.

"Don't say anything. I already feel bad enough," she warned.

"You should."

"It's not that I don't love Julian. I do. Last night was the first time we ever . . . you know."

Craig laughed.

"This is serious, it's not funny," Monica said.

"I wanted you to get the loan. I didn't want you to have to bend over for it."

Monica slapped Craig in the chest. "It just happened."

"I thought only guys used that excuse," Craig said.

Monica put her face on the table.

"I can't believe that he was upstairs last night when you were giving me the whole spiel about Nia. Had y'all done it already?"

Monica gave an odd look.

"Yeah, y'all had already done it. Don't say anything else to me about my life."

"Cool. I hate giving you advice, anyway." Monica sipped her coffee and stared out the window. But Craig couldn't stop.

"What are you going to do about Julian? Are you still going to marry him?" Monica shrugged her shoulders. "Everything I said last night about Julian is true. He does love me unconditionally, and he's good for me. I don't know if I'm good for him, though. I love him, but maybe not in the way he needs to be loved, and I don't know if that will ever change. But if I marry him, I will commit. I will not cheat. I swear."

"How can you say that?" asked Craig.

"Because I won't. I chose to sleep with Mick last night because I knew it would probably be the last time I ever slept with another man. It was completely wrong, but I just had to make sure that—"

"That you weren't missing something," Craig cut in.

"No. Stop interrupting. I had to make sure that I would feel like shit in the morning. So much so, I could never do it again."

"So your plan worked," said Craig.

Monica turned toward Craig while she exited the kitchen. She had a dismal expression as she spoke. "Just the opposite. I don't feel like shit. I don't feel anything." She went upstairs and got dressed for work.

Chapter 22

"Use ta Be My Girl" (The O'Jays, 1978)

Monica's little shenanigans made Craig positive that visiting New York was the right thing to do. He wouldn't attempt to sleep with Henna, but if he spent one last time with her, and felt guilty, then he was definitely ready to commit to Nia. If he felt nothing, then he would have to break it off.

Sure, it was wrong to follow in his sister's foolish footsteps, but it sounded like a sane plan to Craig. By the time Craig got home, Nia had left for work. His timing was perfect. With everything going on, there was no way he could hear her talk about a wedding.

Therefore, he washed a few clothes and packed his bag. Though, he wasn't leaving until tomorrow afternoon, he put his things in the truck and headed for the club. Craig kept to himself most of the day, and he stayed at Monica's that evening. He decided to avoid Nia altogether before leaving town. Again, it wasn't the right thing to do, but he wasn't good at confronting unresolved issues. Going to see Henna was his attempt at resolution. He had to deal with one woman at a time.

Craig arrived in New York early Thursday afternoon. Monica had given him Henna's address, so he quickly hopped a train to Brooklyn. When he arrived, Henna wasn't home, so he went down to Fulton Street and grabbed a bite to eat. Two hours later, she still wasn't there, so he decided to call. Henna didn't answer her phone. Therefore, Craig camped out by her home and waited. After three hours of waiting, Henna arrived home. He saw her walking toward her front door. But he sat and watched her for a moment while he reminisced about their past intimate moments.

As he was about to walk over, Craig saw a man approaching her. The man looked very familiar. Soon he realized it was the porch visitor, Ahmad. He was bringing her a sweater. He watched their interaction. Ahmad lightly held Henna's wrists and pulled her close. She wasn't resisting; in fact, she seemed to be enjoying his attention. He playfully tickled her side and she laughed and played along. Ahmad then followed her into her home. Craig waited for close to an hour, but Ahmad remained inside. He automatically assumed that she and her ex-manager/ex-boyfriend had rekindled their relationship. Perhaps this was why she didn't want him to come to New York, Craig thought, or maybe she had never ended it with Ahmad, and she'd been playing him all along.

Craig's flight was scheduled to leave the next day at 6:00 P.M., and he was still determined to speak with her. So Craig went into the city, got a hotel, and decided to return to Henna's that evening. Close to eight that night, he gave her a call, and she answered.

"I'm in town," he told her.

"What?" Henna said. "When did you get here?"

Then Craig did something rare to his character. He showed a hint of jealousy. "So, are you kicking it with your ex-manager?"

"What are you talking about, Craig?"

"I was going to surprise you, but I saw you and him together. Never mind that. I just wanted to make sure you were fine."

"I told you I was good. So you were at my building?" Henna said, still a little confused.

"Yes. Are you busy now? Do you still have company?"

"No."

"I'll be over," Craig said, and then quickly hung up.

An hour later, Craig was buzzing Ms. James. She gave him a smile as wide as the Grand Canyon. Craig tried to be stern, but he was so happy to see her, face-to-face, that he couldn't help but grin. During their conversation the two worked through many emotions that were left unresolved. They both apologized and agreed that they let their feelings get the best of them.

"We should have known the second time we got together that it was trouble."

"We knew, we just didn't say anything," Henna replied.

"So why didn't you say something?"

"Why didn't you?" Henna wasn't going to be the easy mark.

"You had already laid your disclaimer the first time we hooked up, remember? You said that it didn't mean anything."

"And you said you didn't have time to be with me," Henna quickly countered.

Craig let out a smile. "That really got to you, didn't it?"

Henna didn't answer but rose to make a pot of coffee. "You want some?" she asked.

"Yeah, that's cool."

The two continued to talk, and they even admitted that they cared more than they would allow themselves to admit at the time. Craig didn't mention Nia, and so Henna followed his lead and didn't talk about her either. Even so, this was a huge breakthrough for them both. Over coffee Henna let him hear what Bobby had done with the songs, and they talked about doing shows together.

"Maybe you can perform at the opening of the Righteous Room?"

"I'd like that," she said. "What made you decide to change the name?"

Craig let out a quick chortle, and replied, "I was on YouTube looking at old blues footage, and at the end of the performance, one of the players said that was some righteous playing. Music was virtuous to them. I wanted my place to have that same kind of feeling."

"I feel you."

"You like it?" he asked, deeply wanting her approval.

"A lot," Henna replied.

The two of them laughed and talked into the early-morning hours. Henna's body language was still very stoic, and her guard was high. She was able to laugh and joke, but she wasn't relaxed, not even after she retired to her room and showed Craig to the spare room.

"I suppose I am a guest now?" he said, snickering.

"Yes, you are," Henna replied, grinning.

Just before she walked into her room, Craig gave Henna a tight embrace. "I've missed you," he said, looking into her eyes.

"I've missed talking with you. But . . ." Henna stopped talking.

"But what?" Craig inquired.

"I'm glad we can be friends. I think we work better this way."

Craig didn't respond. He simply nodded, said good night, and walked into the bedroom. That morning Henna and Craig went to brunch and then prepared to part.

Henna kept their interaction extremely platonic. She didn't want him to misconstrue her excitement, and she surely didn't want to confuse herself. She was aware of how easily that could happen. Before Craig left, Henna wished him the best on his marriage to Nia. She wanted to get his reaction, and deep down she hoped he'd say that they had broken up. But he didn't.

Meanwhile, in Craig's mind, Henna seemed to have washed her hands of him and had moved on. She, herself, had mentioned how she often flicked on and off, like a light switch, and so Craig assumed she was in off mode. He wasn't about to chase her or beg her to change her mind.

Henna beamed and gave him a tight hug as they walked downstairs to wait for the cab. "Call me when you get close to the opening. I want to make sure I put it in my schedule," she said. "You sure you don't want me to take you to the airport?"

"I'm sure," Craig replied. When his cab arrived, they embraced once again, and he got in.

"I left something for you in the house," he said just before closing the door.

Henna nodded, and once he closed that door, she exhaled deeply. It was like she'd been holding her breath the entire time to pull off another great theatrical performance. It appeared that if the singing didn't pan out, Henna knew she could have a bubbling career as an actress. Of course, she'd probably be typecast as that light-skinned girl with the good hair who thought she was better than everyone. But right now, she didn't even care. Henna missed Craig tremendously, but she figured there was no reason to say it. Yes, he came to see her, but he was still engaged to Nia. Both of them were once again waiting for the other to make the first move. Craig figured his step was coming to New York. But to Henna, that was only a pawn move. She was waiting for something with more statement. He would have to move his king at least halfway across life's chessboard to get her attention, and if his king was not in check, there was no need for her to move.

Henna had gone into the bodega down the street to grab some juice, and when she walked back into her home, she saw the gift sitting on her bed. Henna opened the flat package and nearly came to tears when she saw its content. It was Etta James recorded live, with the extended version of "Sugar on the Floor". She sat on the bed, staring at the LP single. She pulled the record out and grinned at the shiny vinyl. Henna had forgotten she'd mentioned her old record player to Craig and how much she loved the light scratch of vinyl. She couldn't believe he'd found that song. She put the record on and stretched across the foot of her bed. With the record player set to start over, she listened to "Sugar on the Floor" eighteen times before she rose. Somewhere around the eleventh time, Henna decided she was going to re-record the song. She rushed to her computer and researched the publishing and called Ahmad for help. At the end of the evening, she spoke with Bobby, who wasn't familiar with the song. However, he immediately went on iTunes and downloaded the version. This was the last song she needed to complete her project. Henna was in pure bliss that night before resting her head. She tried to call Craig before falling asleep, but his phone kept going to voice mail. She assumed he was with Nia, and at first thought, it angered her, because she had good news and he should have been available. Yet, soon after, Henna calmed down and accepted that this was the nature of their relationship. She could thank him and let him know in the morning. She started the record again and listened to the song another twenty times. She wanted to redo it with Craig on acoustic, Travis on piano, and two others on strings—a cello and a violin would be perfect. She quickly jotted her ideas down and sent them to Craig, Bobby, and Ahmad via e-mail. Moments later, she was sound asleep.

Henna called Phillip early the next morning and made an appointment to come to the office later that day. She knew he didn't have a record player, so she emailed him the mp3 version from her computer. He'd already heard the acoustic songs, but Henna had to convince him to do a remake, and Phillip was not fond of those. He felt they were cheats. But Henna had never done one, so she figured it wouldn't hurt. It was just her luck that Phillip's mom was a big Elton John fan, and though he wasn't familiar with Etta's version of that particular song, he did love her voice. That was enough to get Henna in the door, and once she explained her vision, he was sold. In fact, for Phillip, the song gave the entire project clarity.

"This should be the first single," Henna declared.

Phillip agreed without hesitation. Henna couldn't believe how easily he was negotiating. She wasn't aware that Ahmad had come in last week and talked to Phillip about the project. With him, he had supporting data on acoustic sales, and showed his marketing plan to complement the mission. As a final point Ahmad said that he had other labels just waiting for Henna to sign with them. He swore that they would hold on to this project, give the label some junk that she'd put together, and then come out with the acoustic one on another label. Phillip didn't want to take that chance. However, when Henna informed Ahmad of her meeting, he let her think it was all her doing. He knew she was more agreeable when she thought she was in control. Plus, he liked her newfound confidence.

Henna made plans to head back soon to Atlanta to record the song. When she went to bed that night, she knew it was her time, and she was about to shine like never before. Since she had recorded her first album, this was the only time she had complete creative control over her project. Usually, either Ahmad or the label, or sometimes both, swayed her. Her gut told her this was going to be a huge success, and though following her instincts lately had led to a whirlwind of antics, she was sure this was the right thing. This project was giving her a new zeal for music, and she couldn't wait to get back to finish it.

Her interaction with Craig was her only concern, but deep down she couldn't wait to get back to see him again as well.

Chapter 23

"Ninety-nine and a Half (Won't Do)"
(Wilson Pickett, 1966)

Craig and Nia set their date. They planned to go to the courthouse on the next Wednesday, which was four days away, and Craig seemed to be content with his decision. Nia was ecstatic. Therefore, the couple went shopping for wedding bands that Sunday afternoon. Craig wanted white gold, and Nia wanted yellow, so they decided to look for combination bands. On their way back from the jeweler's, they stopped by the club, which was really coming along. The look and feel was just what Craig had wanted, and anytime he got the chance to show it off, he did. Nia hadn't been to it much, since she worked as a teacher during the day and taught aerobics in the evening. Besides, she wasn't keen on the idea of opening a club. She knew it would keep Craig out many late nights and she preferred him home. Nia felt the club life was immature, but she loved Craig and wanted to be supportive, and so she didn't say anything. Yet, she rarely visited or asked about its progress. When she walked in, however, she was taken aback by its charm and character.

"It doesn't seem like a regular club," she commented.

"It's not," Craig said, walking her from corner to corner. Nia checked out the pictures on the walls and the exposed lightbulbs hanging from long, linked chains.

"I really like it, Craig."

"I hope so. For the last year I've put just about all of me into it."

Nia continued looking at the details. She was amazed at how old, and yet new, it looked. Craig, too, was still overwhelmed at the progress. Though he looked at the club every day, it looked different at night as the city lights sparkled through the tiny rectangular windows closely flushed to the ceiling. Craig was overwhelmed at his "baby" that was suddenly grown up. He rushed over to Nia and kissed her.

"What are you doing!" she yelped.

"Shhh, just kiss me."

Nia agreed for a second, but then she pulled away. "Let's go home." Craig tried to kiss her again, but she denied him.

"Let's stay here," he flirted, raising his eyebrows. Nia looked around the room and frowned.

"Here, where?" She motioned toward the floor, just as Craig nodded.

"We can't," she whispered, slightly embarrassed.

"It's my club. We can do whatever I want to do," Craig said while attempting to pull off her shirt.

Nia continued to back away. "Let's just go home."

Craig quickly became annoyed. "Forget it!" he bellowed before storming out.

Nia followed behind him, yelling, "What's wrong? I just don't want to do it here! We can do it at home."

Craig stormed to the truck and cranked it up as Nia was getting in. She was quiet at first, but then she became outraged at his sudden reaction. "What is wrong with you?" she hollered. Craig didn't answer. "Craig Lamar Cole. You hear me! I said, what is wrong with you?"

"You're too prissy. Why aren't you more relaxed around me? We're going to be married in a few days and I can't even get you to have sex with me outside of our bedroom."

"You're mad because I wouldn't have sex in your little club!"

"My little club?" Craig said as he mashed his foot on the accelerator.

"You know what I mean. Why is the location important? It's not like I said I wouldn't do it. I just didn't want to do it there. We've been out all day, and I want to wash up, and stuff."

"Wash up? That's ridiculous," commented Craig.

"No! You're ridiculous," retorted Nia.

"Why can't you be more passionate, more in the moment?"

They continued to argue the rest of the ride, and when Craig pulled into the driveway, he kept the car running. Nia realized he wasn't getting out, and so she asked, "Where are you off to now?"

"I'm going to get a beer."

"No, we should talk," said Nia.

"I'm done talking."

Nia sat in the car for a few seconds longer; then after huffing and griping, she finally got out and slammed the door. Craig peeled off as she walked in.

While he was driving down the street, even he couldn't understand the source of his own anger. He knew what type of woman Nia was. She didn't have spontaneous sex in random situations, unless she was extremely excited about something. That had only happened twice in their relationship: the first time he gave her some jewelry, and the first time he asked her to move in with him. Other than that, it had been bedroom, bathroom, and the occasional living-room couch. But even then, she could only have an orgasm in the bedroom. Yet, he was still upset, and therefore he couldn't go home and apologize because it would just become a venting session about everything he didn't like about her. Craig continued toward the bar, went in, and ordered a Bass Ale.

Nia sat at home, frustrated over what had just taken place. She was dumbfounded, and couldn't understand the source of his outrage. She called her girlfriend back home, who insisted that he only started the fight to get out of the wedding. At first, Nia believed her, but then she knew Craig was the type of guy who would say, "I don't want to marry you," so she didn't think that was it. Nevertheless, she did consider it being a possibility when Craig didn't show up, and two more hours had passed.

By the time he returned, Nia had fallen asleep. He stood over the bed, and while looking at her quietly, he apologized for his actions. Obviously, she didn't hear a word. When she woke up the next morning, he was asleep on the couch. She started to wake him, but she didn't want to get into any heated conversation before work; therefore she wrote him a note and left. This is how they communicated. Their relationship was a bundle of sincere but unspoken apologies. But this time Nia was not going to let it ride. The conversation continued to linger on Nia's mind the remainder of the day; so when school was out, she visited Craig at the club. Oddly, Craig wasn't there, but Travis expected him back any moment, and so she waited. Nia tinkered around on the piano, while Travis went to the back. While she passed the time, Nia looked around the room again and noticed all of the hard work Craig had put into the bar. She began to feel guilty about her lack of interest. If this was her man's dream, she should be more supportive. Nia looked at the floor, but she still frowned at the thought of making love on it.

"It's dirty," she whispered to herself.

Just then, Travis's wife sat next to her. She recalled meeting her twice, but they hadn't spent any time together. Therefore, she couldn't figure out why she was staring with a silly grin on her face.

"Hi, Grace, right?" Nia greeted.

"Yes," responded Grace as she continued to gawk.

Nia looked at her and returned the stare with an uncomfortable smile.

"Congratulations," said Grace.

"Thank you," Nia said. "We pick up our bands tomorrow. We had them designed."

"Wonderful. I didn't realize you were getting married too. Well, double congrats."

Nia was baffled, and it was apparent she had no idea what Grace was talking about. Then she realized that Grace was referring to the club opening in a few weeks.

"Yes! The club is amazing, isn't it? I'm so proud of Craig and Travis. I guess I should say congratulations to you too."

"Honey, what are you talking about? I am congratulating you on the baby. Travis tells me that you're pregnant."

"Huh?" Nia said, her baffled look had become even more incredulous.

"You're pregnant, right? Travis said Craig was having a baby."

Just then, Travis came from the back; he was holding a couple of two-by-fours for the base of the stage. He placed them down and looked at the two women who were burning holes through his body. "I didn't do it," he said immediately.

Nia popped up from the piano bench and marched toward him. "Craig is having a baby?" she said loudly. Grace was rallying two steps behind her. Travis backed into the corner as though bullies on the playground were attacking him.

"I—I, um, you need—need to talk to Craig," he began to stutter.

"What does that mean?" asked Nia.

"Yeah, what does that mean? You said he was having a baby. What are you hiding?" added Grace.

"I know you are not saying . . . Did Craig get some girl pregnant?" Nia screamed.

Travis picked up his wooden boards and used them to defend himself from the two angry women. He looked at his wife and pointed. "I need to see you in the back." He gave Nia a sorrowful expression, turned, and hurried to the back.

Nia looked around the room and it started to spin. She became so dizzy that she needed the corner of the bar to keep her balance. After waiting a few minutes, Nia caught her breath and hurried from the club. She went home, and to her surprise Craig was there waiting for her. The argument had gotten the best of him as well, and he wanted to come home and surprise her. As soon as she walked in, she noticed two dozen roses sitting on the counter. Nia lifted them out of the jar, smelled them, and then she looked at Craig, who sat across the room.

"I'm sorry," he said. "I think I just got nervous about the wedding, but I shouldn't have acted that way. Forgive me?"

"Forgive you for what?" Nia said innocently. "Forgive you because you started an argument with me for no reason, or because you got some girl knocked up and forgot to tell me about it?" Nia still held a pleasant, but eerie smile on her face. This look remained until she hurled the twenty-four roses across the room. However, the lightweight flowers obviously didn't express her venom. So she picked up the thick glass vase and it, too, went sailing through the air until it crashed against the wall. The exploding glass fractures sent Craig running to the other side.

"Hold up!" he shouted.

"You wanted me to be more passionate? Well, here it is!" she yelled.

Nia went ballistic. She began picking up books, candles, and anything with a little weight and tossed the items to and fro. Craig ducked and dodged her aim. He tried to subdue his petite girlfriend, but her fury was raging. Just when he got close, she grabbed his guitar and swung it to keep him at bay.

"If you come closer, I will crack this wood across your skull!" Nia roared, holding the guitar like she was about to knock one out of the park. Craig stood still. He knew she was serious. And though he didn't know how much it would hurt, he didn't want to put one scratch on the vintage mahogany Gallagher. It was his favorite guitar, and she knew it. Craig backed up and calmly stood against the wall. Nia stared at him, and though her anger began shifting to anguish, she still held on to the instrument.

Craig saw her melting, but he didn't budge as he spoke. "Baby, I'm not having a baby."

"Did you get some girl pregnant?"

Craig waited a few seconds before responding, but then he answered honestly, "Yes."

Her grip weakened, and the guitar weapon slowly lowered as her hand trembled.

"Why?" she asked.

"I'm sorry."

"Sorry doesn't tell me why!" Nia tossed the guitar on the bed. "Look at me!" she demanded.

Craig eyed the safety of his instrument, and then approached. "I know I should have told you. I didn't know how."

"You're a coward. No. You're a bitch."

"What?" Craig asked. He wasn't use to Nia being so forthright.

"You whine. You're selfish. You can't admit when you make mistakes. You run from responsibility. You lie."

"If I'm all those things, then why do you want to marry me?"

Nia looked at Craig and poured her answer from deep within her heart. "Because I love you absolutely and completely with all that I have." She didn't even bother to wipe away her constant flow of tears. "I can tolerate a lot. But not respecting me . . . that I can't deal with." Nia slowly walked into the bedroom and began packing. She closed the door behind her, and Craig knew not to invade.

He called Monica, who insisted that she'd not spoken to Nia. Next he called Travis, who picked up on the first ring. Before he could ask, Travis blurted out, "Grace thought Nia was pregnant and congratulated her. She took my phone. I couldn't call."

Craig was silent at first and then spoke one word, "A'ight." He hung up. Craig sat on the couch and waited for Nia to walk out of the bedroom. It took hours. But he needed the time to think, anyway, so he waited.

When she walked out, she was rolling her luggage. "Could you take me to a hotel?" she asked softly.

"I will. But you don't have to go."

"I do. You see, if I don't leave, I'll probably forgive you. And if I do forgive you, I may never forgive myself." Nia continued toward the door, and then she looked back at Craig. "Take me now, please."

Craig grabbed his keys and took Nia to a hotel. He reached in his pocket to give her money, but she refused to take it. He turned the engine off and she sat in the front seat and stared out the window.

"Were you ever going to tell me?"

"Probably not," he whispered.

Nia turned and looked at Craig, something she hadn't done the entire fifteen-minute ride. "I hope you find whatever it is that you're searching for." Nia got out of his truck and grabbed her bag. Craig rushed to her side and helped her with the luggage. He made an attempt to grab her hand as she began walking into the hotel, but she wouldn't let go of the suitcase handle. She turned to face him, and the tears were once again running down her face.

"Please don't," she whimpered. He let go, and as he was releasing her, Craig realized this was something he should have done years ago, just let her go.

"I'm really sorry," he uttered again. She nodded and walked into the Marriott. When Craig got behind the wheel of his truck, he felt tears building in his eyes. Unable to cope with the onslaught of emotions, he slammed his fists against the wheel, nearly fracturing a few fingers. The jar caused a couple of those tears to fall as he looked toward the hotel. He'd truly hurt the most sincere person he'd ever met. It was sad to lose her, but it was more tragic to hurt her. Though he didn't feel as bad as he would have hoped when he returned from New York, this was definitely his lowest moment.

"I feel like shit," he said to himself. It took him a minute to crank up and drive away; even then, he drove aimlessly around the city. Finally Craig ended up at Monica's, but she wasn't home. He wanted to talk to her, but he knew she was going through her own mental mayhem and it would be selfish to burden her with his situation. And though Craig's egotistical behavior never bothered him before, now that Nia had so loudly brought it to the surface, it seemed to weigh heavy.

He backed from Monica's driveway and went home. Once there, Craig cleaned up the shattered glass and picked up the other items strewn about the room. He took a shower and went to bed. It was only seven that evening, but he was worn-out, mentally and physically. He didn't wake until four that morning. In his bed he stared at the ceiling, until moments later when he got up and played on his guitar. Craig strummed softly on the instrument, which was just in peril the afternoon before. Emotionally, Craig was torn, between wanting to call Nia, and wanting to see Henna. As far back as he could remember, he had never felt like this. His ego wouldn't allow him to confess how he felt about Henna, and it wouldn't let him come clean to Nia. Now that he had neither woman, he knew justice had been served, but he hated it had come to this. Craig then heard his phone vibrate from the other room. When he picked it up, he had six missed calls. They were all from the one girl he could always count on, Monica. He dialed her number, and she answered.

"Are you okay?" she said.

"Why are you up?"

"I was worried about you. Nia called me."

Craig was quiet.

"Do you want to come over?" Monica asked.

"You know I do. But I need to deal with this on my own. I appreciate you asking, though."

"I love you," she said.

"I love you too, sis."

Craig hung up, and smiled. This was growth, because for the first time, he chose not to lean on Monica's shoulders. Just the comfort of knowing that they were there was ultimately enough.

Monica returned to sleep, but she was so tired the next day that she took off from work, which was extremely rare. Yet, she felt the day would be good to clear up some things. She'd been avoiding Mick since their intimate night, and after seriously thinking things over, she realized that it was never going to happen again. Still, Monica wasn't solely convinced that she should be marrying Julian, and she knew that she needed to come clean to him about her feelings as well. Today was going to be a day of confession. She wasn't strong enough to confess what had happened between her and Mick, but she certainly was going to push the wedding date back. Monica went to Sweet J's and didn't even bother stopping to talk to Cola. She went straight to Julian's office and knocked, but he wasn't in. She called his cell, and he didn't answer. She was sure Cola knew his whereabouts, but she wasn't going to ask, so Monica left the café and called Mick, who was next on her list. He was at the bank, but he agreed to meet her for an early lunch. Monica met him at a twenty-four-hour breakfast eatery near her home. Soon after she ordered her French toast, she laid everything on the table.

"I shouldn't have slept with you. We both know that. I let my emotions get the best of me, and I'm not that girl. I've never cheated in a relationship before. I did because I was running away from the commitments I've made to Julian, but this isn't going to happen again."

"I respect that, I mean, I dig you, but I assumed it was just sex."

"Why would you assume that?" Monica rebuffed.

"Because you have a man, whom you keep saying you love," he said.

"So you slept with me . . ."

"Because you're fine," Mick quickly replied. Monica had nothing else to say.

They finished their brunch and Mick went his way. That was it. No extra flirting. He didn't try to change her mind; he simply nodded and walked away. All of the sexual tension that they'd had since their first meeting was gone. She couldn't understand it. No, she didn't have a desire to sleep with him again, but his nonchalant attitude about her decision made her question his intentions, and her performance. She called Henna to disclose everything, but Monica couldn't even get to her and Mick's lunch conversation, because Henna kept yelling.

"I can't believe you slept with him! What is wrong with you?"

Monica attempted to keep going around her repeated shrieks, and when Henna finally calmed down, she was able to give some sound advice. "Don't let your pride get you back in a situation that you don't even want."

At first, Monica didn't get it. She thought Henna was referring to Julian, but she wasn't. Henna explained further. "You are contemplating why this man doesn't want you, when you don't even want him. Soon the thought will turn into curiosity, and then you'll be calling him up, just to strike up conversation. You still won't want him, but you will want him to want you. And as soon as that sensation takes over, you'll be sleeping with him again. Been there, done that."

Henna was right. Even as they were talking, Monica was thinking about calling Mick just to see if he was ever really interested in her at all. But why did that matter? Only her ego could benefit from that answer.

"Okay, I will let it go," said Monica.

"I still can't believe you slept with him." Henna repeated once more.

"All right, already. Let it go, please," begged Monica.

They continued to talk about Julian, Henna's new CD, and Craig. Monica didn't spill the beans about Nia, especially since Henna had seemed to move on.

"You are coming back for the opening, right?" Monica asked.

"I will be there. Craig and I have some recording to do."

"Recording, huh? That's what they call it these days?"

"Please. My head is screwed on really tight, for real this time."

They laughed and talked for another ten minutes or so, and then Monica's phone clicked. It was her fiancé. She hung up with Henna, and after speaking with Julian, she made plans to see him in an hour. During that next sixty minutes, Monica replayed at least twenty different conversational scenarios in her head. She didn't know how it would play out, but as her doorbell rang, she became nervous, so edgy that Julian automatically knew something was wrong. To make matters worse, he'd brought several island getaway brochures for them to consider for their honeymoon. He laid them out on the table as they sat.

"I wanted to surprise you. But I know how you like your opinion considered."

Monica looked at the blue water, white sand, and smiling couples. She thought she could be one of those people, if only she just shut up. But what would happen once the honeymoon was over? This is the question that festered.

"What if I'm not ready?" was how Monica started the conversation.

Julian, puzzled, as if she'd just spoken in some lost Arabic language, uttered, "Huh?" His back position stiffened as he moved the brochures to the side and reached for her. "Babe, what are you talking about?"

"I don't think I'm ready to get married."

"What happened?" he asked.

This was her moment of truth. Could she risk telling about Mick, or was it best to say, "Nothing. Nothing happened"?

Julian was silent as he leaned back in his chair and pondered her response. After a few moments he looked back at Monica and spoke. "Are you not ready to get married, or is it me?"

"It's me," she responded quickly. "I just didn't want to use the cliché 'it's not you, it's me.' But, for real, it is me. I'm not ready."

"I am," he firmly stated.

It was quiet again. Monica rose and poured glasses of water for them both. When she returned to the table, Julian took her hand. "I can say with everything in my heart that you are the woman with whom I want to spend my life."

Monica looked him in his eyes. She took a deep breath and replied, "I can't say the same."

"Then you're wrong. It's not you, it's me," Julian responded.

"But I don't want to break up," Monica insisted.

"There's nothing else for us to do. If you don't feel this way about me, you never will."

"That's not true."

"Well, let me put it this way. I don't want to wait around and find out."

Julian rose and looked at Monica once again. He glanced down at the ring, and she slid it off and placed it inside Julian's palm. He closed his hand into a fist, and then he put his closed hand over his heart.

"I really was praying that you wouldn't break this old ticker of mine."

Finally she felt like shit, but it came days too late. Monica lowered her head and whispered, "I'm so sorry,

Julian" as he walked toward the door. He opened it, turned, and looked at her. She stood at his side and stared into his eyes, which spoke volumes of sorrow. When he closed that door, she knew it was over. Julian wanted a wife, not a friend. To him it was all or nothing, and Monica had to admit that she couldn't give him all. As much as she wanted a husband, this wasn't it. She recalled Ahmad's statement to Henna: "You're not enough to give you my forever." It sounded cruel at the time, but at this moment she understood it. Honestly, Monica thought, if more people admitted that, the divorce rate would probably decrease threefold. After a few minutes of silent reflection, she called Henna and gave details.

"I feel like a failure that triumphed," she said.

"Please explain?" Henna requested.

"I failed at making a relationship with great potential work."

"So where did you triumph?"

"Over my inclination to settle."

"So they cancel each other out, and you're back at ground zero. Though I think your triumph was much greater than your supposed failure."

"I guess," Monica murmured.

"Go get some ice cream," Henna suggested. "I promise once you start licking, everything will be okay."

Monica chuckled, and they soon disconnected.

Henna had been feeling a little funky as well, and she needed a change, which she was about to get once she got to the salon. Henna originally had an appointment to get her hair colored, but once she got to the shop, she changed her mind. She kept her naturally dark brown shade, but she went for something more dramatic.

Henna had the stylist cut her long, straight hair into a short spiky hairdo. It was very similar to Halle's haircut in "Swordfish." In fact, that's the picture she pointed to in an old magazine just before she said, "Chop it all off."

When the stylist turned her chair around, Henna was shocked at her appearance. Since the age of four, Henna's hair had never fallen short of her shoulders, but now it was standing straight on top of her head.

"You like?" asked her stylist.

A smile bright as the morning sun fell upon her face. "I love it."

Surprisingly, Henna walked out of the shop feeling brand-new. She rushed to Haydu, who barely recognized her. He ran his fingers through her four-inch long locks. "In one day you've gone from next-door cutie to Hollywood sex symbol." he said.

"It's not too Halle Berry is it. I hate when people think you're copying someone else's style, even though I did copy her style."

"Halle, who? You look amazing."

With a big smile, Henna suggested, "let's go out tonight," and they did. Haydu, Henna along with her other bandmates, Todd, and his wife, went to at least five bars and clubs that evening.

Henna was so exhausted that she slept until one o'clock the next afternoon. But when she woke, the euphoria of a new hairdo was over. Unfortunately, most of her joy was temporary these days.

"What is it going to take?" she asked while staring at her reflection in the mirror, and though it never replied, Henna knew the answer.

Chapter 24

"Baby It's You" (The Shirelles, 1961)

Since their breakups, Monica and Craig had been spending almost every night together. Craig came over to eat, and Monica put her cooking lessons from Julian to work. Each had analyzed their flaws over and over, and Monica was convinced they were not to blame.

"It's Dad's fault," she said on this particular night when they'd been drinking. "Our broken home has us seeking unhealthy relationships that we eventually mess up, 'cause we know they aren't right in the first place."

"What? You're crazy."

"Seriously. All this time I've wanted someone who could be faithful, and I had it. Here I am blaming men for my messed-up relationships, but it wasn't them. People use cheating to hide the truth . . . from them, from ourselves . . ." Monica analyzed.

"Well, at least he still respects you. Nia has cursed me up and down the streets of California, I'm sure."

"Hurt is hurt," stated Monica.

"No, hurt is different when you find out the person cheated," Craig insisted.

"Cheating may hurt the ego more, but heartbreak is heartbreak."

"Says the woman who got off easy," Craig commented.

Monica smirked as she rushed to grab her ringing
cell phone. Henna was calling to say that she would be
in town by Friday and wanted to make sure her bedroom was still available. Henna asked Monica not to
say anything to Craig. She didn't want to bother him
and Nia, and she certainly didn't want him to think she
was coming to see him.

"Why are you coming early? It's two weeks before
the opening."

"Bobby is mixing the songs and I want to be there."

Monica didn't say anything. She so badly wanted
to tell Henna that Nia was gone, and to inform Craig
that Henna was coming into town. But she'd promised
them both that she wouldn't say a word. However, she
could still hint. So as soon as she disconnected, Monica
grabbed another beer from the cooler by the patio door
and rushed back to her brother's side.

"That was an interesting phone call," she said, throwing Craig a bone. But he didn't bite. He was in a beer-
induced stupor. Therefore, Monica tried a more direct
approach. "When is the last time you talked to Henna?"

"Close to a month ago, when I was in New York."

"You should call her," said Monica.

"She's no longer pregnant. She said our business was
done."

Monica was surprised to hear those words. "She said
that?"

"In so many words. It was a fling. I'm not calling her.
She's with her ex, anyway."

"Ahmad? No, she's not."

"Yes, I saw them together."

Monica was quiet. She was starting to believe Craig.
Maybe it was just a fling, the one she said she desired.
Perhaps she was simply coming to Atlanta to work on

her CD. Big sister decided to let the conversation rest for now. She'd have to talk to Henna in person once she got to town, but when she sat down, Craig began to cross-examine.

"Why are you talking about Henna so much?"

"Not much. I just wanted to know when you last spoke to her."

"You didn't want us to be together, and we're not, so you should be happy," said Craig.

Monica thought about what he said before she answered. "You know why I didn't want you with Henna?" Craig waited for an answer. "I knew it would end painfully. Both of you are too stubborn and too headstrong to be together."

"For once, you are right," concurred Craig.

"But then again, I don't know. Maybe the saga hasn't ended yet," hinted Monica.

Craig gave her a curious look, but she remained quiet. With fusion jazz as their soundtrack, the two stared into the evening sky and continued to make small talk.

Monica stopped by Sweet J's the next morning to see how the new retiling was going. When she walked in, Cola halted her in her footsteps. "You have some nerve," she scolded.

"I only stopped by to see how the tiling was coming along."

"That's not your job anymore," Cola said.

Monica ignored her statement and tried to push her way past the gatekeeper. Cola pushed back, nearly causing Monica to trip.

"Get your hands off me!" Monica yelled.

Just then, Julian and another associate from Monica's job came from the back. Julian rushed toward the commotion.

"I can handle this," he said as Monica puffed her chest and released a rumble. Julian pulled Monica to the side and whispered, "What are you doing here?"

"I came by to see the tile." She motioned to the workers placing new tiling on the back wall.

"But you're no longer on this project. Didn't they tell you?"

"What? Who are they?"

"I called your office and asked that I get another rep to replace you."

"But—" Monica tried to interrupt.

"Don't worry, I told them you did an excellent job, but that there was a personal conflict of interest."

"Is that why Samuel is here?"

Julian nodded. "They should have said something yesterday."

"I didn't go to work yesterday. I've been using my days to catch up on some rest." Monica stood in the center of Sweet J's and looked at her ideas being executed without her. "But I'm a professional. I can finish the job without—"

Julian silenced her words by placing his hand softly against her lips. "I can't work side by side with the woman who is breaking my heart." Julian slowly turned and rejoined Samuel, leaving Monica, thunderstruck, in the center of the café.

From the left she could hear Cola clearing her throat, and without even turning in her direction, Monica could see the gloating. Cola was beaming heat rays straight her way, and so Monica drew upon her self-esteem and walked out with her head high. She stood across the street and stared into the café window. She could see Julian from her angle, and so she watched him interacting with Samuel and the work crew.

"God, I really like him," she whispered to herself. "Why can't that be enough?" She continued to stare, until she found herself out there for at least three minutes. Monica finally realized that she had to let it go. She got in her car and drove to work.

Craig had signed up and paid for a full tango session, and was now in his last week of classes. He was very proud of himself. He'd started taking them because of Henna, but now he was actually enjoying them. According to his teacher, he'd become quite good. Of course he had nowhere to display his skills, but the teacher mentioned signing him up as a dance partner for hire. Many women students came to class and looked for male partners to learn with. Craig didn't know how he would fit it in his schedule, but he knew that might be a good way to pick up some extra money, especially since he would have to help Monica pay back the loan. When he mentioned the opportunity to Monica, she said it sounded like he'd be a gigolo. At this point Craig had no problem with that either.

Monica mulled through her job the next few days, but on Friday she rushed home early to meet Henna, whose flight landed at 4:00 P.M. Monica was there close to an hour before Henna arrived, and when she opened her door, and saw her friend's new look, Monica's jaw nearly dropped to the floor. Henna stood at the door with a strapless, flowing sundress, big silver jewelry, and her brand-new haircut.

"Oh my God! You look incredible!" Monica screamed.

Henna embraced her friend, and they hugged as though they hadn't seen each other in years.

"I've missed you so much," said Monica. "I don't know how we went two years and didn't see each other. Now I feel like I can barely go two weeks."

"I've missed you too," added Henna, who hurried in the house and put her things upstairs.

After an hour of catching up with Monica, Henna's first stop was the studio. As she walked into Bobby's office, she was surprised to see framed magazine tear sheets of the two of them.

"What is this?" Henna pointed to the pictures.

"You hadn't seen these?" he asked.

Apparently the press photographers released the pictures from Diddy's party to several tabloid papers. Henna wasn't a tabloid follower, so she hadn't seen the articles. Obviously, the couple wasn't "hot" enough to make front-page news, but the pictures were covered in at least four tabloids. Henna giggled as she read the clichéd headlines underneath: HENNA JAMES AND BOBBY-B MAKE MUSIC IN AND OUT OF THE STUDIO.

Henna quickly called Haydu to have him run out and grab any of the tabloids he could find. This way she could frame them as well when she returned home. Bobby thanked her again for the attempt to redirect people from the truth about his sexuality. He admitted that a few artists stopped calling after the first paper was released. However, since people found out he was working on her latest project, his artist roster had expanded. He was now getting calls from R & B and jazz performers.

"I thank God for the day you walked in my studio," he said, smiling broadly.

"Oh, and I think the label is going to let me be on Wayne's song," Henna added with a chuckle.

Bobby ran his hands across the tops of her hair ends and grinned. "There's a new Henna about to break out. I hope they're ready."

She and Bobby went over all of the music and narrowed the project down to ten songs. Thankfully, Phillip was involved with the process, so Henna knew that this project would get play. Each of the artists involved had submitted and signed all of the proper paperwork, and Henna was looking at a late-fall release. The plan was to tour a couple of months to promote the CD. Though Henna was not excited about getting on the road, she'd be traveling with her new musical friends, so it wouldn't be too bad. The label agreed to pay for the seven artists to tour with her and the band, so this tour would be much easier to swallow.

Henna literally spent the next three days in the studio. She left Monica's house around ten in the morning, and she didn't return until close to two the next morning. She'd never been so involved in the process before. This project was becoming her baby. She now understood what Craig was saying when he referred to his club as his "baby." Bobby's goal was to win Henna a Grammy; a nomination wasn't good enough, and he was convinced she could win this time. He'd planted the seed. Now Henna was also pushing toward the same goal. Normally, she approached a project with the intention of simply making good music, but since this project came from a true and pure place, it needed to be as good as it could be. There was no harm in desiring a Grammy, and winning it would be Ahmad's job. He knew the right contacts, and the perfect marketing plan to get that nomination.

By day four she and Bobby decided to take a break. They were both exhausted, and Henna needed a day without music. She simply wanted to relax and hang out. Therefore, she took her iPod and went to the park. After an hour of walking around the track, Henna took a seat near the swings. She was surprised to see the same old woman she'd had the conversation with two months ago. The woman waved but didn't recall Henna.

"Ms. Audrey?" Henna called out.

The woman smiled and walked closer. She peered into Henna's eyes, but she still couldn't recall how she knew her.

"I'm sorry, I don't remember you."

"It's okay. We met here in the park a while ago. You just made such an impact on me that I remembered your name."

Audrey took a seat next to Henna, who struck up a conversation.

"How's your grandson?"

"Oh, he's fine. He's in school. I'm here walking with my husband today." Audrey motioned toward an elderly gentleman making a lap around the track.

"I just love to watch him walk. He still has that same strut that caught my eye thirty years ago."

"Wow, that's a long time to be with somebody."

"It passes like no time at all, when it's the right one," said Audrey.

"The one? I don't believe in magic."

"Oh, there's no magic in it. No spells. You just got to have your eyes wide open, 'cause he's not coming wrapped in the package you expect. And he's not going to act like you want him to act. But when it's right, there is no denying how he makes you feel."

"I guess," Henna said doubtfully.

"No guessing in it. Trust me, Otis and I have been through some hard times. But look at him. I love that man. He gives me a smile from deep within. You can't teach that. That's the type of stuff that makes thirty years pass like thirty days."

Henna watched as Otis walked off the track and toward the woman. She glanced at Audrey and saw a sly grin build on her face.

"You ready, Mama," Otis said as he stood over Audrey.

"I'm ready." Audrey rose and looked back at Henna. "You take care of yourself," she said to Henna just before she and Otis walked away.

Henna watched them playfully poke at one another as they trotted across the grass.

"Thirty years?" she whispered. Henna sat in the park and soaked up the sunshine for another hour before heading to the house. That evening she made an Asian chicken salad for her and Monica. Amazingly, she hadn't run into Craig since she'd been back, and she wasn't sure if he even knew she'd returned. But she needed to talk to him about recording "Sugar on the Floor" and they needed to practice. For some reason it proved difficult to call him.

After dinner Monica and Henna decided to go out for dessert. It was close to ten that night when they walked into Intermezzo and ordered their sweets. They sat in the back room, and as they nibbled on their desserts, they simultaneously looked up at each other and spoke.

"I miss him." Both women grinned at the uncanny timing of the statement.

"You should call him," Monica told Henna. "I don't stand a chance with Julian, but it's different with you."

Henna paused for a minute, but then she replied, "He's with Nia."

Monica couldn't take it any longer. She had to say it. "Nia left."

Henna looked up.

"I was hoping Craig would say something to you, but he said you were with Ahmad."

"I'm not with Ahmad."

"That's what I told him. Please call him."

Henna sighed a few times and then replied, "Craig is a lot of work. I don't know."

"You said when it's right, there's no denying how he makes you feel."

"The angel said that, just before she strutted away with her husband of thirty-some years."

"Wow. I want to be with someone that long and still be happy. What's the secret?"

Henna shrugged her shoulders. "I wish I knew, sister." They each took several bites of each other's dessert and finally Henna continued to speak. "Your brother gets me. He gets me like no one else ever has. He makes me crazy, but at the same time he makes me smile this uncontrollable smile. And it comes from inside. So even when I try to stop, I can't. And it's not just the sex. I get goose bumps whenever he's in the same room."

"That sounds like love," said Monica.

"It feels like I'm at the top of the roller-coaster hill, and my seat belt is loose."

Monica reached across and placed her hand on top of Henna's. "It will be okay," Monica promised.

When Henna spoke again, the tone of her voice was one that Monica had never heard. "I don't want to get hurt," she said. Henna gazed at Monica with eyes as sincere and vulnerable as a child's.

Monica gave a sly smirk and commented, "Well, well, the rubber lady's elastic has finally worn out."

Henna gave a tiny smile and replied, "Indeed, it has."

The two finished their treat and went home.

Henna tossed and turned that night in bed. She picked up the phone several times to call Craig, but she hung up at each instance. She decided that she would go see him that morning, so she got dressed while Monica was fixing breakfast. She made her statement as though it were a grand announcement. "I'm going to see Craig today."

"Finally!" Monica said.

"I've got to stop by the studio, pick up the demo, and make sure Bobby e-mailed Phillip the tracks, and then I'm going to the club."

They ate breakfast and parted.

As soon as Monica got to work, Craig called. He was on his way to the club. The food and beverage orders were coming in and he was invoicing and stocking most of the day. He could detect a certain devious tone in Monica's voice, but she managed to get through the conversation without mentioning Henna.

Craig got to the club, walked to the back, and began working. An hour later, one of his carpenters came to the back and told him he had a visitor out front. Craig walked to the main room and stopped in his tracks when he saw Nia. She was standing in the center of the room; there was a peculiar smile on her face.

"Hi," she murmured, with a tiny wave.

Craig didn't speak. He was shocked. He had thought they'd truly never see each other again. Sure, they'd broken up many times before, but he'd never seen her so angry as the last time. He slowly approached her as she extended her arms. They held each other tightly.

"I'm sorry. I never meant to hurt you," he said.

"I don't want to live without you, Craig."

Craig still held on, but he didn't reply. He cuddled Nia in his arms as they moved toward a table and sat. She revealed why she was back.

"We have too much history for me to throw it all away. I still love you."

Craig then blurted out something very surprising. "Let's go get married."

Nia was shocked. But then the gasp turned into girlish giggles as she answered, "Okay, let's do it." She looked at her watch. "We can go to the courthouse and get the license and do it today. It's still early."

Craig looked around the club and looked at the time too. He immediately responded, "Okay."

Chapter 25

"Ain't Too Proud to Beg"
(The Temptations, 1966)

He'd finally committed, and Nia was going to become his wife. He searched his gut for that bubbly, passionate emotion that he so deeply wanted to feel. Though it wasn't there, there was a true longing, and a loving feeling, and it was enough. He didn't want to lose her again, and he felt like God was giving him a second chance. Then Craig suddenly felt like he was having an out-of-body experience. He could hear Monica's words about settling: "She's not strong enough for you." But he also saw himself continuing to walk toward this woman who was willing to give him the rest of her life. Craig's heart rate started to rush, and he broke into a sweat.

Suddenly, he heard the words from "Sugar on the Floor", You're a stranger to me. Still you give me your life. I toss it to one side, Still you're sweeter to me When will I be sure.

His breathing pattern increased, and by the time he actually made it across the room, he was faint. Craig took a seat.

"You okay, baby?" Nia asked.

Craig looked up into Nia's eyes and nodded.

"You still want to go?" she questioned. Craig nodded again. Nia knelt and embraced him tightly. They rose and began walking out of the club.

As they were leaving, Travis was walking in. He was surprised to see Nia, and even more surprised when she told him they were on their way to the courthouse to marry. He didn't have time to pull Craig to the side, but he did make eye contact with him.

"You good?" Travis said to Craig.

Craig smiled, and though his nod said yes, his eyes silently screamed, "Man, I don't know!"

However, Travis knew this was a decision that his boy was going to figure out the hard way.

"Well, congratulations," he said as they got in the truck and drove off. Before they could get down the street, however, Craig's phone rang. It was Henna. Craig answered on the first ring.

"Hey, I'm in town," she said. "I was thinking we could link up to practice."

"It's good to hear from you," Craig said, trying not to sound too excited.

"So, are you at the club? I could stop by."

"No, but tomorrow we could link," he answered.

"Oh."

Craig could hear the disappointment in her voice, but he didn't know what to say. Nia was sitting next to him, eavesdropping on his every word. "Call me this evening. I can come by the studio."

"Okay. I will." Henna hung up the phone.

Craig's heartbeat raced again. He knew that once he just went ahead and married Nia, everything would be all right. Once he'd done it, then that was it. He'd have a woman to care for him the rest of his life. Wasn't that what a man needs? She was supportive, nurturing, giving, sweet as pie, and attractive. He was lucky that a woman with all of those attributes not only loved him, but was willing to put up with all of his crap. Craig began smiling, and then his phone rang again. It was Monica.

"Hey, whatcha doing?"

"I'm on my way to get married."

Monica laughed and replied, "Damn, you and Henna move fast, don't you?"

"What?"

"I already know about everything, I talked to Henna. You don't have to pretend."

"What are you talking about? I'm with Nia. She's back, and we're on our way to the courthouse."

"Noooooo!" Monica squealed. "Nia! She is too dependent. You can't marry her. Henna's back, and she misses you. She was coming to tell you. She wants to be with you."

Craig couldn't move. It wasn't until the cars behind him started to honk that he realized that his light was green.

"Is everything okay?" asked Nia, but Craig didn't answer.

"You can't go. Turn around," demanded Monica.

"I can't," he said.

"You have to," she begged.

"Monica, I know what I'm doing." Craig hung up the phone and continued forward to the courthouse.

Monica grabbed her purse and rushed from work. She had held her tongue long enough. It was time to put an end to the madness. She peeled from the parking lot and headed downtown.

Meanwhile, Henna was still at the studio with Bobby. She and Zion were working on another song that wouldn't be included on the album, but something they would do on the tour. She basically was killing time until she was able to see Craig that evening. Henna decided to call Craig and ask him if he wanted dinner.

Now that she'd decided to give in, there was no need to pretend like she didn't want to see him. She was just going to tell him.

However, when she called, Craig didn't pick up. He and Nia had just gotten to the courthouse; he was in the restroom, gathering his thoughts. Henna called right back, but this time Nia picked up Craig's phone that was left in his seat. She was taken aback by the woman's voice. Henna didn't speak until Nia said hello for the second time.

"Um . . . is Craig available?" she asked.

"No, he isn't. May I take a message?"

"It's Henna. . . ."

"Oh, hi, Henna," Nia said cheerfully. Ironically, she had no idea of Henna and Craig's involvement, and so she gladly shared their news. "Craig's in the restroom. We're downtown at the courthouse."

"Is everything okay?" Henna asked.

"Yeah, we're getting married!" Nia exclaimed.

Henna's stomach immediately knotted up. Her body went numb, and she dropped the phone. Bobby immediately knew something was wrong. He grabbed the cell and whispered, "You okay" as he covered the receiver.

"Henna! Henna!" Nia called as Craig was coming from the bathroom, and so Nia handed him the phone.

Henna put her ear back to the receiver. "Will you tell Craig that I called?"

"It's me, Henna." There was silence on the phone.

"Congratulations," Henna finally said.

"Um, yeah. Is there something you wanted to say?" Craig asked. There was an apparent underlying tone with his question. Henna picked up on it, but she refused to say anything.

"I was calling about your dinner plans, but I assume you will be eating with your wife," Henna said, nearly running out of breath to speak. Her line clicked, and so she hurried off the phone.

"Hello," Henna said.

"It's me," said Monica. "Have you talked to Craig?"

"He's at the courthouse getting married," Henna fussed. "You said Nia was gone."

"She was, but don't worry, he's not marrying her."

By now, Henna was almost in tears. She couldn't explain her hurt, but the thought of him actually going through with this marriage was causing her stomach and head simultaneous pain. Though he'd decided to marry her before, Henna thought that day would never come, and that consideration held more weight than she had realized. Yet, she didn't want to fight for a man who didn't want her.

"Let it go, Monica."

"I will not!" Monica hung up the phone.

Craig and Nia were waiting, because the court official who issued licenses had just gone to lunch, and so this gave Nia and Craig a moment to talk. In this moment they said absolutely nothing. Nia stared fondly into Craig's glazed-over eyes. He seemed as lost as Dorothy in the poppy fields, and all he wanted to do was sleep, but he was in too deep to turn around. Just before the court official returned from lunch, Monica came rushing around the corner and found Nia and Craig sitting in the room. She gestured hello to Nia, while pulling her brother into the hallway.

"Monica—"

"Hush. You don't want to marry this girl. I'm not saying you have to be with Henna, but you are doing this for the wrong reason."

"I'm never again going to find someone who loves me like this."

"You don't know that, and who says she loves you so much? Nia is crazy. She's a glutton for punishment. She's obsessed with you, and she would rather have an unhealthy relationship than be alone. Is that love?"

"I don't know, Dr. Phil, is it?" With a sarcastic expression, Craig folded his arms and waited for her response.

"All I'm saying is wait for someone you know you can't live without, and not someone who's going to be there just because."

"What if that someone never comes?" Craig asked.

"Then you can spend your life with your spinster sister." Monica grinned. Craig gave a tiny chuckle, but then looked away.

"I know you don't think I love Nia, but I do. I'm tired of 'ho-ing.' I'm tired of being out there. It's time I settle down. Most of my boys have wives who don't support them. They nag, and make their lives miserable. Nia is not that woman. Yeah, I may find someone that I'm passionate and crazy about, but she may be hell to live with. I don't want to take that chance, when I can have a great life with Nia. And it's not settling. It's growing up and realizing good for what it is. And I will be good to her, I promise."

Monica heard his words, and the first time, she understood. She had many friends in relationships with that one person they'd fallen head over heels for, and most of those relationships were turbulent, unstable, or on the brink of divorce. In the long run, was it better to settle with a friend, who would be there through the ups and downs, or wiser to substitute sparks for substance? Monica had no idea, but she respected her brother's maturity.

"I had your blessing once. What happened?" asked Craig.

"That was when Mick was upstairs in my room, I didn't have time to do much evaluating. I just want the best for my little brother."

Craig took Monica by the hand and proposed a question. "Answer this honestly. If I got in a crash tomorrow and became paralyzed, do you think Nia would take care of me?"

"Definitely," replied Monica.

"Would Henna?" he asked. Monica couldn't give him an answer. "I want a wife who is going to be there through thick and thin." He then took a step back and looked at his sister before stating, "I'd be crazy to let that go."

Monica looked him directly in the eyes. She saw he was serious. She didn't see the flighty, crazy-eyed baby brother she was accustomed to. "Go," she uttered.

Craig embraced his sister. "Thank you for understanding," he whispered. "You coming in with us?"

Monica shook her head. "No, I have to go back to work." Monica slowly walked down the hallway and out of the courthouse. Craig took a few deep breaths and walked back into the room to meet Nia.

It was around six-thirty that evening when Henna finished up with Bobby. They were still thinking about places to tape the live concert, and Bobby was convinced that the Righteous Room was perfect. Henna finally agreed, but she didn't want to have to interact with Craig any more than necessary. They'd have to work together to record the song, but after that, she simply wanted to go her way. Her emotions were sliding on a seesaw. One minute she was going to confess her love, and the next she wanted to walk away and never see him again. The mere thought of getting hurt made her want to run for the hills. That vulnerability window was only open for a second, and after hearing Nia's voice, it slammed shut and locked automatically. Henna went home and had plans to be in the house for the rest of the night, until Craig called around seven and wanted to meet at the Righteous Room. He wanted to go ahead and go over the music. She declined a couple of times, but eventually she gave in to his pleading.

When Henna arrived, Craig was already there. Travis came down to let her in, but he barely recognized her wearing a big, floppy cap pulled down close to her eyes. However when he saw her face, he smiled and gave her a hug.

"Glad you're back. Craig told me we were going to record next week."

"Yeah, I'm excited about it."

"Okay, talk to you later." Travis left as she entered. Henna walked upstairs, but by the time she got halfway up, she heard Craig playing a tune on his guitar. He was singing. She'd heard him talk over tunes, but never really sing. She was surprised at his baritone voice. It was a little raspy, but very sexy. She wasn't familiar with the song, but she listened to the words. They were simple, straight to the point. She especially liked the verse, "She tossed in her chips, hope she wasn't bluffing, 'cause I'm throwing in my hand, and I hate to lose in vain, but just to see her smile, I'd fold a thousand times, one thousand times, over again."

Henna continued walking up the steps, and stood against the wall where they'd once shared a kiss. She gently touched it and reminisced. The Righteous Room had completely transformed, and it was beautiful. Craig only had a few lights on, and the stage was dim, so he didn't notice Henna at first. When she sniffed, he looked up and stopped playing. Henna gave him a pleasant smile.

"I really like your song," she complimented.

"Thanks," he replied.

"You really love her, don't you?"

Craig gave a crooked nod, and replied, "I think I do."

Henna swaggered over to him. "You better do more than think. She is your wife."

Craig smirked.

"Your voice is nice. Why don't you sing more?" Henna asked.

"I leave that to the professionals, like you."

"Well, I say that we make 'Sugar on the Floor' a duet."

"No way. I'm playing, and you're singing." Craig hopped up from his seat and grabbed a few music sheets from the piano. "I was thinking of this for the arrangement—two violins, a cello, guitar, and maybe some horns."

"It's too much. I want something simple. I don't even want a piano anymore. The words are confusing enough." Craig nodded in agreement and Henna continued. "I want it like the song you were singing. It was perfect, just three chords and the truth. That's all we need."

"I wish relationships could be that simple, you know. Just . . ." Craig strummed three chords on his guitar and sang, "Hey, I love you."

"It can be. . . . Not real life, but the song can be . . . right?"

"Why can't real life be that way?" Craig asked.

Henna sighed, for she really wasn't into having a deep conversation and only wanted to rehearse, but she answered just to push things along. "Because it can't. People aren't made up of song lyrics and notes. We have emotions and feelings, pride, and other complicated stuff. Anyway, I'm thinking that 'Sugar on the

Floor' can have a string intro only, nothing too dramatic, but a simple classic lead-in. What do you think?"

"I think I love you."

Henna, really not listening to Craig, kept talking. "Good. So you'll be playing acoustic guitar, right? Is that going to sound right with strings? Maybe we should do a harmonica. Yes! A harmonica would be perfect. Let me go get the music." Henna turned around to get her iPod from her purse, but Craig grabbed her hand. "Did you hear what I said?"

"When?"

"Just now," he replied.

Confused, Henna paused. Craig didn't know if she was playing with him, or if she truly didn't get it.

"Craig, what are you saying?"

"What did you say to me when you first walked in about that song I was singing?"

Henna thought for a second to recall her words. "I said I like your song."

"And then," Craig continued.

"I said . . . I said, 'You must really love her,' and then you said, 'I think I do,' and—"

"The song is about you, Henna." Craig forced her to make eye contact as he came closer and removed her hat from her head. Suddenly the tender moment froze. "Where's your hair!"

"I cut it off. I was looking for something that was going to pep me up. I just needed a change." Craig ran his hands through her flattened spikes. Henna tried to do a quick fix as she pulled the locks upward with her fingers.

"It's supposed to stand up."

"I like it, I think," Craig said, trying to envision the style. Finally Henna and Craig locked eyes and each let out a tiny smile, but then Henna's expression turned troubled.

"You're married."

Craig shook his head.

"You're not married?" asked Henna.

"I couldn't do it. I had the pen in my hand, but then I realized that although she was perfect for me, I'd have to become someone else in order to be perfect for her. That wouldn't be fair to either of us." Henna's stomach began to churn. "I want to be with you," Craig admitted.

Henna's face grew anxious and she became fidgety. "You can't just jump from relationship to relationship, Craig. That's not good."

"Oh my God, I'm sitting here telling you that I love you, and you're chastising me like you're my mother."

"I'm just telling you what I know," Henna remarked as she took her hat and placed it back on her head. "Look, I can't work with you if you're going to keep going back and forth with me like this. I just want us to be friends," Henna stated.

"No, you don't."

"What? Yes, I do. I knew we should've just done this in the studio." Henna backed away and walked toward the stairs. Craig picked up his guitar and called Henna's name. As soon as she turned, he tossed the six-stringed instrument to her. Henna nearly fell flat on her face, trying to catch it, but she did.

"Have you lost your mind? This is a mahogany Gallagher."

"Nope, I haven't lost my mind. That's just how much I trust you. You're going to play three chords, and I'm going to tell you my truth."

Stomping her legs like a spoiled toddler, Henna yelled, "I don't want to play some stupid game!"

"Yes, you do. If not, you wouldn't have caught the guitar."

"I caught it so it wouldn't fall."

"That guitar is an extension of me. You caught it to show me that you wouldn't let me fall."

Henna wrinkled her face and grunted, but she knew he was right. Frustrated, she stood on the floor and nervously tapped her sneakers against the perfectly vintage-finished hardwood.

"Three chords, Henna," Craig insisted.

Henna strummed the guitar.

"That was one chord."

Henna rolled her eyes and strummed again; this time she chose E and D chords to complement her first one, which was A.

Craig began: "Henna James and I met. We had lots in common. We hit it off, talked, laughed, had great sex, and laughed some more." Craig looked at Henna to strum again, which she did. "I didn't tell her I had a girlfriend because I didn't want to stop spending time with her, but she found out and wouldn't talk to me. That's when I realized I had already fallen for her, but I thought it was too late." He paused again, she strummed, and this time her chords complemented each other. "She got pregnant; she pushed me away; I let her. I was scared. I wasn't ready to be a father, and I had no idea what kind of mother she would be. She seemed flighty, which was fine for a lover, but not for the mother of my child." This time Henna strummed forcefully and gave an angry glare.

"It's true," Craig said, glaring back. "But as it turns out, God was just testing us and we failed. We claimed to be honest with ourselves as artists and speaking about what's real. But neither of us could admit that we'd met our match. That was too scary. We're fine, we're popular, we're musicians, and we don't take well to rejection. Anyway, I ran to my old faithful girlfriend and she took me in, promised to never leave, and love me with all of my faults. Henna ran to her career, it took her in, promised to never leave, and so on."

Henna began playing behind his words. Her three chords had turned into a whole song, and Craig continued to talk over her music. "Somewhere in all of the confusion, I realized that when Henna was around, I felt different. I felt powerful, confident, and nervous— all at the same time. I wanted to spend all of my time with her, but it was too late, she was gone. She was older, more mature, or so I thought, and I figured if I actually gave my heart to this woman, she could really hurt me. No woman's ever hurt me. But Henna's love made me vulnerable. She exposed me, and it left my heart defenseless. I think the only way you can love someone unconditionally is to put yourself out there on the line like that. You know, defenseless, just to take your heart from your chest and say, 'Here it is, hold it, squeeze it, cover it, drop it, whatever. I don't care what you do with it because it's yours.' And you gotta trust that the only thing they want to do with your heart is protect it. I don't know if I ever handed Henna my heart. I think she just reached in and snatched it out. But, um . . . it's going to be kinda hard to live without her close, because she still has it."

Henna stopped playing, but Craig continued to talk. "So, if she doesn't want me, I hope she gives me my heart back. It may never work the same, but hey, you gotta roll with the punches, right?" Craig chuckled.

Henna stood in the center of the floor and stared at him. When he matched her stare, she became embarrassed and looked away as she spoke. "She only took his heart because he didn't need two." Henna felt Craig approaching, so she turned toward him. He looked confused by her statement. Henna continued in third person. "He'd already stolen hers, so she figured, she'd take his. . . . You know, tit for tat."

By now, Craig was a few feet away. Henna held out the guitar to thwart him from moving in closer. As he continued to move, the guitar poked him in the chest. Her arm stiffened. "Don't come any closer."

Craig stayed positioned for a second, turned, and rushed toward the stage. He flicked on a couple of switches to turn on the sound system, leaned into the microphone, and spoke. "Door number one, or door number two?"

Henna laughed. "I'm not playing with you."

"Yes, you are, come on. Trust me, you want what's behind these doors."

Henna finally caved. "Door number one."

Craig grinned, went to the sound system, which was hooked into his iPod, and played a song. Blaring across the speakers was "Vida Mia," the perfect song for a tango.

"May I have this dance?" Craig asked as he approached. Henna placed the guitar on a table and let Craig take her into his arms. They began to dance. He led her around the room and she felt light as air. Henna melted in his arms. "See, girl, I told you I could tango." Henna giggled like a child as Craig spun her to the left, placed his arm on her waist, and pulled her so close that their noses touched. She overheard him whisper, "I pray I never get in a car accident."

"What did you say?" she asked, but he dismissed her comment and spun her one last time. Craig then stopped dancing and stood still; she followed his lead. Now the two dancers were standing motionless in the center of what had become their dance floor. Henna looked into his eyes and asked, "What was behind door number two?"

Craig motioned across the room toward the bar. Henna squinted to see it, but couldn't make it out.

"A pecan pie with your name written all over it. See, I knew you would finally come around, and I wanted to be prepared."

"That's very arrogant of you."

"Is that some sort of compliment?" Craig asked.

"Yeah, a little arrogance is sexy, and lucky for you, sexy happens to be my weakness."

Before she could finish the sentence, Craig brought his face closer and they kissed. Henna felt a fire inside her body, and she literally broke into a sweat. When they parted, Henna couldn't believe how overwhelmed she'd become.

"Oh God, you do have my heart," she whispered. It was one thing to say it, but at that moment she knew without a doubt that it was true. Amazingly, the kiss only led to a night of creating good music. Henna and Craig wrote the notes and worked out the melody for their version of "Sugar on the Floor." Henna even convinced Craig to sing. It was a night of firsts: Craig's first singing duet, Henna's first single off her project, and the first time they both agreed to let go, and let love do her thing. But they still had trust issues, and Henna refused to leave New York, so could this long-distance love truly work?

Epilogue

"Three Chords and the Truth"
(Sara Evans, 1997)

The Righteous Room officially opened its doors on a Friday. It was for family and friends only, and Craig had the meal catered. Monica brought Mick along as her date, but she insisted it was only because he'd help make everything possible. She admitted that she'd never seen Craig so excited about anything, and he had a good reason to be. The Righteous Room looked like a step back in time. It was a 1940s juke joint, with modern nuances, such as a high-tech sound system, a fully stocked bar, and valet parking.

Currently, downstairs was an art gallery, but he still planned to turn the space into a lounge area. Most everyone's juke joint reference was from The Color Purple scene when Oprah knocked out Rae Dawn Chong, and so all night people continued to quote the infamous line with Squeak's voice and all. It was cute at first, but after two hours of that, Craig decided to ban anyone he caught quoting anything from the film. Other than that, the night was a huge success, and all admitted that they'd never been any place quite as vintage, exotic, and sexy. Henna and Craig both knew it would be the spot that would attract all of Atlanta's tastemakers and its visiting superstars.

Henna stayed late after everyone left and wanted to discuss the official opening, which was the next night. She'd be playing songs from her latest project, and Bobby-B had arranged to videotape it for marketing. Craig honestly couldn't think about the next evening. He was still riding high from earlier, and he wanted to wait until tomorrow. Henna insisted they discuss it tonight.

"This is our first argument as a couple," he said.

"We're not a couple," she said. Craig looked surprised. "I live in New York, you live here. You don't do well in long-distance relationships. I'm witness to that."

Craig still looked at her in astonishment. "I just assumed—"

"No, don't assume," she interrupted.

"Henna, shut up," Craig demanded.

"What?"

"Shut up! I would say 'be quiet,' but that won't work for you." Henna surprisingly settled down. Craig began his speech. "You will move here. You will work out of Bobby-B's studio, and we will create music. When you're not on tour, you will help me run this place, and when I'm on tour, you will run this place without me. We don't have to live together at first. We don't even have to have sex. . . . No, take that back, we have to have sex. But you can be on top most of the time."

"You have this all worked out, don't you?"

"I do," Craig insisted.

"Were you going to discuss this with me?"

"I just did. You have a problem with it?"

Henna paused, looked around the room, and finally murmured, "No."

"I didn't hear you," Craig said.

"No," Henna said louder.

"That's what I thought. Now, come give me a kiss."
Henna shook her head. "I'm not giving you shit."
Henna took off running, with Craig close behind. That
night they christened Craig's office, the back room, and
the stage.

That fall Henna's brownstone sold, and Three Chords
and The Truth peaked to number one on the adult contemporary charts, and was there for six weeks. Henna
got two Grammy nominations for the single "Sugar on
the Floor" and for best album. However, the most exciting night for her was August 25 when she performed to a
sold-out show at Madison Square Garden. She only did
one song; after all, it was a hip-hop concert. Yet, when
she walked out onstage to join Lil Wayne on "I'd Bust
Your Guts," the crowd went wild.

Henna toured again, and this time she loved it. She
helped her man run his club, and she loved that too.
She finally admitted that she was strong enough to submit, and she loved that most of all.

That following spring, when Henna stood onstage
with two Grammy Awards in her hand, her speech was
perfect. After thanking the fans and the label, Henna
turned to her team.

"I want to thank Ahmad for managing with just the
right amount of guidance, Haydu and Monica for caring with just the right amount of compassion, Bobby-B
for producing with just the right amount of creativity,
and Craig for loving with just the right amount of song.
I share these awards with all of you."

Henna never imagined that her music would lead
her down the path to her own healing, but as it was oc-
curring, she embraced it, knowing that was exactly how
it should be. Healing begins at home, and what's more
at home than something fashioned from within. It was
a surreal moment on that Grammy stage as she stared

into the sea of strangers, clapping and cheering over her presence. She took in that brief second and for the first time she knew she could finally stop running. Her course had led her back to the place where she began, and there she'd finally found what she didn't realize she was looking for, that skinny light-skinned girl from Mississippi who simply wanted to heal people with her song.

Henna James had finally learned to respect the journey, even if all of its purpose was still misunderstood. She felt accomplished and, more important, worthy.

That award-winning night, Henna performed like never before, and when she was done, her tears were flowing; yet her smile was brighter than the almost-blinding stage lights. With closed eyes, she humbly bowed her head and then slowly looked up to face her new journey. The crowd was on their feet. Still, her low, sexy whisper made its way through the screams and the ovation.

"I'm Henna James. Peace and blessings to you, thanks and good night."

Notes

Notes